J A ANDREWS

Secrets Among Thorns

A shocking thriller packed with secrets and lies

Copyright © 2025 by J A Andrews

All rights reserved. No part of this publication may be reproduced, stored or transmitted in any form or by any means, electronic, mechanical, photocopying, recording, scanning, or otherwise without written permission from the publisher. It is illegal to copy this book, post it to a website, or distribute it by any other means without permission.

This novel is entirely a work of fiction. The names, characters and incidents portrayed in it are the work of the author's imagination. Any resemblance to actual persons, living or dead, events or localities is entirely coincidental.

J A Andrews asserts the moral right to be identified as the author of this work.

Designations used by companies to distinguish their products are often claimed as trademarks. All brand names and product names used in this book and on its cover are trade names, service marks, trademarks and registered trademarks of their respective owners. The publishers and the book are not associated with any product or vendor mentioned in this book. None of the companies referenced within the book have endorsed the book.

First edition

This book was professionally typeset on Reedsy. Find out more at reedsy.com

This one is for all the Kindle readers out there, thank you for reading...

Prologue

Ten Years Ago
Carol

This unbearable heat beats down on me, scorching my already sunburnt skin. I've been slaving away in the garden for an hour, too distracted to even think about sunscreen. My mind is a chaotic mess, reeling from bad news that has left me on edge and unsure of how to react. I'm terrified to tell Darren, but he'll be home soon from work and I haven't even started dinner yet.

Usually, Fridays are reserved for fish and chips, but in this heat, the thought of standing over a hot oven is unbearable. Drenched in sweat and grime, I haven't even had time to shower before I hear the key turn in the door. Panic sets in as I frantically rush back to the kitchen, pretending to prepare something.

We've been married for years and I know our usual routine - he'll explode at first but eventually calm down after an hour or so. But in this moment, as I stand there trembling with fear, I can't help but wonder if this will be the time he finally snaps for good.

'You alright there, Carol?' Darren asks, his boots covered in mud that he's dragged halfway through the house. 'You look. I don't know; you look worried about something. Anything happened whilst I've been at work?'

'Dinner is going to be late. I'm sorry, I was going to do us both some fish and chips, but I thought you might like something different tonight?' I respond, stumbling over my words. 'Do you want me to prepare us a salad, pasta, maybe? I thought it was a bit too warm for us to have a hot dinner like that?'

I grab a cold beer from the fridge and hand it to him. He pulls the ring pull off, takes a swig and grits his teeth slightly. His face showing me an expression of distaste I recognise every couple of days. He's not happy.

'How many times do I have to tell you that I don't eat any of that crap.' He snaps, still walking the mud through the kitchen. 'You're going to have to clean all that up. You know I don't like a dirty fucking house. Get the mop and bucket, will you.'

I put my head down and rush to the cupboard in the hallway, get out the mop and bucket and run the kitchen tap to fill a large jug with some water. I'm trying to think of things to talk about over in my head as I play with the taps.

'What would you like me to do for dinner instead?' I ask, changing the subject and watching him glug down the can of beer. He's drank the lot.

'How about a takeaway, my treat? I still have some of that money my mum lent me the other day. How about a pizza, Chinese, or Indian?'

'I was expecting fish and chips. I was looking forward to that all day.' He says with a tone. 'Fish and fucking chips, like I always have on a Friday. I'm starving hungry and was expecting it when I got in through our door. I'm always home at this time on a Friday. You know what I want.'

I don't mutter another word, I finish filling the jug of water, empty it into the bucket. Pre-heat the oven and take out the frozen chips, with a frozen piece of fish from the freezer. I don't see any tins of mushy peas in the cupboard, which will make him angry.

'I'll have a shower in a bit and get myself cleaned up since it'll probably be ready in forty minutes, now.' Darren says, his words make me on edge. 'Where's the kids? They should be back from school, shouldn't they? Kieran's long face is usually looking at me by now.'

I look at my watch to check the time, it's almost six. Lauren didn't go to school today because she was fretting over her A-level exams and Kieran was staying at a mate's house paying computer games, he went there straight after school.

'Kieran's at his mate's house, you know the one with that war game he's been banging on about that he wants for his birthday. And, Lauren, well, she's upstairs in her bedroom studying for her A-levels. Her exams are next week.'

'They're both good kids really, aren't they?' He says, before shouting, 'Lauren? Hey, come down and speak to your father for two minutes. I want to tell you something.'

I put the dinner in the over, look out of the kitchen window and admire that the garden is really starting to take shape now. The shed has seen better days, but we can't afford a new one yet.

'Lauren?' Darren shouts, walking his muddy boots now to the hallway. 'I said come down here for a minute. I've got something to tell you.'

Finally, Darren takes off his boots and leaves them on the mat by the front door. I don't know why he couldn't have done that as he came in.

'Get us another beer from the fridge, will you, Carol.' He asks, this time nicely. 'One from the back this time. The other one didn't feel very cold. You know how I like them cold. Why give me a warm one?'

I'm still walking around tense, on edge and fretting about if he's going to kick off. He hasn't even asked me about his dying brother. I seem to be the only one in the family who is decent enough to visit him in the hospice.

'Darren?' I ask, but he's not listening. 'Darren, we need to speak about something, it's important.'

He ignores me and goes running up the stairs. I walk slowly to the hallway to listen. My heart is pounding, and I wish there was an easier way of saying it.

'Darren?' I shout up the stairs. 'Can you please, fucking listen to me for a second?'

I take a deep breath, prepare myself as I hear him walking around up stairs. The heavy thuds making me shake with nerves.

'Darren?'

'Where the fuck is Lauren?' He says abruptly. 'She's not here. She's not anywhere. I thought you said she was studying, where did she go?'

'I don't know. She didn't say.' I say rushing up the stairs, 'she was here earlier. She came to the hospital with me, we saw your brother and she came back up here. She's seventeen, Darren. She's not a kid anymore, you can't ground her. She's practically an adult now, a grown woman. It was just a date with a lad from school, leave them be.'

He huffs and mutters something I didn't quite hear. He's not ready for his little girl to grow up, but I daren't tell him that she's old enough to make her own decisions, especially when it comes to lads.

'Darren. It's your brother and it's important.' I say with a solemn tone. 'Lauren and I, well, we went to see him today and it's not good news. It's not good at all.'

'What?' He snaps, and I keep my eyes fixated on his hands. 'I know he's dying of cancer. We both know that already, but he's not dead yet is he?'

'We need to prepare for it soon. That's all I know, I don't know exactly when. He's been given a lot of just-in-case medicines. His blood pressure has really dropped, his blue mottled feet have gotten worse and it's not good.' I explain, wanting to comfort him, but afraid of turning his emotions sour. 'He might not last the weekend; we were told today it's days now, not weeks. You should go see him, tonight?'

Darren stares right at me. He has always found it difficult to manage his emotions, but he needed to know. Someone had to break it to him.

'Where's Lauren? She must have said something?' He demands, completely ignoring the facts about his brother. 'I wanted to tell her that I saw that waster lad from school she fancies. He was hanging around the yard at work wanting a job.'

'I've not seen her since we got back.' I say, concerned. 'I'll call her mobile. Actually, I'll text her, you know how that phone lives on her twenty-four-seven, but she never picks the damn thing up. She might have popped to the shops.'

I call her but there's no answer. I text her and there's no reply.

'I don't want that lad anywhere near her.' Darren says, heading into the bathroom for a shower now. 'She's going places that girl of mine; she's got a smart head on her shoulders.

I'm proud of her.'

He never gives me any credit for bringing her up, taking our kids to school every day when they were little. Making everyone's lunches, dinners, and doing all the shopping. It's not like I want any thanks or expect it. I've forgotten what it feels like to be needed, loved and wanted. Our lives changed when we had kids and that financial strain added extra pressure. Darren works most days; I work part time and keep the house in order.

This is meant to be a marriage, not an existence.

Chapter One

Sunday, 4 June 2023
Brenda

I am fixated on the haunting image of a woman's face in my local newspaper. She is a mother, tormented by the unknown fate of her then, seventeen-year-old daughter who vanished ten years ago in Plymouth - a city not too far from me. Despite only vaguely recalling the initial news coverage, this recent black and white photograph grips me with its raw emotion. The mother's eyes are dark, sunken, and filled with an unending sorrow that resonates deep within my psyche.

I can't tear my gaze away from her desperate expression, feeling a strong urge to reach out and comfort her in some way. As I continue to study the image of this poor lost soul, a strange sensation begins to wash over me - a sense of connection and understanding that defies logic. It's almost as if I can feel her anguish and hear her silent cries for help. This inexplicable bond between us is familiar to me - my late grandmother possessed the same gift.

I can't imagine what pain and suffering she must be going through with the torment of fear and uncertainties surrounding her daughter's disappearance. I can read every detail of her face, but her widened eyes and that stare hook my interest. I can't stop thinking about her.

The more I concentrate and focus, the more intense my need to cry develops. I don't quite reach the point of tears, but the emotion is heavy and heartfelt. I feel it. I've read the article over and over and my emotions intensify with every read.

'Carol Cooke.'

Even when I say her name out loud, I get goosebumps all over my arms. In this article, she is pleading for her daughter to return home. I don't want to keep thinking the worst because she has mentioned sightings, but nothing more has come of it. No one knows if her daughter is dead or alive; I don't want to second guess it.

I rub my hand over the page whilst closing my eyes. I see flickers of light, all shades of colours, but most of all, it's as though I can feel a hard, heavy breath behind me. I wonder what ever happened to that girl, but all I see now is darkness. My heavy gut feeling makes me think I'm nervous, or maybe it's fear. If I was Carol, and my daughter had been missing for ten years, I don't think I could ever sleep at night until I knew where she was. I don't know how she copes.

'Are you at it again, Bren?' Alan disturbs my train of thought. I open my eyes and squint a little. My cup of tea is going cold on the table by the sofa. My husband is the only person who ever calls me Bren. He has this habit of shortening names.

'I thought you said you were going to watch the telly?'

'There's something about her I can't let go of. I can't stop thinking about her?'

'Who?' He asks. 'The girl or her mother?'

'Her mother, Carol.' I reply. 'It breaks my heart thinking about what she must be going through. All that love you must have for your child to lose them. Not knowing if she's dead or alive. I could cry for her.'

'You've always been oversensitive, Bren. Just let it go,' Alan replies. 'Teenagers run away from home all of the bloody time. What makes this one any different?'

'Those eyes.' I say, holding up the newspaper. 'Take a look at her. That distress?'

'I don't see anything in her face. It's black and white; you can barely make her out. It's not the best of images, and the print quality is shit.'

'I feel drawn to her,' I reply. 'She was in the paper last week too, but again today because someone thinks that they saw a recent sighting of her daughter out near our way. There was sighting reported in Salcombe.'

'I don't like to judge people, but sometimes when these kids run away from home, you never know what trauma they might have gone through. Bad parenting, schooling issues. Who knows what the hell was going on in that household?'

'I feel like it's something sinister. Something bigger than all of that.'

'Leave it for the police, Bren.' Alan shrugs his shoulders. 'Most kids from Plymouth who run away from home, don't come to Salcombe, do they? It's either London or further up north? I'm sure they'll find her. People can't hide forever.'

'She's not a kid anymore, Al.' I reply, irritated. 'Lauren Cooke would be about twenty-seven years old now. Ten years missing is a long time; she might even have kids of her own too. I'm surprised anyone would recognise her after all that time. We could have bumped into her if she's near us over the years.'

'I blame your grandmother for all of this, you know.' Alan

laughs at me. 'You and your gypsy heritage; you'll be knocking on all the neighbour's doors next with handfuls of heather.'

'I don't like it when you mock me.'

'It's only in jest; you know that Bren.'

'I have my beliefs. I know what I know. I feel what I feel, and I trust it. I trust that there is more to this life than just the end.'

'It's that energy thing again, isn't it?' He asks. 'You think we all get absorbed into the energy of the universe. If that's the case, how come you think you're getting messages from ghosts?'

'I don't talk to the dead, you know that.' I snap. 'I don't for one minute believe that dead people are trapped on this earth as ghosts, but I do believe in signs, and some things that happen can be more than just a coincidence. I feel things, even if I can't fully understand it.'

'Alright, I'm sorry if I offend you. But I believe in my views too.' Alan replies. 'There's no real evidence anywhere to support life after death. I believe more in science and everything that's real in front of my own two eyes. I'm not alone in my way of thinking.'

'I'm very spiritual. I can't help but feel connections. You know when you walk past someone and you get a vibe. It's like that for me, but I try to read into it further. I try to feel what kind of vibe, whether negative or positive. What energy is that person giving out? Then I get a sense of who they are, and I feel like I get to know people really easily too.' I explain. 'My grandmother said I've got the gift, just like she had, and I feel like I have some kind of spiritual connection, but I'm not in tune. It doesn't come as natural to me.'

'Drink your tea before it gets cold.' Alan dismisses me. 'I think it's all a load of crap. You know my thoughts on death. It's the end, and nothing else exists after it. We become nothing.'

'I'm going to the spiritualist church in Plymouth next Saturday. I've not been in a while.'

'If it's that one about higher thought, I won't be coming with you if you don't mind. It's definitely not my kind of place. Do you remember when I went that one time with you, God knows when. I hated it, it's not for me, Bren. Please, don't ask me to come with you.'

'I never expected you to put yourself out. I was only saying what I was planning. I'm curious, and I want to go back.'

'When was the last time you went?' He asks. 'Wasn't it after your grandmother passed away? I don't think I've heard you say you've been again since?'

I sip my tea, but it's already too cold. I pull a face to show how awful it tastes.

'Yes, just after Gran passed away. That's about thirty years ago.' I reply, not acknowledging his criticisms. 'I knew from their messages that she was with me that day. They told me things no one else could have known. When she took me to the fair, I tore a hole in my favourite pink dress. The medium could not have known that. She was precise with every detail. I believe in it, Al. I can't fully explain it, but there's something in it.'

Al is still doubting me, I can tell.

'I feel things. I sense things. I can't stop ignoring it now that I'm getting older. I'm convinced I could be putting it to good use. Making other people feel warm, trusted that after we die, there are other ways we exist.'

'Do you want me to make you another brew?' Al asks. 'Let's change the conversation, shall we? Plymouth is a small town, there's always someone who knows someone, and I wasn't convinced.'

'I know you don't believe anything about the afterlife.' I reply. 'But don't forget that we all live in this small world together that spins around a giant ball of fire. Somehow, we float in a universe of nothing, and I'm sure there's a lot more out there that we have no idea about. All our energy is absorbed into the universe; that's not a mystery. We do live on, but not in physical form.'

'I'll let you get back to staring at that newspaper now, Bren.'

'Gran used to tell me it was like fine-tuning a radio station. You meet some people and get a signal or a sign. Then you fine-tune into it until you're on the same wavelength. I never understood that until I got older myself. It's only recently that I've started feeling things. Things my Gran said would happen.'

Alan takes my mug before leaving the room. He sometimes mocks my spirituality, but we accept each other's views. My grandmother used to have the same criticism all of the time from people she knew too. Eventually, she gave up being a medium and focused on tarot cards. I grew up relatively poor in her care and never had the best of everything, but I never went without food, water and warm clothing. Gran wasn't very materialistic either, she never had savings, nor never owned anything of high value. Her words to me as a young girl was to live each day with happiness, forgiveness and an open mind.

'Never forget where you came from.' Gran would always remind me. 'Your Romany Gypsy heritage is in your blood. It will never leave you. Trust it. Trust yourself, and don't let others sway your instincts.'

For years she never charged for her tarot reading. I remember her card decks; she told me they were handed down to our family from our Italian relatives hundreds of years ago. The neighbours would always be over at the weekends where my Gran would tell them their fortunes and, in some instances, misfortunes.

It wasn't until word got around about Gran's talents that we would have random strangers knocking at our door with money. Often, these were women who had gone through relationship breakups, families who had lost loved ones, or their jobs, hoping to know what the future might hold.

Gran was deeply religious, a Christian who went to church every Sunday, but although I inherited my family's spiritual views, I've never felt very religious. I respect all religions and everyone's right to believe in what they want.

'Here, be careful; this one is boiling hot.' Alan puts a fresh cup of tea down beside me. 'Go on then, tell me what you're feeling. Is she dead or alive?'

'Lauren?'

'Yes, of course, I mean Lauren,' he says. 'The missing girl, what are all your instincts telling you about her?'

I feel a cold shiver down the back of my spine. I take a deep breath, only this time, it's not because of the arthritis in my knee.

'I can't call it, Al.'

It wasn't until I said it out loud that I felt a tear rolling down my cheek.

'What if she's dead?'

Al shakes his head and grabs the newspaper from my lap. He pulls open the pages and stares at the image of the mother.

'I don't like it when you get too invested in these things.' He says. 'You should keep your emotions for those dramas on the telly instead. You've got too much time on your hands. If she's dead, they'll find her eventually. If it's not the police, it'll be some poor dog walker, they're always found in the end, aren't they? In bushes or some rural marshland.'

I wipe my eyes with my sleeve. I'm shaking and emotional.

I want to find her.

Chapter Two

Monday, 5 June 2023
Brenda

The sun glares through the windows like a blinding spotlight, stinging my eyes as I try to make sense of it all. The missing girl consumes every thought, keeping me awake all night with her haunting presence. How is it possible that she's been sighted in my quiet little town of Salcombe? I would have noticed her by now, wouldn't I? But none of the locals are talking, and it's driving me mad. Why haven't the police taken action, knocking on doors and searching for her? And if she's really here, why is she not coming forward, revealing herself and demanding to be found? The puzzle pieces don't fit together, and it's eating away at my sanity.

Al was right; we talked over breakfast, and I admitted I have been obsessing about her and focussing on the situation too much. She's not my daughter. I don't know her mother, although I hope and pray that she's found, but I need to move on from that family's situation. I feel torn over it, like I know that family's situation is nothing to do with me, but it's like I have no choice over the thoughts in my head. I try to shut them out, but they return, time and time again.

I should go back to the Spiritualist church in Plymouth and talk about what I've been thinking and feeling there with my thoughts. Address what's going on in my own head before I worry about other people. The only explanation I can think of was that seeing that missing girl, gave me a calling. I connected with it in ways that I can't fully explain or reason in my own head yet. If my Gran were alive, she'd help me with my understanding, but I also have that niggling doubt. Am I being stupid? Do I need to take up a new hobby to occupy myself. Is it all down to boredom?

'I need a sign. Anything?' I say out loud as if there's someone who can hear me. Maybe there is, maybe there isn't, but I believe in signs. 'Where are you, Lauren? What happened to you? I feel like you're in my head all the time. Please come through.'

I stopped still in my tracks, unsure what I was waiting for, but there was nothing. I look around, and the world around me is as busy as ever. A sign that life moves on.

I've strolled along the seafront to clear my mind and to catch the sunrise before I begin my cleaning shift at Southleigh Holiday Cottages. I've taken my medication and my antihistamines. I'm raring to go.

I sip my bottled water because I'm trying to reduce my caffeine intake; my bladder can't tolerate it. I'm at that age where it all starts to go downhill, so I've been told. I still feel like I'm in my twenties, but my body tells me otherwise.

'Sixty is the new forty,' they tell me at work. I'm the oldest cleaner there. 'You don't look a day over fifty, Brenda.'

'These creaky old knees of mine will tell you otherwise.' I joke. 'And sometimes I'm up twice in the night to pee. You'll know what I mean when you get there. It'll come to us all.'

CHAPTER TWO

The news channel correctly forecasted the weather to be glorious today, with a very high pollen count. I love the sunny weather this time of year, but I hate sneezing constantly with my hay fever.

I stroll past the picturesque harbour. I always smile when I walk here because I appreciate the beauty of where I live. Salcombe is a small idyllic little coastal town nestled on the Kingsbridge estuary. There's something magical about sitting on the benches here, the sun beaming down on your face, and fishermen working from their boats. Many tourists go out on little fishing trips. It's always been a quaint little community for those that live here all year round. I couldn't imagine living anywhere else now. My own little heaven.

I take a slow walk beyond Little Cove Beach, facing the small uphill struggle to the holiday cottages via a small lane. I've not had arthritis for long, but it feels like someone is stabbing my knee with a sharp pen. I get a sensation constantly that I need to click it. I can manage my walking with constant starting and stops. I used to get frustrated, but it's now part of who I am. It's not getting any better, but it's not getting any worse, either.

I've given up driving since I received my bus pass early on medical grounds; the only perk to being sixty. I'm not quite state pension age, but I took an early retirement pension package from my old workplace, which helps. It's not quite the same as having the freedom I used to have since I now rely on the local bus service, but I can manage my day around it.

I stand at the entrance to Southleigh Holiday Cottages, waving at some of the guests who have decided to leave early. If it weren't Al's day off, he'd have dropped me here himself. He's been a maintenance worker for years now on this site, but he volunteered to pick me up when I'm finished today. He deserves his rest, my turn tomorrow for a lie in.

I'm sure those guests recognised me from when they arrived last Friday. I hope they've done their dishes, cleaned their kitchens, or stripped their bedding. Any little thing that saves me some time in this heat will help me today.

This time of year, these cottages are always fully booked with all the Londoners and northerners travelling down to Devon. I dread cleaning today because of the heat, but it keeps me busy since I'd only be bored at home. I'm not the kind of woman who wants to take up knitting or cake baking for a hobby.

Around thirty cottages of varied sizes are scattered across the holiday park. Some sleep only two, and some sleep up to sixteen people. They must make some serious money here when I see how much they charge online. I don't know who has that sort of money. I bet the guests don't realise how little the cleaners get.

This site was once some old farmland until the land was sold by the daughter of the farmers that used to operate in this locality. There were many protests that day; I was at one of them too, standing there with my sign opposing the development, but now working here tops up my pension. I'd be bored if I were sat at home with nothing to do every day of the week. It makes me feel such a hypocrite at times, but now that I can see the boost to the local businesses, and all the extra families that get to enjoy the beauty of Salcombe, I don't mind anymore.

It does get quite lonely here in the Winter months when all the second homeowners and the holidaymakers stay away. Shops close, the bus services reduce, and around forty per cent of the town remains here during those dark, cold nights. No one barely goes out. A few young families live here, but not many. It's not quite retirement central, either. Salcombe can be a warming, energetic, activity filled place in the height of the season. It's a dystopian looking, derelict world when the leaves start to fall from the trees in the Autumn months.

I wave at John at the reception desk as I walk past the window; he's busy with welcome packs but smiles and nods back. The housekeeping building is right down the far end of the site, but I'm almost there. I hear those who have arrived before me laughing whilst a few others are standing outside holding their buckets.

'Have I missed something funny?' I ask Liz; she's grinning and listening to the others. 'Can't be having that much fun on a Monday morning?'

'No, nothing. It's nothing much.'

'Well, everyone else is laughing?' I reply.

'No, you know what I'm like. Just a nervous laugh.'

I walk on through to housekeeping, and bunches of keys sit on the housekeeping manager's desk. I don't always see eye to eye with Tina, but she talks to me at times like my whole career as a civil servant before I took early retirement was non existent, and I have no idea how to change bedding properly or clean for the sixty years I've been alive.

'Morning, Tina.' I say, as the whole room goes silent. 'Are any of those keys for me?'

'Morning, Brenda. Good weekend?'

'Not bad. The usual. You know, telly and a good book. Thought about going to the car boot sale in Kingsbridge on Sunday but never got round to it.'

'Oh, I have put you on Kingfisher Cottage this morning. The guests checked out late last night, and the new arrival has called to say they would like to check in early. We're treating this one like it's a VIP.'

'Who is it?' I ask. 'A celebrity?'

'Something like that,' Tina replies. 'No, not really, but if you could you treat it like a deep spring clean would be great. Give it a bit of extra attention. You'll have fewer keys, but it'll not affect your wages. Don't worry.'

'It's no problem for me. I don't mind at all. I'll grab my little hoover, and away I'll go.'

'Thank you.'

As I leave the housekeeping yard, I hear the other women talking about me behind my back.

'Do you reckon her spirit friends will help her clean today?'

'Shh, she'll hear you from outside.'

'At least she isn't carrying that crystal round her neck this week.'

It doesn't bother me; I've heard it all before. Part of me wanted to turn around and remind them that negativity breeds negativity. If they don't believe that there's an afterlife, I respect their choice, but I wish some people would respect my views too. THAT crystal belonged to my gran; it has so much sentimental value. Whenever I hold it, I think of her and how much love she gave me during difficult times. I'm connected to her when I hold it, this crystal has been passed down mother to daughter for centuries.

Growing up in the sixties without a mother or father wasn't easy for me. Gran used to take me to school on her own every day and back again. The other children in the class would call me the girl who lived with the witch. She was known for being quite open with her spiritualist views, more-so than I am. She was known for talking to voices that she heard in her ears.

CHAPTER TWO

'They're only little whispers.' She'd tell me. 'I have to listen hard and clear my thoughts away for them to come through.'

I've never heard whispers or seen a ghost, but with me, it's an intuition I can't describe. I have gut feelings and many coincidences that I can't ignore. It's as though someone out there is looking after me. I can't see them, I can't hear them, but I know they are there. I feel guided by an unexplainable presence at times.

Maybe it's the spirit of my mother for feeling guilty that she walked out on my father and me when I was two years old. My father then developed depression, and my grandparents looked after me. At the same time, he continued to drink himself stupidly. I was told he killed himself with an overdose. I have vague flashback memories of him, but nothing substantial enough to invoke any reminiscent pleasant memories. I was only two, nearly three, when he died. I never did know what happened to my mother; she could still be alive now for all I know. She'd be well into her eighties, but I don't intend to fix all that lost time.

My gran hid her emotions well, she put all of her energy into nurturing me and watching me grow, that by my late teens we never talked about my mother anymore. I think we both accepted that she'd cut all of us out of her life and there was no point going over it. She was a firm believer in focussing on the future.

'It's all about tomorrow,' she'd say. 'No point talking about yesterday, that was then.'

My mother made her choice and abandoned me. There's nothing I can do or say to change that. Life can be cruel at times.

Chapter Three

Monday, 5 June 2023
Carol

The mere thought of travelling on days when my mind and heart are at odds with each other makes my stomach churn with dread. My fears, anxieties, and desperate hopes merge together, creating a roller-coaster of emotions that leaves me on edge. Every breath I take is a struggle as we try to hold onto the flickering flame of hope that Lauren is out there somewhere. I cling to Darren's words because he is constantly reminding me to never give up on finding her.

'Darren, are you ready? We should have left the house about an hour ago.'

No response, which does my flipping head in. Typical bloke, probably looking for his car keys. I know where I last saw them, so I'm bracing myself for the questions.

'Darren?'

'What?'

'We got to get a move on. Hurry the fuck up, will you?'

A few thuds down the stairs, Darren enters the kitchen holding out an old sports bag. It doesn't even look full. I knew I should have packed for him.

CHAPTER THREE

'Is that it?' I ask, but he looks vague. 'You have managed to fit four days worth of clothes in that little sports bag?'

'It's enough. It's only a few days ain't it? I can wear the same jeans more than once. It's only really boxers and t-shirts.'

'But what if it rains?'

'It's not going to rain; I've checked the weather app on my phone. It'll be fine. Trust me.' He smiles.

'You always ask me to trust you?' I joke. 'I trust that you don't consider all possibilities.'

I lean in close to Darren and stroke his arm. We are embracing each other for a cuddle, and I rest my head on his shoulder. He's almost a foot taller than me.

'What if this time we really do find her?'

Darren pats my back, pulls away and looks me right in the eyes.

'Then we will tell her how sorry we are.' He replies. 'Sorry for not listening if she needed help. Sorry for those times she couldn't talk to us about what was going on in that head of hers. Sorry for not being the parents she wanted, but we will spend the rest of our lives making it up to her.'

'Do you think that sighting of her near Salcombe was real?' I ask, taking a breath. 'I wondered if she might be working out there. It would be awful to thinks that after all this time she was right under our noses and not that far away from home.'

'I don't know. There's been a few people on and off over the years claiming to have seen our little girl, hasn't there, but more than one recently out that way. I guess we can only go and find out for ourselves.'

'Do you think she is still alive?' I ask, holding back my emotions. 'Or do you think she's, you know. Dead somewhere?'

Darren lets go of me, turns his head away, and we aren't even looking at each other.

'I've told you before not to do this.' He shouts. 'We will find her. Of course she's alive. Don't ask such stupid fucking questions. This is our daughter you're talking about, not next doors fucking cat. You remember what we said all those years ago? She's not dead until they tell us she's dead.'

He's shaking, but I know he's holding back more of his emotions too. I'm calm, but it's a miracle I never had a breakdown. The inner emotional strength and resilience I have to conjure up sometimes to get through the day makes me so lethargic. I have to be strong for my family.

'Our little girl is out there. I don't know where, but she's out there somewhere. It's the guilt that upsets me. All the questions I ask myself why she couldn't speak to us.' Darren says through his tears. 'Every day, I think about her and what must have been going through her mind to run away from home. I don't know if it was all those times back then I worked away from home or was there a time I shouted at her. I blame myself, but I will never ever believe that she's dead. Not our little girl.'

'I know, I know.' I say, trying to comfort him. 'I'm not giving up hope either.'

'If we ever believe that our own daughter is dead, then we've given up on her, haven't we?'

'Come on, let's make a move. Get out and away from here for a few days if nothing else comes of it.' I reply. 'I called the holiday park early this morning, and they've agreed we can get in our cottage early. They're going to prioritise it for cleaning. I don't want to waste time, so we'll head to Little Cove later. Lauren might be working in one of the restaurants, or someone might recognise her. I've put some old pics we took on the tablet device. It's in my bag with the charger.'

'I already feel like a failure.' Darren explains. Head in his hands. 'I failed her as a dad. Why couldn't she have left a note or made some kind of contact? Sometimes I get angry that she could walk out of that door and leave us like this, knowing nothing.'

'Darren.' I say firmly. 'There could be a million different reasons. She could have met someone and fell in love. Or something was going on she never told us about. Whatever made her runaway from home, and never so much as phone, text, or email. I hope we find out one day. She obviously had her reasons.'

I walk closer to Darren as he's pacing the kitchen.

'All I want her to know is how much we love her.' I reply. 'Whatever happened in the past is in the past. When we see our daughter again soon. She will know just how much we love her. I miss her so much.'

Darren pulls himself closer towards me, and together we sob. I didn't want to cry, but our emotions are running high.

I've been dreading this trip because as much as I am a mother with a missing daughter, I have had to rebuild my life whilst trying not to crumble and succumb to depression. There were days I was angry with her, and other days angry with myself.

Although he doesn't talk about his sister anymore. We have a son, Kieran. He didn't have the best years growing up after Lauren went missing. He went off the rails, got involved in drugs, and most of his mates ended up in prison. Others moved away, but I'm thankful that Kieran managed to turn his life around since he got an apprenticeship with a firm of builders. He's a plasterer by trade now and earning a decent wage living in his own rented flat with his new girlfriend. I don't see him as much as I used to, but he's got his own life, and we couldn't be prouder of him.

I drag my small suitcase to the car whilst Darren carries his sports bag. I glance back at the house and remember the days when both of my kids lived here. The place felt alive and vibrant, with two teenagers causing chaos. Lauren would have her music on way too loud, and Kieran would be a nightmare to get off his video games. We laughed, cried, had arguments, had trips out, went shopping, shopped online, and were a family. Now Darren and I exist in the remnants of a former life with nothing but memories to keep us going every day.

St Budeaux isn't any picturesque village. Locals call it a concrete jungle and although the crime rate is high, our little street is a community in its own right. The police might not support us or take us seriously, the local council may have abandoned us and treat us all with the same contempt, but we survive in this area with what little money we have. We look out for one another.

Our house is now solemn and empty; it needs decorating. Lauren's room is exactly as she left it. I felt close to her in that room when she left. It still has posters of her favourite bands on the wall, the same bedding, and all her clothes in the wardrobe. Some days I go in there and shut the door to try and smell her. Neither of us can bring ourselves to pack away her belongings, but I've cried myself to sleep countless times on her bed, clutching hold of the teddies she still kept that I got her when she was a small child. We often took the kids to Paignton arcades. She loved those claw crane machines and the countless near misses.

Nothing has changed in the ten years since Laurens disappearance. Our marriage almost never survived, but we endured

CHAPTER THREE

some problematic years together.

'Do you remember how much grief we gave the housing association when they asked us if we wanted to downsize and move away to a smaller house?' I ask Darren as we place our belongings in the boot.

'I'll never forget it.' He replies. 'I don't think I ever swore so much in my entire life. Why would we want to give up the house where we created so many family memories together. It's also the last known place Lauren can try to reach us. I will never leave here. Not unless we find her.'

'Nor me.' I reply with a smile. 'This is our home. Always has been, and it always will be. I know this street is frowned upon because, let's face it, it's not the best of places to live in Plymouth. The crime we've witnessed, the drug problem with the teens, the constant loud music in the Summer, but it's still our home.'

'I love you.' Darren says. 'You've been my rock.'

'I love you too.' I reply. 'Now let's go and head to our little cottage. I've also got the small posters I printed of Lauren in my case. Hopefully, some of the shops out that way will put them in the window.'

'You never know. I'm sure they will.'

The car engine starts, and I look out of the passenger window. I take a few deep breaths to steady my anxiety, but we're off.

Salcombe, here we come.

Chapter Four

Ten Years Ago
Carol

The fear, nausea and panic are so overwhelming I'm convinced I'm going to pass out. My hands are shaking, and I keep shivering as if I've come down with a nasty bout of flu. My nerves in tatters and my head is a confused mess of emotions.

I've opened the windows to let some air in, I can't breathe. Darren keeps pacing up and down the floor, looking out the window, then opening the front door and walking up and down the street. He keeps wanting to drive to look for her, but he's had too much to drink. He won't listen to a word I say.

'She can't be at her friend's house, can she? This isn't like her at all. Where the fuck is she Carol. You're lying to me, aren't you?' Darren shouts, his face in mine, the smell of beer pungent as he talks. 'She's met some filthy boy hasn't she. She's at some lad's house being taken advantage of, isn't she?'

'She's seventeen, she's nearly an adult. We should start to treat her like one.' I reply, knowing he won't like it, but it's true. She isn't a child. 'I don't know where she is. I honestly don't know. I'm not lying to you. I'm not keeping anything from you, either. She was in her room and now she's not.'

CHAPTER FOUR

'We need to ring the police.' He snaps, gritting his teeth. 'You better not be lying to me because if I ring the cops and you have known all along where she is, making me look and sound a right twat; I won't be impressed.'

'I don't know what to do.' I shout. 'I'm her mother and I don't know what to do. She's not been gone twenty-four hours yet, you know that. We need to wait, she's not a child, Darren. She's not a kid anymore.'

The tension and stress has me bursting into tears. I'm tired, drained, emotional and yes, I'm her mother, but he treats her like she's an infant. I called all the friends I know, we've been through her bedroom to see if she was hiding anything, but nothing. No one has seen her.

The door knocks hard, twice. We both run to answer it as fast as we can, banging into each other on the way out to the hallway. Darren beats me and opens the door to be greeted by Kirsty, who lives next door.

'Everything alright, we heard shouting?' She asks. Which is odd because we do have the occasional row, but we've been more tense than ever with Luke being on his deathbed. 'I saw your lights were on, and I was worried.'

I was waiting for Darren's aggressive reply, but he is good friends with her husband, Tony.

'No, everything's ok, you know.' He replies, more polite than I expected. 'Lauren's gone missing. We've not seen her since dinner time. No reply on her phone, no message, no one's seen her. Not a thing.'

'I saw her this afternoon.' Kirsty replies, looking surprised. 'She was getting out of the car with you, Carol. She looked well and truly pissed off though. Normally she's all smiles isn't she. She looked absolutely upset.'

'It's Darren's brother. Luke.' I reply, 'he's got cancer. It's not good news.'

'Oh, I'm so sorry.' She replies and gives that solemn look the nurses throw at us when they see me. 'I didn't know.'

'I'm sure I told Tony, you know.' Darren pipes in. 'But if you see her, or here anything of her can you let us know?

Kirsty assured us she would and returned to her own house. Darren doesn't seem as tense as before and all the mud is still around the house. It's dried in now, but I'll have to deal with that another time. I can barely think straight now, let alone clean the house. If he moans at me, it was all his fault anyway, and I'll tell him to clean his own mess. I'm sick of doing everything.

Darren grabs another beer from the fridge, one for both of us. I open it to be polite, but I don't really want any. He watches me take the first sip before he drinks his own. For a few minutes neither of us say a word to each other. He checks his phone, I check mine. It's dark outside, it's cold and I'm scared, worried and tense.

'What time was Kieran meant to be back from his mates house again?' Darren asks, even though I've told him multiple times already. 'Where's my boy, gone. Has he upped and fucking left us too? I've not seen one of my kids at all today, not once.'

'I called him to see if he's ok to stay over at his mate's house. He put me on to his mate's mother, and it's fine. They'll be all night on their games console.' I reply, explaining it all over again. 'He hasn't left too. It's better under the circumstances until we know where Lauren is, that he stays at his mates tonight. He's worried, but thinks she'll come back soon. I'd already asked if he heard anything, and he didn't either.'

CHAPTER FOUR

I can tell he's drunk now by the way he's walking and talking. I'm always the level-headed one, the one in our marriage trying to keep this family together.

'Maybe she's gone out with her friends and ran out of battery.' I suggest, 'or, maybe she's been drinking. Do you remember what it was like at her age, I was always over my best friend's house, sneaking some cider?'

'She isn't anything like you, is she? She doesn't even drink. Kieran on the other hand, I caught him red handed the little prick at times.' He snaps, I shut up and don't maintain eye contact. 'If she was anything like you, she'd be out cleaning some toilets, wouldn't she?'

I forgive him because he's angry. I don't rise to the bait because I will end up worse off. He will calm down soon, I hope. He isn't thinking straight, and he loves her. I love her too, and he isn't thinking about me and my emotions. He doesn't care about how I feel. I'm lonely at times, but I know this will pass and he'll be himself in the morning.

'It's nearly midnight. This isn't right is it. I don't know how long we can keep looking out of the windows. I'm sick of walking up and down that street.' Darren announces, 'if you don't ring the police, I'll do it myself. Shall we do it?'

'You do it. I can't. I'm too emotional, I'd be a mess.' I reply, holding up my hands showing him they're trembling. 'I can't speak to them, you tell them. I want to hold out hope that she will contact us soon. This isn't like her, but I keep thinking, she's not a child anymore. Maybe give her some space?'

There's a tight feeling in my throat; I'm struggling to swallow my saliva as the panic is getting stronger. The thought of the police being involved, the reality of Lauren being a missing person and the neighbours all wanting to get involved.

I've seen these things on the television, this can't be my life. It can't be our reality.

'I bet it's that fucking lad who wanted a job, who I told where to get off.' Darren says, pulling out his phone. 'I'll fucking kill him. And her, for putting me through this stress.'

Darren stumbles, swigging his beer.

'Lauren, it's Dad, again. Come home, you're not in any trouble.' He says on her voicemail. 'I love you. Here's your mother. Carol, tell her you love her too.'

'I love you too, love.' I shout across the room. 'Come home, please. We are worried sick as you can tell.'

I feel sick to my stomach, so sick that I've had to sit down. Tears streaming down my eyes as Darren hangs up the phone.

'Something bad has happened, hasn't it?' I say, worried, 'I wish she'd come home. I don't know what to do. How do people cope? Who do we speak to?'

'Hello. Police, please. I'd like to report a missing person.' Darren says, he's dialled the emergency services. 'It's my daughter, Lauren Cooke. She's vanished.'

I listen as Darren explains the best he can what happened. I know she had her mobile phone on her, we called the hospital already and gave a description. My mind has gone blank and all I do is stare and listen to Darren's every word. He's making more sense than I would.

'They're going to get someone to call us back, it might be a few hours.' He says after hanging up the phone. 'They're assessing the level of risk, but because she's seventeen, no mental health issues that we are aware of, it's been around six hours since we said last contact. I don't think it's urgent.'

'I knew it.' I reply. 'A different story if she was six or seven, but at seventeen they expect it don't they. Teens go out all the time. Maybe we should stay calm and think about reasonable explanations to where she could have gone.'

Darren glances at me but doesn't say a word. He's looking at me, oddly.

'What?' I ask, 'what is it?'

'Someone from the local police station will call us back soon. It may take a few hours whilst they allocate an officer.' He says, 'they are taking it seriously, but it's not high risk. I gave them her phone number, maybe they're looking into where it was seen.'

'I'm too worried to think straight.' I reply, tired, hungry, unable to have eaten dinner due to the stress. 'I hope they can find her.'

'They will find her. Of course they will.' He snaps at me again. I know he blames me. He blames me for everything. 'Why the fuck wouldn't they. They have all kinds of technology out now, don't they?'

'Do you want anything to eat?' I ask, changing the subject, not wanting to think about anything other than Lauren. 'Those fish and chips are burnt to a crisp, cold now. I should bin them. I can make you a sandwich if you like?'

Darren shakes his head, puts a hand over his face and starts to cry. I've not seen him cry in years since we had to have our little Jack Russell put down.

'Don't say it. Don't you dare.' I say, emotional and crying too. 'Don't Darren, I mean it.'

Darren wipes his eyes and comes over to comfort me. He wraps his arms around me, and we stand here in the middle of the living room embraced in our fear and emotions.

'She not dead. It's only been six hours and look at us.' I say, 'I'm a quivery wreck, you're crying. When she comes through that door, she better have a good explanation.'

'I wasn't going to say she was dead.' He replies, stepping away from me, now crossing his arms. 'No chance do I think our girl is dead. I'd never think that. I was about to say, what if she's pregnant and ran away with that fucking lad.'

We're both startled as the phone rings. Darren answers it immediately and it's the police again.

They're sending someone round to the house. I get an immediate panic and stumble with the shock. What if she is pregnant?

I hadn't noticed any changes in her behaviours or who she was hanging around with after school. Lauren was very normal in that sense, she's sensible, hardly talked about who she fancied as she's always been quite shy.

No, she can't be pregnant, if she wasn't a virgin, I'm sure she'd tell me at least I am her mother, we have had those conversations. I even bought her condoms when she was sixteen just in case. Darren flew off the handle, as you'd expect an overbearing father, but its better that than not have them.

'She's going to have sex one day, Darren.' I'd told him whilst she was out of earshot. We'd given her the necklace she loved and wanted, as well some cash to buy herself something nice. 'I want her to know that we're ok with that, she's growing up into a young woman.'

He hasn't spoke about it again from that day to this.

Chapter Five

Monday, 5 June 2023
Carol

For most of the long drive from Plymouth to Salcombe, neither Darren nor I spoke to each other, except for when we stopped off for a quick coffee at a local service station. The prices were extortionate, but we had no choice. It's that or take the free tap water.

It had taken us just over an hour through the countryside and through many narrow back lanes, but we had the radio on for most of that time to distract us.

It's been a morning of mixed emotions; happy one minute, smiles the next, and almost a different reality as though we haven't had an awful past, then occasionally the reminder of why we are travelling seeps in. This isn't a holiday for either of us.

We have a few moments of awkward silence and occasional laughter, then is followed by an overwhelming sense of guilt. It doesn't feel natural to have fun when everyone knows my daughter has vanished. The sadness that follows a flicker of normality is my punishment. I question myself and what others might think of me every time someone catches me smile.

I don't often feel like the old me. I'm not allowed happiness; otherwise, what will people think?

'It didn't feel like we'd been on the road all that long, did it?' I ask Darren, who turns to face me. 'I wonder what the next four days will bring, don't you? I hope the weather is decent at least.'

'I really want to see our little girl again.' Darren replies, 'her disappearance has left nothing but a gaping black hole in our lives. Don't you think?'

'I do, too. No one else really knows how we feel, do they. Unless they've gone through this pain themselves. I wouldn't wish it on my worst enemy.' I reply, 'I'm scared I might not even recognise her beautiful face if I see her again. Ten whole years is a long time to be away from home. She could have changed so much in that time. Changed her hair, her dress sense, I wonder?'

'You're her mother, of course you'd recognise her. Don't be so fucking daft.' Darren snaps at me. 'You don't half talk some shit at times, you. I'd recognise my own daughter anywhere, anytime. I'll never forget how my little girl looks. Not once. I don't believe for one minute that you'd walk past her and not know that was her.'

Darren turns off the radio, and I sense an atmosphere in the car. We're parked on a small side road, looking straight at a sign that says Welcome to Salcombe. I don't want another row, another talking to, another day of explaining how I feel. All that makes me so fatigued and fed up, as always. I wish he'd just let it go.

I peer to the left of me and take in the vast green countryside filled with hills, sunshine, and steep valleys. It feels a million miles away from home because we live in what would best be described as an urban concrete jungle. We live from one payday to the next, trying to make ends meet and whilst giving our kids the best we could afford. To have lived anywhere like this would be heaven in comparison; it really is like visiting a different country.

'Feels like we're visiting a whole different planet here in this little remote part of Devon, doesn't it? Can you smell how much cleaner the air is out this way?' I say, 'I bet everyone says that when they drive out here. So close too on our own doorstep, we never venture out of Plymouth much.'

'I'm still looking at the map on my phone, trying to find the best route to the holiday park.' Darren replies. 'What was it called again? South something or other, wasn't it?'

'It's called, Southleigh Cottages. You must have heard me talking about it and saying it all week.' I reply. 'We can't be much further away now. Salcombe is only meant to be a small little place. This map on my phone makes it look as big as London.'

Darren pulls out his phone, and I glance in his direction as he uses the search function on his map app. As he scrolls and zooms in. The sun has reached the perfect point where it shines and reflects on his face. I admire his ruggedness, and I love him so much. Despite the circumstances from all those years ago, I know he loves me, I know I am his world, but he doesn't half look like his brother at times.

We both met each other when we were in our early twenties; he was the friend of an old neighbour I've since lost touch with. Apart from the noticeable frown lines and the hint of grey in his stubble, some slightly thinning hair, he's not changed all that much.

'Do you remember when we first met?'

Darren rests his mobile phone on his knee.

'You mean that time I fell over your shoes when I was pissed in the pub. I fell flat on my arse, and you laughed at me.' He says, grinning to himself. 'Blimey, that was so long ago now, and at least I can handle my drink better as I've gotten older.'

We both laugh, but I know he means it.

'You make it sound like we're in our seventies.' I joke, 'we aren't quite drawing our pension, yet.'

He really believes he can handle his drink better. I don't feel comfortable telling him any different. Those mood swings, the temper and aggressive remarks, all forgotten memories every time. He's dealing with it, the best he knows how. I am too.

'Yes, but don't you feel like we've both aged a million years since then?'

'Well, it is coming up thirty years now, isn't it?'

Darren takes my hand.

'I love you so much. But who the hell takes their heels off in the pub and leaves them where anyone could trip over them.' He says. 'That's a massive health and safety hazard if ever there was one.'

'Those heels found me a husband.' I reply, looking into his eyes. 'They did their job.'

We both laugh again. I've never been a fan of high heels, and I remember my feet killing me that day. I wasn't even meant to be at the pub, but my neighbour had dragged me out because she didn't want to go alone. I strongly believe in fate and that I was meant to meet Darren that day. Something just aligned in our worlds to make it happen and for us to be together. I have no idea what happened to those shoes. They were patent black leather, but I probably threw them out soon after.

'I love you too.' I reply. 'I know we've had our moments, but

CHAPTER FIVE

I couldn't imagine ever sharing my life with anyone else.'

'Good.' Darren says. 'I'd kill him. And you know I mean it.'

I smile, of course I know that he means it. He can't go anywhere without a fight.

Darren put his phone back in his pocket, started the car, and we took a short drive down another set of country lanes. I feel like this is some kind of fresh start, knowing that when I return home in the next few days, life might change.

'We're not lost, are we?' I ask, 'I'm sure it wasn't as rural as this in the pics I saw online. Do you know where we are, or where we should be at least?'

'It's the right direction, trust me. It's definitely the right route. We should almost be there.' Darren snaps. 'You don't need to question my organisational skills when it comes to travelling. Just trust me and shut up.'

A minute later, the Southleigh Cottages sign came into view. 'At last. We're here.'

I take a deep sigh, another one of those moments when I'm reminded about Lauren and why we are here. I glance at Darren, and hope he behaves himself on this break.

My stomach is in knots because I know at some point on this trip, I will always have to explain to people that we are the family with the missing daughter. Everyone will look at us with their sad expressions, but no one can understand what it feels like unless it happens to them. I wouldn't wish these emotions I feel at times on anyone and explaining everything opens old mental wounds.

'Do you know what number cottage we are?' Darren asks. 'We could park the car straight outside, maybe even drop our bags in, then head off down the pub?'

'They didn't put it on the email I got back. I've got no idea, but I'm sure that reception will know; they must have allocated one for our early check-in. I'll ask them if you want to stay in the car. I know you hate doing all the talking and what-not. I don't mind showing my face in there.'

'Thanks. You're shaking? Look at you, are you alright?'

'It's because I have to do that thing. I hate doing that thing.' I explain. 'It makes me on edge.'

'What thing?'

'That moment when I stand there and explain, I'm THAT woman with the missing daughter.' As if he doesn't know. 'Everyone then treats you differently. They look at me with sadness, pity. They give me a look that I absolutely hate and it takes me right back there, right back to the day she vanished.'

'I can do it if you want me to, and you stay in the car?'

'No, I said I'd go in. I'll get it over with.' I say. 'I'll go now and you just wait here with the car and bags.'

There was a row of empty parking spaces outside the reception hut. I'm not sure what I expected, but the site itself was smaller than I had imagined. There are rows of cottages, some bigger than others but very close to each other. I look around, and there's a sense of busyness. Families putting their kids and dogs in cars, staff wandering around.

I hear the slam of a car door; it startles me. I jump slightly because I'm always on the edge of my nerves.

'We'll do it together. I'll come in with you.' Darren says, 'I wonder if Lauren has ever been here? She might have even worked here once, it's quite remote.'

'You never know.' I reply. 'She was meant to have been spotted down near the fishing port. Where all the bars and restaurants are. I can't imagine her as a waitress though, can you? She hated doing as she was told.'

'I know, but she might not have had any choice if she wants money to live on. I wonder what she's doing right now. I have a good feeling about our time here. If our little girl is in the area, we will find her. I know we will.'

'Me too.' I reply, taking Darren's hand. 'Let's go get our cottage key and see what home will look like for the next few days.'

I'm not feeling very much in the best of moods today because I'm apprehensive and nervous about our time together. We will be stepping out into an environment where I know I will be handing out leaflets for the next four days, explaining who we are, and talking about Lauren. Then will come the issues I have with Darren, and all the explaining. It takes me back to the day Lauren left. The most distressing day of our lives, and that's all before Darren hits the pub.

It's going to be a difficult few days.

Chapter Six

Monday, 5 June 2023
Brenda

The state of cleanliness in this cottage when I got inside was shocking. Not one single pot or pan had been cleaned by the last filthy guests, and the kitchen was stinking of old bacon fat. Rubbish left all over the floor, mud up the walls, it's a right state. They never think of leaving it in the same condition they found these cottages. It's the same every year as we approach summer and the kids aren't even off school yet.

I always aim to clean each cottage with the same standards I maintain in my home, but I never feel appreciated for it. Every time the supervisors complain about how slow I am, I remind them that it's quality, not quantity. They've hardly ever had any complaints with my cleaning, not that I get much thanks. This holiday park treats us all like dirt sometimes, but without cleaners, they'd never get away with charging the prices they do to stay here. A bit of appreciation now and then wouldn't go amiss.

How difficult is a thank you now and then? I've never even had a bonus, in all honesty, Al doesn't even know why I still work here, and I'm sick of explaining that it gets me out of the house. I get to meet people, talk to people. I feel energised, more positive and healthier for it.

It looked like a family of four had been staying here for a week, looking at all the beds they've used. I bet Tina gave me this one on purpose. She knows what she's doing that one. I'm not stupid, she wants rid of me by trying to make it as difficult as possible. She won't win. I'll do my best to get it as clean as possible, and I'll stand there and smile when the next customer puts in their cleanliness report.

I'm nearly done; only the living room to go through, and then I'll make up the double bed. I'm exhausted. I need to sit down for a minute to stop my dizzy spells. Between that and the arthritis pain in my knee, I don't know why I put myself through this cleaning torture.

One of my biggest fears about slowing down in my later life is that I'll seize up altogether and end up housebound. I can't imagine Al looking after me; he can just about look after himself. He says I nag him enough as it is. I have this motto of use it or lose it. I don't want to lose my mobility, so I convince myself some days that the pain is worth it. I have to keep on moving these knees of mine, I'm not old yet.

I see a woman walking towards the car park in the distance through the living room window. It's her. I'm in awe, and shock, and can't believe my eyes, but it's definitely her.

I know exactly who she is and I'm overjoyed to the point where I am a little bit tearful. I look again, and my jaw has dropped to the floor as I see Carol Cooke walking out of the reception building with a man, who I am presuming is her husband, waiting for her. It's definitely them. I wasn't expecting this today, but here they are. In my sight and on my place of work.

My mind is being flooded with the image of their daughter, Lauren. I can't get that newspaper picture out of my head either. I want to run at her and ask a million questions, but I'll find out from reception why they are here.

Is this some kind of sign?

'Is someone trying to communicate with me?' I ask, looking upwards, analysing my feelings to see if they are mine. 'Is anyone there? Did you bring her to me, is this for real?'

Nothing but silence. I think about my emotions and the aura of the room. Still nothing to go on. I can't believe that she is here.

I'm fixated on Carol, and she hasn't even seen me. I can't stop staring at her, and my heart is racing. I don't even know what I'm feeling. It's a mixture of anxiety, happiness, and excitement, but the one that hits me the most is nausea. I feel really sick to my stomach with nerves now. That emotion has overpowered the others because I might have an opportunity to meet her.

Over the last few months, I've been trying to connect with the gift my grandmother always said was in my blood. I know I should go back to the Spiritualist Church, and I did ask for a sign, so maybe this is exactly the sign I needed. Fate has had its way and put us in the same location. It must be a sign because every time I look at that poor young girls face in the paper; I feel a connection to the case. I want to find her, I want to know where she is and help that family.

Life was always the same routine until I retired from my old job. Get up, go to work, make it through the day trying to balance a marriage, and my own well-being, watch the television, make dinner, go to bed. Life is full of routines, and although I have strong beliefs in spiritualism, I never started to feel separated from my own feelings until recently.

'It's this bloody missing girl, isn't it?' I say out loud to myself, spotting myself in the mirror and noticing how tired I look from all this cleaning. 'You're drawing me in, aren't you?'

Or maybe it's my grandmother. The feelings and emotions don't feel like my own; it's as if I'm going crazy. I remember my grandmother explaining this to me when I was a young girl.

'Their emotions and feelings will wash over you like a wave, and you will have to find the tide to make sense of it all. Know what is your own and learn to identify the flash of emotions that hit you.'

I remember nodding and smiling, thinking it was irrelevant as I didn't connect with her gift of communicating with the spiritual world. I was only seven years old, so why would I? I watched her on many occasions talking to herself and was fascinated by her talents. The world back then felt very magical as a child, I was brought up with immense love and positivity, my gran never had a bad word to say about anyone, not even my mother.

'Can you see them, Granny?' I very clearly remember asking. 'Are they in your head? Are they around me. When can I get to play with them?'

I was often afraid at night that some will come and get me as though they were monsters, but my gran always assured me that spiritual energy is almost always positive. There was nothing to be afraid of. Once you accept, learn and feel it, they are there to help and guide you.

'No, but I can hear them.' She replied. 'It's like a radio. At first, there are some scratchy sounds, but the more I concentrate, the more I can make sense of the words if I listen in very carefully. It's like whispers, some are so quick I can barely keep up, but then others are slow and take their time. You will get your turn when you become an adult.'

It was lost on me at the time. I've spent my whole life believing in the spiritual world but unable to connect with it. I often wondered if I misread the signs, ignored any voices, or signals. For years I heard nothing, saw nothing, but then little things came out of the blue. Random circumstances that felt too coincidental to be anything other than spirit. Times when I'd think of my gran and her favourite song would come on the radio, and times when I'd remember my grandfather, and I'd get the scent of his aftershave hit me. I feel them with me at times. I get comfort from that too.

I remember other times when I think back on my life, when I used to help my grandmother set up the kitchen for her readings. We had immaculate lace tablecloths that she used to bleach once a week to keep their pristine whites, many old, melted candles that looked like something out of a horror movie, and her collection of crystal balls. It was all about the ambience.

I used to help her count the money after she'd been reading all weekend. She was never great with maths, and I miss her laughter. I'll never stop loving her and for taking care of me. She was my world for a very long time.

Since my grandmother died, I've always wondered if there would be more signs, but there's been nothing. I haven't smelt her, heard her, seen her, which I will admit questioned my beliefs. Maybe it's me. Perhaps I've shut everything out of my life except for my career, and it's been sitting there dormant, waiting for me to reawaken my curiosity about the spirit world.

What I can't seem to understand is why now? Why is it now that I'm in my sixties that I'm experiencing deep thoughts of the afterlife that I can't shut away? I don't want to ignore it because I believe there's more I need to explore.

As I keep the image of my grandmother in my mind, I ask the question again.

'Gran, are you with me?'

'Gran?'

'Gran, give me a sign. A tap, a knock. Anything, my love?'

There was nothing.

I tried to clear my mind, but I'm still excited about Carol being on this site. I can see their car driving towards the cottage. If they stop here, do I take that as a sign I need to follow my intuition? I try to remember more of my grandmother's wise words.

'Don't look for the signs. They will come to you all on their own.' She'd say, as we used to sit by the coal fire. 'Your gift is in how you interpret. Symbolise the meaning, for the dead cannot speak, but you can be guided.'

I do miss her. I used to shrug my shoulders and roll my eyes at half the stuff she used to say to me. I never understood it then, but I am starting to wish I listened more.

The sound of the car parking outside distracts my thoughts. I hear the thump of two car doors being slammed shut, putting me on a heightened state of alert. I'm still excited as I compose myself and walk towards the door. I spot Carole taking a large bag from the boot, confirming that this is their rented cottage.

Somehow, we are about to be brought together in our two separate worlds. She may not know my name nor ever recognise my face, but I know this is something that is meant and strong. This has to be something stronger than fate.

It's definitely a sign.

Chapter Seven

Monday, 5 June 2023
Carol

The young, smartly dressed lad at the front reception desk explained to me multiple times how our cottage wasn't ready yet. He was sharp and dismissive, not allowing me to explain that I wasn't all that bothered. I never once complained, but I'm wondering if I had a particular look about me. Either that or they are used to other people often turning up early. He was very defensive, which wasn't great for a first impression of this site. I'm sure he was judging how I looked and how I talked.

'It's fine. I totally understand it.' I stated. 'I know the cleaners will have a difficult challenge at times. I get it, but I only want to drop our bags in quickly, then leave. I will literally be straight in, then straight out. I don't want to fully move in right now. I know check in is later in the day.'

I explained further that I, too, was a cleaner myself, but for a hotel chain in Plymouth. I don't think he really cared. He did that smile and nod thing before changing the subject to something else. There was some kind of welcome pack discussion, but it was all going over my head. I'm only here for a few days, so I don't need all the bells and whistles that come

CHAPTER SEVEN

with it.

I don't doubt the cleaner has a difficult day ahead on changeover days. I know how it feels to be up against the clock, changing bed after bed, scrubbing bathroom after bathroom. Cleaning floor, after floor for hours on end. He did at least explain that our cottage had been prioritised for an early check-in. He handed me the key, and now here I am. It looks clean from the outside, and a better accommodation than our own home.

I knocked on the door twice despite having my key; I didn't want to look rude. Darren is parked in the allocated parking bay outside. He's still in the car. I hear the footsteps and murmurings but cannot listen to what the cleaner on the inside is saying. It's not loud enough. I don't want to walk inside, so I wait a minute longer. The lock catch clicks, and the door opens.

'Hello. Sorry about that.' Says the woman standing in front of me, holding her cleaning cloth. 'Can I help you, my love?'

The cleaner seems gentle, less annoyed with me than I expected her to be. I was sure someone would open the door, pissed off that I dared to bother them. That's how I react in the hotel. I don't cope well with the pressure. I can't deal with stress anymore.

'Hi. I'm sorry to bother you. I know you're really busy, but would you mind if we dropped our bags off inside? I won't be long, it's just that we can leave them here and head out for the day. I don't like leaving them in the car.'

'Sure, come on in.'

'Thank you. I really appreciate this. I know you're not finished yet, so I will rush back out again.'

'It really is no bother.'

She smiles and walks away. I pick up the bags I'd left by the steps and head inside. The cottage is better and bigger inside than I had imagined. It has a warm, homely feel to it too. I fell in love instantly. I spot the modern wood and steel fittings, the large screen television, and a kitchen with its own island in the middle. I don't think I will ever want to leave. She has done a great job. It smells so fresh.

'What a stunning property.' I say with my eyes peering around every corner. 'I love it. I'm in awe, honestly, it's absolutely stunning.'

'I won't be too long now.' She explains. 'Just the vacuuming and a few other bits and bobs, my love. I'll be another twenty to thirty minutes if that.'

'It's ok, we're heading out soon. We've not got any food yet and can always walk around the site anyway or try to find some local shops. Darren will want to check out the bar; I can guarantee that much.'

'I saw your photo in the local paper recently.' She said. 'I'm so sorry about your daughter.'

For that split second, I could feel myself stopping my breath. I wanted to sigh, drop my bags and brace myself for explaining that I was the mother with the missing daughter again. I've rolled out that explanation so many times now, and never does it fail to make me emotionally distressed.

'It's fine. You don't need to explain anything to me.' She says before I even have a chance to reply. 'Would you like a cup of tea?'

'No, no. I can't stay.'

'I'm so sorry, I haven't even introduced myself properly, have I? I'm Brenda. I live locally, and welcome again. Sorry, I shouldn't have mentioned anything.'

'Thank you.' I reply with a sigh of relief. 'I'll just drop my bags off upstairs. I've assumed that's where the bedrooms are. Then I will leave you to it. It's ok, you don't need to keep apologising.'

'Let me help you. It really is no trouble.' Brenda asks. 'Is that all you've brought with you?'

I smile and nod. I've got my handbag over my shoulder filled with toiletries I stuffed in it from home and the bags we've used for our luggage in each hand.

As I walk past Brenda, we softly clash in the hallway. My handbag falls off my shoulders, and some of the contents fall to the floor.

'You brought cleaning stuff with you?' She says looking surprised, 'and even your own shampoo?'

'I can't help myself when I go away.' I reply, 'I know it's clean, but sometimes I feel better going over a few things myself. I don't mean any harm.'

'Don't worry about it.' Brenda says, bending down to pick it all up. 'I've got it. I'll just stick it all up here on the side.'

As I was about to thank her and offer my help, I saw her holding my house keys, but her eyes were fixed on the keyring of Lauren. She's holding the keyring and rubbing it gently. Brenda looks engrossed but also, she seems sincere. It's a moment of awkwardness between us and I don't know what else to say to her.

'Is that Lauren?' She asks me, more softly spoken than before. 'Is that her? She's so beautiful. She has your eyes. I can see the resemblance, what a beautiful photo.'

'Yes. She was only ten years old in that school photo.' I reply. 'I remember it like it was yesterday. It was the start of a whole new term; she didn't want to go to school that morning and tried pulling a sickie. Like all kids do, but I didn't even want to buy the bloody photos because the schools charge so much. But now, all I do is look at it every day. I never knew then how precious this was to become.'

'I don't have any kids myself. We tried, my husband and I, but it was never meant to be.' Brenda says, still smiling. 'Are you sure I can't tempt with that tea?'

'At least you've saved yourself a lot of expense and heartache.'

I keep walking towards the staircase, talking as I go.

'I will only be a minute, but you've done a wonderful job. The place is absolutely spotless.' I say to distract her from wanting to talk about Lauren, some more. 'I'll get out of your hair and return back in an hour or so. If that's ok with you?'

The main bedroom was twice the size of ours at home and has an en suite with a walk-in shower. I'm sure we've been upgraded, it didn't look as grand as this in the pictures, but they haven't said anything. I'm in awe of the modern décor and fancy silver finishings. The furniture is divine, it's all so posh compared to what I'm used to.

I'm lost for words, and the smell of cleaning products is a little strong, but I open the bedroom window to let some air in. I hate feeling enclosed, no matter how big a room is, you can't beat the fresh air.

I head straight back down after texting Darren that I'll be two minutes.

'I can't get over her big brown eyes. She's beautiful.' Brenda says, this time sat on the living room sofa, still clutching my keys. 'She's so adorable. It's really sad what happened.'

'She's just like her father, that one.' I reply. 'Adorable, but with an attitude. We're only here because of the sightings people are reporting to the police. We have some posters to hand out to some of the local bars too, and we still have hope.'

'I thought as much.' Brenda replies. 'I haven't seen anyone that resembles her, but I did see the news article the other day. I know I would have recognised her, but I will keep an eye out for you.'

'That was going to be my next question.' I say. 'We're keeping an open mind but have been left disappointed in the past. I don't know how to explain it, but something feels different this time. We both felt we should just head on out here immediately, despite what the police say. My husband was really insisting we drop everything and head straight here. So, here we are.'

Brenda looks up at me. Her eyes are teary and she looks devastated. I know what containing your emotions looks like. I glance at her chest as she's breathing more heavily.

'I'm so sorry. This must look so weird, my love.' Brenda explains. 'It's so overwhelming. The sadness is so awful. I can't imagine what you're going through. The poor little love, it's like she's just vanished. I remember the news all those years ago.'

Rather than stand there and explain the emotions, the anger, the pain, the grief of not seeing my daughter for what is now ten years. I hold out my hand to take back the keyring. Rather than give me back the keyring which I was expecting, Brenda takes my hand and that surprised me.

I assumed she thought I wanted a handshake, yet this is starting to feel strange. This woman doesn't even know me, or my family and there's a whole sense of awkwardness about her. I'm feeling uncomfortable and I want to get away from her. I have to get back to Darren, he'll be coming here and kicking off if I don't head out soon.

Brenda hands me back my keys, stands up, straightens her top, and is still breathing heavily, looking at me strangely upset.

'It's both sides of The Empress. This is so weird. I can hear it.' She says. 'There are two sides. I can't explain it, but I see it, hear it.'

'I don't follow.' I reply, confused. 'Empress, who? Feel what? Hear what? Am I missing something? Are you ok?'

'Sorry, I'm really sorry. I shouldn't have said anything. I was talking out loud; I do that sometimes.' Brenda continues. 'I'm getting a funny old fool in my older years. It's just standing here with you. I remember something my grandmother used to say. She used to read tarot cards.'

'Oh, ok.' I reply. I returned my keys to my bag and wanted to head out the door. 'I must head off but thank you for doing such a great job of cleaning. I don't envy you.'

I turn around and head back outside. I feel a little dizzy, but I'm unsure what happened then. How strange of her to be that upset.

This is the weirdest experience.

Chapter Eight

Monday, 5 June 2023
Brenda

Al is looking at me as if I've gone insane. He picked me up from work, as he said he would at around four o'clock, but we've now argued all the way home. I say argued, but I really mean that sarcastic ranting we do when we try to bite our tongues and hold back. I know he has my best interests at heart, but he doesn't understand anything spiritually; he is a closed book.

I was excited about meeting Carol earlier. I was only explaining how we met by chance and Al, would have it that I was somehow stalking her. I explained until I was blue in the face that it was sheer fate that had me cleaning her cottage. I didn't choose my own cottage key to clean, I had no idea. That too was on my mind, our paths crossed, and I don't believe it's sheer coincidence. It was meant, somehow.

I don't know what my next move should be, there are so many questions I'd like to ask, but it's not my place. It's none of my business, but there's a gripping feeling that is driving me towards them. I wish I could knock their door right now and spill every detail that's swirling in my head. What were their last conversations with their daughter?

I didn't get a chance to speak to her husband, but Carol was enough to awaken the thoughts that I tried only this morning to shut down and close off.

'I'm telling you, I felt something. I heard something, I know what it was.' I explain, as Alan is looking at me with annoyance. 'It was a sign. I can't help what I believe in, Al.'

'I can't believe that you still believe in those things.' Alan said, shaking his head. 'I've got to the age of almost sixty-five and I've not seen one ghost, not heard one spirit in my head, and never seen anything out of the ordinary. I just think that death is the end.'

'I don't like it when you mock my belief's. We've had these conversations many times over God-knows-how-many-years we've been together now, and I have witnessed far too much in my life not to believe.' I rant further, 'just because you don't believe in it, doesn't mean that my spiritualist views should be swept under the carpet.'

Al for once shut up. He continued to peel the potatoes for the mash we're having for dinner.

I wish at times he would keep his mouth shut and try not to force his views on me. I don't force him to believe in any form of afterlife. Being a spiritualist and coming from a family where generations of us taught and practised our belief's, it's embedded in my way of life. I've known no different. All I have ever asked of him is to keep an open mind and stop treating my views like I'm going insane.

'It's not a spiritualist church you need to visit.' Alan used to say, 'it's a bloody doctor.'

We agree to disagree and as of late, he's quieter about his opinions on it.

'I heard my Gran's voice. I heard her loud and clear. It was as if she was standing right next to me at a time when I asked for a sign. I'm not going crazy. I know what I heard.'

'And what did she say?'

'She shouted at me loud and clear about both sides of The Empress.'

'What the hell is that?'

'Tarot cards, Al.' I explained. 'I mentioned this already in the car. The Empress is from memory, a card that signifies feminine strength, it's about maternal feelings, I think.'

Al is still shaking his head which is really frustrating me because I'm trying to have a serious conversation. Hearing my grans voice made me go stone cold. It was short, brief, but not like she was talking right next to me. It was like listening to a faint radio.

'I think it's all a load of old shit.' Alan replies, putting down the knife and potato. 'Have you thought about how much stress you're under. Your knee, maybe your work. Get a fucking grip Bren. Listen to what is coming out of your mouth.'

My mouth drops in shock. I'm angered.

'Take time off work. Why don't we go away somewhere?' Alan continues. 'I'm concerned about you, Bren. This isn't you?'

'What do you mean, this isn't me.' I snap. 'I was brought up with tarot cards my whole life. I still have my Grans up in the loft. And no. I don't need time off work and I don't need a damn holiday.'

There was an awkward silence between us both. I didn't know what else to say, and Al said nothing. He carried on peeling the potatoes, whilst I pre-heated the oven for our evening meal.

I've always known Al was a sceptic and I respect his views because he hasn't had the same upbringing as I have. It's only now that I can't ignore how I am feeling and what I am hearing. I have gone almost my whole life ignoring the signs. He can call me bat crazy as much as he wants, but I recognised that voice in my head. I heard her.

'I'm sorry for snapping at you. I shouldn't have.' Al says, coming over to stand next to me by the kitchen door. 'I'm worried about you, that is all. The more you poke your nose in that poor family's business; I'm telling you it won't end well.'

'I'm sorry too.' I hold his hand and give it a tight squeeze, all the while I'm looking out at the sky, the clouds and everything that nature brings us. The birds, trees and the sunshine. 'I can't help what is going on in my head right now. I need to follow my heart, my instincts.'

'What do you expect to get from this?' asks Alan.

'I'm not even sure.'

'I'm at some kind of crossroads.' I explain. 'I have a sense that I either have to ignore everything and give up thinking about Lauren, or the alternative.'

'What alternative?' Alan interrupts before letting me finish. 'Shouldn't the police be dealing with all this?'

'The alternative is that I follow my instincts even though I don't know what path it will take me down. It's just something strong. It's the first time I've felt guided, the first time that for once I think my gran is connecting with me, and meeting Carol today was like confirmation that I shouldn't drop this.'

I look at the concern in his eyes.

'I know what you're thinking, but can I ask you to let me have this one opportunity to trust it.'

'I remember when Lauren first vanished ten years ago. I remember that clear as day. I remember how I felt when the newspapers brought it up again. The way I can't stop looking at her picture. There's something I feel inside me that wants me to find out the truth.'

'How are you going to do that?' Alan interrupts me again. I'm holding back not to snap.

'Of all the places, her mother is literally up the road from us as we speak. I spoke to her, I saw the loss in her eyes, and the softness in her voice. I need to help her. That's the only way I can really describe my constant feeling. It's to help and offer support. She needs some kind of closure; she is desperate to find her daughter.'

'Why you?'

'I don't know why me.' I reply. 'I don't have any answers for anything. Not right now, but I have an opportunity. I asked for a sign and now today Laurens mother is as close to me as she'll ever be.'

'I don't think we should intrude on their business, their loss, their grief, their lives.' Alan says. 'Like I keep saying, it's none of our business.'

He still doesn't understand what I am saying.

'Is it about helping them, or just you trying to find some kind of connection to your Gran?' He asks. 'Please, can we stop all this?'

'No.' I reply, firm and sharp. 'I'm not letting this go. I've committed myself. I felt her keyring, I know this is something that I am meant to do. I don't expect you to understand it, I barely even understand it, but I'm not going to drop it.'

'You don't know what you're letting yourself in for.' He continues. 'Don't blame me if you end up falling out with a lot of people.'

'I know you won't support me on my spiritual feelings, but again, it's something I am drawn to and have to do. I'm going to visit the spiritualist church in Plymouth at the weekend, talk to them about it.

'Ok, Bren.' Alan replies. 'I'll drop it now, but I think you might be intruding on what is their loss, their daughter, not ours. We don't even have any kids. I can't get my head around why you want to intrude. I'll drop you off and pick you back up from that church. I can always visit my mate John and see what he's up to in Plymouth.'

'Appreciate that.' I respond but thinking about where I have my Grans old tarot cards. 'Do you think you could have a look up in the loft for my Grans tarot set?'

Al nods.

'Yeah, can do it later on if you want. Didn't we keep all her belongings in a separate box up there, she had some old brown trunk from the eighteen hundreds didn't she?'

'She did.' I smile and remember it. 'It's probably worth a small fortune on its own. Thank you.'

As Al heads into the living room, I smile at him, but inside that smile is a feeling of pain and hurt. The emotions that have struck a chord from nowhere on the back of him saying we don't have any kids. Why did he need to bring that up out of nowhere?

Sometimes I wonder if he ever has any resentment.

We tried and tried many years ago, but enduring those miscarriages when I was younger was an emotional drain. I don't think my body can produce any children, I blamed myself, but I've since learned to live with the reality. We could have done more maybe, medically, but we decided to let nature take its course.

Sometimes I feel guilty for not trying more, but we gradually accepted we were never going to be parents. There were times when we argued about it, and my thoughts and feelings were on the tip of my tongue.

   He would never forgive me.

Chapter Nine

Ten Years Ago
Carol

We're both sitting in the back garden; we've been out here an hour and not said a word to each other. We haven't left the house in days and had constant visitors, whether it was the police, the press, friends and neighbours. Only now does it feel like it's just my husband and I alone. I'm on edge when he shouts, nervous when he's quiet. I can't imagine my life without him. Where would I go?

I've finished planting some of the last rose bushes and we're now fixated on the plants. Staring into thin air whilst our minds wonder into a world of their own. It's as though there's lots to say, but we don't know exactly what to say, so we say nothing. Darren is lost without her, we both are.

Kieran's being very quiet about it. Every time we mention his sister he tells us that she'll be back when she's hungry, back when she needs money, is probably hiding at her friend's house, but he's only fourteen. He doesn't understand the seriousness of the matter. He's keeping out of our way, and Darren was convinced at first that he knew something. After two hours of being questioned by his own father, Darren accepted that

CHAPTER NINE

Kieran genuinely has no idea,

The weather is cooler with a light breeze every few minutes. I've drank my soft drink, Darren is having a coffee for a change, but it's gone stone cold. I can see the layer of film on the top, he hasn't touched it. I'm praying he stays off the beer, I'm too tense for another day like yesterday.

'It's been three whole days and there's still nothing. I feel so helpless.' I say to Darren who looks depressed. 'I can't stop seeing her over and over in my mind telling me she's going upstairs to study. That was the last time I saw her.'

'It's driving me up the wall.' Darren replies, 'I'm sorry for blaming you. I know you couldn't have stopped her, but I wish I knew why she did it. What did we do to upset her, what could we have done to make her stay?'

'The police aren't really helping much, are they?' I interrupt, 'Her social media doesn't show anything. I can't get in to look at any messages. We don't have her phone, but they made it sound like we didn't really know her.'

'I know, they said the same to me. I had the same treatment.' Darren replies, looking down at the cold coffee, a few flies landing on the table. 'I told them that I know my little girl and she would not run away with some boy from school. She didn't keep secrets from us, well, at least I thought she didn't anyway.'

'I'm tired of all the questions. I really want answers now.' I say, holding back the emotion. 'I gave the local paper a photo of her, it's the most recent one we have. I can't believe that nobody saw anything. They went round the whole street and not one person saw a single thing. How many people live in this street? There's always somebody out and about no matter what time of the day or night. How the fuck did nobody see anything. They're lying.'

'That's really winding me up that is. If that fucking Ian's kid from across the road had run away from home and I'd have a really hard think about it.' Darren says, his body language more aggressive. 'No bastard likes talking to the police round here, but this is my daughter. It's different from that family across the road who's always selling drugs to the lads the next street over. This is one of our own. They should speak up if they saw something, even if it's just to me. I'd take care of it; they know that.'

'I'm sure they would have. That, nobody likes a grass mentality doesn't count when someone is missing. I'm sure if they had seen something, they'd have let us know.' I defend the neighbours, to save him going knocking on doors. 'It's because this area is notorious for trouble isn't it. There's always some drug related incident, police smashing doors in. Couples arguing in the street, fights, but somehow, we all get along and accept each other. If they saw something, there's no reason for them to lie, Darren. I think it's the truth.'

Darren nods, turns away from me and pours his coffee down the drain next to his feet.

'They've been a godsend to us some of our neighbours, they really have.' I continue. 'Rod, well he's been out driving all over town to see if he can find her. Rich and Julie from number ten; they've been printing posters and putting them on lamp posts. A few in the Post Office window too. Also, the police are doing their job. I know they can do a lot behind the scenes. They'll find her, they will.'

'If someone's taken my daughter, I'll kill them.' Darren snaps, standing up. 'I'd smash their fucking face in. I'd die for Lauren; I would absolutely die for both of my kids.'

CHAPTER NINE

'I would too. Believe me, I'd join in.' I reply, hoping I don't have another night of him on the beer. At least he's eaten and has spent most of the day drinking coffee. 'Our kids are loved, and they know they're loved. They have been allowed to have freedom of speech, growing up with more than I had as a kid, they're lucky and they know we love them so much.'

I get emotional again, the shakes have kicked in, and the breathing is back. I am sure this is the onset of a panic attack. I've never had any to know, but this from what I read online sounds like it. I take slower breaths to manage the feelings and the trembling. It's my nerves. I'm going to speak to a doctor about it.

I've been trying to approach the subject all afternoon, but not sure how to ask him. He's sobered up at least, not touch a drop of booze since yesterday and maybe he's more rationally minded.

'Darren, can I ask you something? But don't kick off.' I say nicely, approaching it with caution. 'The day before Lauren vanished, I remembered something that I'd forgotten about. I didn't tell the police anything, so don't worry. And please don't lash out at me. This is only something I remembered today.'

'What's that? Why would I lash out?' He replies, 'do you think you might have remembered something that could lead us to where she is? I'm not sure I follow you?'

'No, it was something I saw and heard. It was you and Lauren.' I explain. 'I saw you and Lauren whispering something to each other and I didn't really think anything of it, but she was quiet for the whole of that day. She was fine on the day she disappeared.'

He looks, sucks in his bottom lip as he always does when he's remembering something and thinks about it.

'I don't remember any of that. I mean. What's wrong with talking to my own daughter anyway?' He says, 'what time would that have been? I came in from work, I was early, I remember that much. It couldn't have been anything that pissed her off with Kieran, she'd have shouted the rooftops about it. You say whispering like it's something secret and sinister. That's not what I'm like at all and you know it.'

Darren walks away from me, takes his coffee cup inside, it's the one Lauren bought him. I know when he's not telling the truth, he can't look me in the eye, his tone of voice is higher and he tries to act normal. He didn't overreact which isn't like him. He's been weirdly calm all day.

I get up and follow Darren inside; to see him standing in the kitchen holding an old photograph of Lauren he's taken off the wall, it's the same school photo I have on my keyring.

'She really didn't want to go to school that day, did she?' I say, smiling and remembering that day well. 'She hated any kind of attention on her and never liked being in photos. She begged you to let her stay at home, do you remember?'

'I remember a lot from that day.' Darren says, slamming the photo down on the side. 'I was fucking awful to her that day. If anything has happened to her, I won't forgive myself.'

I'm shocked, as though I've been left out of the loop. What does he mean.

'Do you want to explain that a bit more?' I ask, stern. 'I don't remember you being awful to her, in what way?'

I can forgive him for the way he's spoken to me at times, but I am desperate now to hear him out. I'm angry.

'Tell me, what you mean by awful.' I demand. 'What are you not telling me. I'm your wife for gods sake. I'm her mother.

What happened.'

'Calm down, it was years ago.' He explains, 'it's nothing bad, something I had forgotten about.'

'What?'

'I smacked her on the back of her leg. It was hard.' Darren admits. 'She was arguing with me and shouting back. You know she was about ten, or eleven, but I hit her. It's the first and only time I ever raised a hand to any of my kids.'

I'm tearful, I can't imagine how she must have been feeling.

'I never wanted to bring my kids up like the way my parents dragged me up.' Darren says, 'I was so sorry. I apologised to her straight away, but then.'

'Then what?' I snap. 'What the fuck, Darren. Why did I not know?'

'While you were at work, I caught her standing at the bottom of the stairs with a bag of clothes and a pair of shoes in her hand.'

Darren covers his eyes to sob. His cheeks are glowing and I'm standing there wondering if this really was the only time.

'She wanted to leave home.' He sobs. 'She was leaving us because she didn't want to live here.'

I turn around because I can't look at him. This whole situation seems a fucking mess. The whole drama we're under with Lauren, Luke is going to die any day now, and I'm not even sure if I love my husband, on top of finding out he could have been beating the kids behind my back.

It's all my fault; I should have been a better mother.

'I've remembered.' Darren says, alert. 'I remember what we were whispering about now upstairs.'

'Go on,' I reply, intrigued. 'I'm listening.'

'It was all about you, actually.' He says, 'she told me that she never wished she had you as a mother.'

I feel my jaw drop.

'I didn't want you to hear that. I said it's not your fault you're useless.' He told me. 'You're not the best role model, are you?'

I start breathing heavier and have that sinking feeling in my stomach again. I shouldn't be putting up with this.

I'm his wife.

Chapter Ten

Monday, 5 June 2023
Brenda

The bright white light from the moon is shining through the living room window. I've been trying to remember the actual name for the moon's appearance for about ten minutes before I remember it's in a waning gibbous stage. Gran was into her spiritual beliefs and astrology, but it was my grandfather who was more obsessive over planets and astronomy. He hoped one day to have lived long enough to see humankind landing on Mars. Every time I look up at the moon, I remember the times he once told me about the man who lived up there. I believed him, but I was only a child.

The skies are crystal clear and the stars are twinkling in every direction I glance. It's magical. The more I stare, the more I wonder how this planet has ever survived with what must go on up there in space. It must be so volatile.

I don't even feel remotely tired, despite it coming up to midnight. I still stand here looking at the moon, having fond memories of my gran sitting me down as a teenager and talking to me about the balance and harmony that celestial object can have on our lives. I know I laughed at her back then, but every time it was a full moon, she was right. I couldn't sleep at all.

I used to be more agitated and unsettled on those nights, but maybe it was a coincidence. Her words of wisdom went in one ear and out the other, but I was a teenager, I couldn't go around talking to my all my girlfriends about the spiritual connections we have with the moon and its orbit around the earth. I was bullied enough as it was. Everyone thought I lived with a witch.

Al went to bed a couple of hours ago. He was kind enough to bring down my gran's tarot kit and spiritual box from the loft after dinner; it's covered with dust and cobwebs. I've not opened that box in years, I kept meaning too, but looking at it now makes me feel emotional. I've cried already and dried my eyes over the tarot set. I can't count how many people she sat down with over the years with these exact same cards.

I know she has advised women on breakups, predicted pregnancies, career moves, changes of luck. Her visitors were mostly always women, I don't know why, but there were the occasional men now and then. My gran always used to say that females were more sensitive and open minded spiritually than men because they are life givers.

My grandfather although he too was spiritual and mildly religious with his regular visits to church, he would rarely do readings, he always connected with others through objects. It was once in a blue moon, but his gift was being able to decipher symbolic images that he'd see in his mind. My gran had met him at some old travelling circus when they were in their late teens in the nineteen-forties. It must have been a very different world back then.

Growing up I thought my grandparents were special. To me they were gifted, and for all the abuse, taunts and negativity they endured sometimes from neighbours, or people who knew what they practised, more often than not, the love, joy and thanks from the positive experiences made it all worth it for them. I really miss them both, and the last thirty years without them haven't been easy.

As I grow older, some of my regrets was not listening to them enough. I distanced myself from their gift in order to keep my own life as normal as possible. I believe in it but rarely voiced my views publicly for the embarrassment. I didn't want to be mocked, laughed at, shouted at like my gran had in her experiences. Maybe because I'm older and wiser now, I'm more resilient, but I've never sat down and tried to connect with the spirit world. Tonight, I am going to try my best.

I cross the curtains to block out the moonlight before walking to the bottom of the stairs to check that Al is still asleep.

'Al, are you alright?' I whisper. 'Al?'

Nothing, but the sound of his snoring.

Wandering back into the living room, I look at the deck of tarot cards on the table in the centre of the room. They're faded, but they're still all there. All seventy-eight cards, a little rough around the edges, some stained with old tea, but still all in one piece. Every single one of those cards took a battering in my gran's hands and have been presented over and over multiple times for many years. Before her, they belonged to her mother, and before that, I am to believe that they were gifted to a member of the family by the Romany Gypsy community sometime in the eighteenth century.

I turn on the tall lamp before switching off the main lights. I don't have any candles here which my gran swore by for improved ambiance.

I'm shaking a little with nerves because it's like the unexpected.

Will I hear her voice again?

Will the cards present me anything that should be considered negative?

Will anything happen at all?

I can do this, I know I can. I'm nervous because I haven't tried reading my own cards in over thirty years. When I close my eyes, I can remember my gran spreading them in three rows of seven. Top row for our past, middle row for the present, and the bottom row represents the future. I can't remember exactly what the seven columns signify, but the gist of it was that the beginning columns are more about yourself, leading through to the final column supporting a representation of your destiny and long-term future plans.

I pick up the deck of cards, shuffle them briefly, sigh a breath to relieve my anxiety, and then one by one I lay the cards out on the table exactly as I remember it. Three rows of seven. I look at all twenty-one cards spread across the table: my eyes immediately drawn to the centre of the present row. The Empress card is directly in the centre piece, it's upside down. I don't think that's a good sign. I'm anxious about that card because of what I heard in my head earlier in the day.

Is this another sign?

I look down to the row that represents the future. My future, and I see The Temperance card, also upside down. Another bad sign that indicates risky behaviours. I wonder if I am even doing this correctly, did I shuffle them for long enough?

'Come on Gran, where are you?' I whisper into the air. 'I need you. I need you more than ever right now. Teach me. Did you choose The Empress card?'

I listen in the silence, closing my eyes tight. If Al could see me, he'd think I was daft for trying this. I'm desperate for something. Something that tells me I am right to carry this on, and that I am right not to ignore my instinctive behaviours. I'm focusing as hard as I can in my minds eye. I see dark shades of red, but no objects, nothing unusual or out of the ordinary. I open my eyes and close them again, just dancing flickers of light reflections. I try to concentrate on the background noise instead.

Nothing.

'How do you do it, Gran?' I remember asking when I was a child because I couldn't make sense of it. 'How is it possible that spirits can talk to you? Are they standing next to you?'

'It's clear hearing.' She replied, 'I clear my mind as best as I can, then it's a verbal thought process. If I'm not conscious about what I am thinking about, it opens the flood gates.'

I keep my eyes closed, trying to clear the thoughts in my mind.

Still no voice. Nothing as clear as it was earlier. I can still faintly hear Al's snoring.

Am I being stupid?

I open my eyes and look at the far right of the row indicating the past. The Tower card is upright, meaning that I've endured a tragedy and loss. That is true, but is this about me, or this about Lauren? Am I blurring the lines with my own thoughts and fears?

When I look across all the rows, I don't see much positivity. Loss, difficulties, tragedy and risks. Maybe I'm only seeing what I want to see?

How would Gran interpret these cards?

The Empress, the Ten of Pentacles, Ten of Cups, Six of Cups, Page of Wands, and lastly The Sun. I keep glancing over the cards again and again. Over and over, I keep concentrating on their meaning, their significance and I'm heavy breathing now as I make the connection. My eyes are teary with the realisation of what's staring at me all this time. All those cards can't be a coincidence, I remember now. I remember it clearly. I watched my gran explain it in the past, but I've never seen all these cards on the reading lines all at once.

I place a hand over my chest. I've made the connection.

'Thank you, Gran.' I say. 'Thank you for connecting with me.'

All those cards symbolic of children and their childhood. The Empress upside down has to be that feeling of emptiness, the Page of Wands is also upside down which is a sign of bad news. I'm starting to get a sense of what the cards are showing me. It's becoming clearer in my mind now. I'm no longer teary, but I am relieved. Everything is confirming this has to be about missing Lauren. All those child orientated cards cannot be a coincidence. I pick up the remaining deck of cards from the table.

'One more, Gran.' I say. 'One more, I'll give it another shot. What are you trying to say?'

I shuffle the pack hard a few times and place the deck face down on the table. I don't know what spurred me to carry on, but I want the next card to tell me something.

'One more for luck.'

'Give me a sign through the cards.' I say, again feeling more confident. 'I'm thinking of Lauren. Where is she?'

As I keep that thought in my mind, I think about the photo of Lauren in the newspaper. I turn the card over and gasp. I fall back down on the sofa, patting my chest, a rush of emotion and a feeling of slight shock.

'No.' I shout. 'Not in hells chance.'

CHAPTER TEN

The Death card is in my hand, I drop it to the floor and I can barely breathe.

She can't be dead. No.

'No. No.' I say. 'She can't be dead. This isn't true.'

I keep shaking my head. I'm confused and don't know what to believe.

Could it be true?

'What's going on?' Alan snaps at me, standing at the living room door. 'You were making a right racket down here.'

I didn't even hear him walk down the stairs.

I walk towards him and put my arms around him.

'I think Lauren's dead.' I cry, now a little emotional again. 'I pulled out the Death card from the pack. I asked for a sign, and its.'

'It's nothing.' He shouts. Interrupting me. 'Nothing. Stop being so ridiculous with all this nonsense.'

'The cards all represent children, and then I turn over the Death card.'

'Do you honestly believe the cards are telling you something?' He asks, 'seriously, take a step back and calm down. Your Grandmother certainly brainwashed you, didn't she? It's all bollocks.'

I shake my head. Wipe my eyes and struggle to understand my emotions right now.

'If she was dead, they'd have found a body by now. I've told you many times. Teenagers run away from home, or some people just don't want to be found, Bren.'

'I know. I know.'

'It's none of our business, now why don't we let them just get on with their lives while we get on with ours.'

I don't know whether the cards represent my thoughts

towards Lauren or my own past.

It could be about my own secrets which makes it harder to understand. I need to talk to someone about this. I have to go to the spiritualist church on Saturday.

Maybe I should confess?

'Are you coming up to bed now, Bren?'

'Yes, give me five minutes. I'll have a glass of water and tidy up the lounge.'

Al heads back up the stairs whilst I grab a glass, fill it with chilled filtered water from the fridge and I return to the lounge. I turn on the light, pull back the curtain and look up at the moon.

'What is it all about?' I ask out loud. 'Life. What is our purpose?'

I cross the curtains tight, place the tarot cards back into the box that Al had taken out of the loft earlier and I close the lid down.

As I brush my hands over the box, I'm not sure what those cards have awakened within me tonight.

It feels dark.

Chapter Eleven

Tuesday, 6 June 2023
Carol

The oppressive heat of Salcombe presses down on my skin, suffocating me as I check my phone. It's a scorching twenty-two degrees and the sun sears the back of my neck, a painful reminder of what I've lost. Tears burn in my eyes as I stare out at the picturesque hillside, feeling guilty for even allowing myself a moment of enjoyment while our daughter is no longer in our lives. The ache in my heart is constant, threatening to consume me if I give into the overwhelming grief. It's like I'm trapped in a hellish club with an exclusive membership that no one wants, reserved only for those who have experienced this level of trauma. My mental health is already fragile, and dwelling on the loss of our daughter feels like sinking into a never-ending abyss.

We're not all that far from Plymouth, but it could be a million miles away when comparing the differences in the two locations. You don't get stunning views like this in St Budeaux, that's for sure. I look out of my windows most days back home with the semi-detached houses opposite with their broken fences, boarded up windows, and the occasional burnt-out car in the street.

The green hills on the opposite side of this pub are what the location sign is calling, Batson Creek, and the ferry has been going back and forth for an hour or more. I'm not sure what that area is called, but it has a stunning scenery. I can't keep my eyes off it. There are sheep casually walking and eating the long green grass, tractors over the hills and little detached country houses that seem tranquil. Nothing we could ever afford or dream of living in. I can't begin to imagine how much they must cost to buy. A small fortune I reckon, at least close to a million maybe, or more.

'At least your work was kind enough to let you have the time off for this break last minute.' I say to Darren who's downing another pint of beer. 'That was kind of them. I practically had to beg the hotel to let me have time off. My manager was a right bitch about it. I've told you about her before haven't I. Always depends on her moods or not.'

'It's pretty chill, where I am, ain't it.' He replies, scratching his head. 'This fucking sun is burning me today. Do you have any sun cream on you in that bag of yours.'

I scramble around picking up my bag from beside my feet. I rumble my hands around inside and I can feel my keys. I pull them out, place them on the table, delve deeper into the bag. My hands are shaking a little, I can see the changes in his mood already.

'I must have left it at home on the kitchen side.' I reply. 'We can grab some from a chemist or shop maybe if we see a decent one later. The holiday park might have some in that little market shop of theirs. We were in a rush to leave yesterday, sorry.'

'You can imagine the bloody cost of it in that shop.' He

moans. 'Did you see the fucking price of bread in there last night. It's daylight fucking robbery. Those convenience stores take the piss because they know you have limited choice and it's a mile walk to the best shop. We aren't paying their prices; I'd rather burn to death.'

Darren picks up my set of keys, he rubs the keyring with the school photo of Lauren.

'Look at our little girl.' He says, teary eyed. 'She is so beautiful. She has your eyes, my smile. She's perfect in every way. I miss her.'

I clutch his hand and take back the keyring, admire the photo of her myself and put the keys back down on the table. I have a sense of imposter syndrome in this location. I hope everyone isn't looking at us. I hate that.

I close my eyes and I know I'm going to have to say it.

'Darren, do you think you've had enough now?' I ask. 'It's barely even lunch time. We aren't here on our holidays. Remember why we are here?'

All I'm interested in now is moving from bar to bar, shop to shop asking anyone if they might have seen Lauren in the area. I've been sat in The Fox & Ferry for two hours and he's done nothing but drink. I'm anxious because I know what behaviour follows and I'm not here for an argument. We're spending money hand over fist, wasting time already and I know how the evening will pan out if he keeps on drinking at the rate he's going. We've all been through difficult times, but I have to be seen to be doing something. I don't want the papers or anyone else thinking we are giving up on our little girl.

'Shall we move on?'

'No.'

'Darren, we've been here for two hours. We've put out just

one bloody poster of Lauren. I have so much more to do, and we're wasting time.'

'No.'

'Darren, I really want to move on. This isn't some jolly.'

Darren slams his fist down on the table, leans in closer.

'I've already fucking said no, for fucks sake. How many more times. Are you fucking deaf? Let me finish my pint. We've got a few more fucking days yet.'

I'm embarrassed but expected nothing less. I shouldn't have allowed him to stay here this long. I should have suggested we leave after his first drink. I thought this one time he might have been able to control himself better. It's my own fault.

I don't even want to look behind me, or around me. I bet everyone is looking at us.

'Do you have to do that?' I snap, but not as aggressive. 'I bet everyone will be looking at us now.'

'Who cares what they all think?' Darren replies. He takes another gulp of his beer. 'Good enough to take our money. Good enough to mind their own business.'

'I thought we could move on to the restaurants further down the road. They must be opening for lunch, and we could hand them some of our flyers.' I deflect the situation and encourage him to move on. 'Come on, drink up.'

I still clutch my keyring with Laurens school photo and I close my eyes. I have a brief flashback of her dancing around her room to her favourite boy band. She was so full of life as a child, so energetic.

'Mummy,' she once said. 'I want to be a dancer when I grow up.'

'Waitress.' Darren shouts raising his hand.

The memory of our little girl stirs emotions and feelings of happier times.

'Darren, can we just go?'

'One more.' He says, hand still in the air. I turn to see the young waitress heading our direction. She has a look on her face of dread, and I'm trying to give her some eye contact to prewarn her that I'm dealing with the situation. A long stare and a subtle nod might do it. 'One more and we'll move on.'

'You said that an hour ago.' I reply through gritted teeth. 'We need to hurry up and move on. How many times, Darren?'

The waitress is now standing by the table. I can't look at her in the eye now through the shame and embarrassment of my husband who is being loud and aggressive.

'How may I help you both?' She politely asks, her hair tied up, and her nails perfectly manicured. 'Would you like the same again?'

'Yes please.' Darren slurs. 'I'll make this the last one though. Can we get the bill too. We're paying on card if you get that little machine thing, saves you coming back twice.'

I sigh with discontent.

'No.' I interrupt, now making eye contact with her. 'We don't need any more drinks. Can we just have the bill please.'

Darren turns and stares at me. I stare back at him. Our eyes locked, but he's had enough to drink. If he dares say one more word, I'm going to get up and leave him here on his own.

'Ok, just the bill, then.' Says Darren.

The waitress heads off in the direction of the bar. The back of my neck still burning with the heat of the sun.

'Did you see her perfect nails?' I ask, to lightly bring the mood back down. 'She's so pretty isn't she. I barely remember my twenties now.'

I look down at my hands. Hands that are constantly scrubbing tiles, washing the inside of showers and forever changing bedding at the hotel. My nails will never look like hers.

'I didn't notice.'

'Probably because you're half cut.'

'I'm fucking not.'

'You are. You always turn aggressive. I don't like it.'

'You never fucking listen to me anyway.'

The waitress comes back over from the bar with the card reader and our bill. I glance down and try not to look shocked at the price.

'Thank you.' I say and tap the machine with our joint account card. 'And thank you for taking the poster of Lauren and putting it up behind the bar.'

'Not a problem.' She replies. 'I hope that someone recognises her and calls you.'

Darren shakes his head. I already know what is likely to come out of his mouth. I want the waitress to get a move on and leave us in peace.

The waitress hands us our receipt and walks away.

'Like she fucking cares.'

'She's only trying to be nice.' I reply. 'Do you need a hand?'

Darren stands up straight, stumbles slightly, and I put my bag over my shoulders. I rub my keyring and throw my keys back in my bag.

There's a whole row of shops, bars and restaurants we can target.

As we walk further down the hill, slower pace until Darren starts to sober up. He stops, places his arm around me and pulls me in closer.

'I don't half love you.' He says. The smell of alcohol on his breath is strong. 'I hope she walks back through our door one day.'

'I love you too.' I reply. 'I hope so too.'

'You've forgotten, haven't you?' Darren continues as we start to pick up the pace. 'That was another thing that fucked me up a bit. Do you remember?'

Do I remember? Like I could forget.

'Of course I remember. That's coming up for ten years now too isn't it.' I reply, showing I care. 'We should visit your brothers grave when we get back to Plymouth. We've not been there for a few years. We could lay some flowers, give it a tidy up.'

'Thirty-six was no age to die of colon cancer, was it?'

'No.' I say shaking my head. 'It affected us all in different ways.'

'We had our ups and downs over the years, but I wasn't the best brother to him.' Darren slurs, still drunk. 'I loved that man. I never told him. I wish I had.'

'I'm sure he knew.' I comfort him. 'You were there when it mattered.'

'And you.' Darren says. 'You are my rock. I fucking love you.'

Hand in hand we walk to the next bar. I'm not prepared for him to get on a drinking session. I don't want the drama. I know a lot has happened over the years, but I wish he could reign it in for the next few days.

I don't want to talk about his brother, Luke.

That's a whole new dilemma.

Chapter Twelve

Tuesday, 6 June 2023
Carol

Darren is struggling to keep his balance as he staggers closer to the waters edge. I keep my eye on him, although I've already imagined him in my head falling into the water, struggling to swim in his intoxicated state. I see him, in my head drowning, gasping for breath, choking to death. What's wrong with me?

All I want to do is scream. I snap out of it because these obsessive, over the top thoughts I've experienced through missing my daughter must be some kind of post traumatic stress disorder. I've never really spoken about it, but it's as though I now see the fear in absolutely everything.

We managed to spend a couple of hours moving from one bar to the next, and although he had a drink in every single one, he's still in a reasonably good mood. For now. I can't bring myself to drink, I haven't been drunk in over ten years.

When Lauren vanished, my whole life changed. Part of my personality is missing with her, but no one I know understands what is like to be a parent with a missing child. I still get invited to work nights out, I still get invited to parties, I still am expected to be the singing, dancing, smiling woman with friends, a husband, who live in a community that have forgotten about my daughter, but I haven't.

Every day I have the same thoughts. The same conversations with myself. All the what ifs, the buts and the maybes that no one else I know other than Darren can possibly comprehend. He has his moments, but he's her dad, and he is experiencing the same. All he wants to know is where his daughter is.

It's not we stop our normal routines that we realise what an impact her loss is in our lives. When we're busy getting up each morning, showering, going to work, making lunch, coming home, making dinner, going shopping, that we realise everyday life is distracting. Without structure and daily routines, I am fearful of my own thoughts leading me to dark places.

I must have handed out about fifty posters to random strangers in those bars and restaurants. I'm not sure how many of the smiles and sad faced expressions were genuine, but I'm exhausted today. Now that my mobile number is on every single one, I wonder if I'll get a text message or a phone call. I'm nervous. The local papers are adamant she's been seen in the area; the police weren't of much use. I understand though, without any concrete evidence or people coming forward, she will still remain missing.

I slap more sun cream on my arms that we bought from a local chemist as we've both now moved slightly back from the water to a nearby bench, still facing the waterfront with a bag of chips he's holding to share between us. There's nothing quite like the aroma of hot, fresh chippy chips, but I'm not that hungry.

'Do you think anyone will recognise her.' Darren slurs, 'it's been ten whole years, hasn't it, but her face couldn't have changed that much. I know we'd still recognise her.'

'We can only hope, can't we.' I whisper, still looking at the ducks on the water. 'That's all we can do. Just, keep hoping.'

I wipe my hands with a tissue and grab one of his chips. I'm hoping some food in his stomach sobers him up. Sometimes I don't know what I see in him, but I know he loves me. I couldn't ever imagine my life without him. He's been my rock, as I know I am to him.

Our marriage seems to have been cemented now by our missing daughter, we've just kept going with every anniversary overshadowed by emotional loss.

'You can have the rest. I'm not that hungry.' I say, tapping his knee. 'They're all yours now.'

'Excuse me.' A voice startles us in the background. 'Hello.'

We both turn our heads on hearing her voice. A young woman, with her brown hair tied back comes running towards us. She's holding what I've assumed is her son's hand. He appears to me to be around five years old, and not very happy about the fast-paced walking.

'Mr and Mrs Cooke?'

It's a been a long time since we've been addressed as Mr and Mrs, but I spot the flyer of Lauren in her other hand. My eyes drift back and forth from the flyer to her face.

'Hi.' I reply, 'Yes, that's us. Didn't we meet about an hour ago? I can't remember which café, but it was definitely within the last hour?'

I remember seeing the young boy in one of the local café's we wandered into. He was kicking his legs and banging his hands on the table whilst his mother was trying to drink her coffee. I remember how difficult kids can be at that age.

'Your daughter. I think I might have seen her. I'm not sure, but it's been playing on my mind since we left.' She says, hardly catching her breath. My eyes widened as I turn to glance at Darren. 'I'm not certain, but I needed to tell you in case it was important. I'd never be able to live with myself otherwise.'

The woman walked closer to stand beside us, both Darren and I say nothing as we eagerly wait for her to speak. I want to scream and snap at her to hurry up and tell us what we need to know, but I smile and wait patiently.

'I thought I might have found you here.' She continues, the young boy is tugging on her hand. 'Josh, keep still for a moment. Mummy is talking.'

I smile at the child.

'I saw you heading into the other bars, so I assumed you might be closer to end of this strip by now.' She says, 'If I hadn't had found you, I would have called your number. I should have called it anyway, but I thought you might be busy.'

I'm starting to shake a little with the nerves and anticipation of what she is about to say next. I notice Darren place the chips on his lap as he sits up, paying attention.

'Seen her where?' Darren says. 'Our Lauren, are you sure? Are you absolutely certain?'

'Do you want to sit down?' I ask, interrupting her. 'We can move up?'

'No, it's cool. Thank you, though.'

I'm staring at her, still desperate now for her to hurry up and tell us what she knows. If she doesn't hurry up, I swear I'll grab her by the neck.

'It was earlier in the year. I was doing a work's charity fun run for their nominated cancer charity. Sorry, I need to slow it down. I'm Sarah, nice to meet you both.' Sarah says holding out her hand.

'Can you, please, just get on with it. Darren rudely snaps.

'What run, and where about exactly?'

Sarah's face changes, it's now awkward, but I was thinking the same thing. Her child is still jumping about, pulling on her hands. Both of them look frustrated.

'I got talking to a woman called, Jennifer. She looked a little like the girl in the picture, but a bit older. She must have been older than me, and I'm twenty-five.'

Darren and I both nod.

'I'm sorry for snapping.' Darren says. 'It's been difficult, as you can imagine.'

'I can imagine, but what I remember is that every time I asked questions, she didn't really want to answer them. She said she wasn't from round here but moved into rented accommodation.'

'How did you get chatting?' I asked, intrigued. 'Do you both work at the same place?'

'No. I don't work with her. I'd never seen her before and haven't seen her since.' Sarah replies. 'She was next to me in the line, but she's the spitting image of the girl in this picture. The more I keep looking, the more it reminds me of her.'

'Jenny?' Darren asks. 'Are you absolutely sure it's her?'

'I think so.' Sarah nods. 'The more I look at this flyer, the more I recognise her facial features too. I can't be one-hundred-per-cent certain, but I'm about ninety-percent sure. She said she had a family member who died of cancer.'

'Why would she call herself that god awful name?' Darren slurs, still affected by all the alcohol he's been drinking. 'She never looked like a Jenny in her life.'

'Look. I'm sorry. I have to rush off. I've got to take my little man here to the optician.' She says. 'He's all excited he's off from school, but it'll be a struggle to keep him sat still for more

CHAPTER TWELVE

than five minutes. You know what kids are like.'

'Thank you.' I say, being polite. 'It's nice to have met you. You have my number on that flyer there if you can think of anything else.'

'I will message you. That's for sure.' She says, as she starts to walk away. 'Good luck with the search, I hope it's something you can start with at least. You know, other people might come forward with the same name. You never know.'

Sarah is now completely out of sight.

'Well then, what do you think of that?' I ask Darren, who is now eating the rest of the chips. 'Does she seem genuine to you? Anything in it?'

'I think it's her who needs to see an optician, not that kid of hers.' Darren replies. 'I don't know what to think. It wasn't much to go on really was it. Luke died of cancer, didn't he, but why would she do something like that. I don't know, it could be a coincidence. We should tell the police?'

'It's not enough to go on, is it?' I sharply snap, frustrated. 'How many times have they been nothing but a waste of time?'

I sigh and think of Lauren. I'm not sure she'd ever like the name Jenny; it sounds too old fashioned. Doesn't seem like a name she'd pull out of thin air. We don't, nor to my knowledge, ever knew anyone called Jenny either.

'Shall we head back to the holiday cottage?'

'No. I want another drink.'

'Darren, I'm being serious. I'm tired. I can't do this.'

'It's your fault we're here, isn't this what you wanted?'

'What?' I snap. 'What are you moaning about now?'

'I've just been told my little girl could be called Jenny, and is running around those hills for charity, while me, as her father, is left out in the cold. Why, Carol? Why?'

I don't know what to say. I sit staring at the water, watching the ducks again with the sun still burning my arms. I'm sure they're going red.

'Why?' Darren snaps at me. 'Why did she have to run away from us? What could we have done differently?'

I remind myself that he's been drinking, he's upset and I purposely say nothing so as not to rile him any further. All I need now is some peace.

'Fucking Jenny.' He continues. 'As if. What the fuck would she know. Barging in on our conversation, telling us she's now called Jenny.'

'She wasn't sure. Was she?' I reply, trying to calm him down. 'She was trying to be kind and tell us something useful.'

'Look what you've gone and done to my fucking head now.'

'What?' I shout to defend myself. 'This isn't just all about you, you know. She was my daughter too. Stop shouting at me.'

I'm breathing heavier, trying to calm my emotions. The was an awkward few seconds of silence, and we both appear calmer.

'It was the local paper that said she was seen in this area.' I remind him. 'It's not my fault we are here. You should want to be here, looking for her. Turning on each other won't do us any good.'

'She disowned us.' Darren says, tearful. 'She fucking hates me, doesn't she.'

I don't say another word. I'm sat here wondering how I'm going to get him home without walking past the pub.

I'm certain everyone around me is looking at us again.

Chapter Thirteen

Ten Years Ago
Carol

Death feels so final. One of the cruellest parts of living in this world is our journey out of here. Watching Luke deteriorate, unable to travel, work, barely eating and constantly sleeping is not living. I'm glad his suffering is over and I'm not sure if there is such a thing as an afterlife, but whatever there is that does exist after our death, should there be anything; I hope is a better world than this one.

In the months before Luke passed away from his cancer, there was a build up of tension in our house. We were living on the edge of our nerves, surviving on adrenaline alone. His death came as no shock, we were all prepared for it. There's something to be said for having a heart attack or stroke where you're taken out in one, quick hit. No one has to suffer the gruelling challenge of their body trying to fight an inevitable end.

When cancer is terminal, and no means of treatment can eradicate every evil cell, the battle is hard, and emotional. Emotional to the point of despair where you sink so low you end up walking around every day in a constant state of void.

You talk about death and funerals as if it's emotionless because you've exhausted every emotion you can think of.

What I wasn't prepared for, was Lauren, and as we are sat here during Luke's funeral, one of us is missing. Darren insisted on leaving an empty space for her. Not that he expected her to walk in and make an appearance, but for him, it felt like she was included in some small way. I agreed it is a lovely gesture.

I can't stop thinking about her. She's on my mind the minute I wake up, and the moment I fall to sleep. I picture her loving smile; I remember things I had forgotten about from when she was a young girl. I sit in her room, still able to smell her there, and I'd cry on and off for hours.

Over the last week even sleeping was a challenge. My brain not willing to shut itself off from the constant wondering about all the what if's. I picked up the sleeping tablets in the week from the doctor and they're helping. Nothing can switch off the constant thoughts, but I manage to fit in some sleep in between. Every day feels like the same routine over and over again.

'He wouldn't have wanted any of this boring crap, would he?' Darren says, head lowered, 'we're not that much of a religious family, are we? He hated hymns, so does Dad. I bet this was all Mum's doing, wasn't it?'

I'm not even sure he knew his brother well enough over the last few years to know what he would have wanted or not. They had fallen out that many times over the years, lost touch, lost their connection and their family bond, but sorted out their differences in the end. They had said all that was needed to be said, no regrets before he died either. He barely made the effort to visit him in the last few weeks, but that's a choice he made and one he will have to live with.

There's still a disconnect between the two families; our kids never grew up playing together, we were always very separate, but it's what Darren and Luke wanted. They were chalk and cheese as the saying goes, but life can be so cruel. I'm sad for everything Luke will miss out on, sad for all the years he's been robbed of and upset for the way our families will likely take two steps backwards. I know we will continue to go our separate ways after this, it's such a shame.

Every now and then I see someone looking over at us. No doubt we're known as the family with the missing daughter; distracting the attention away from why we are all here in the first place. It's hit the local news and everywhere I go, I'm being stared at. Everyone knows who we are and I don't like it. It's as though I'm famous for something absolutely heartbreaking.

'He would have preferred one of his favourite indie bands, banging out a nineties tune, and all of us sat here in holey t-shirts and baggy jeans.' I reply, knowing exactly what Luke would have preferred. 'These formalities are traditional though. It helps with the grieving process. It's not like Luke had no say in it though. He did pick some of these songs.'

'Oh, I didn't know that.' Darren says, 'ok, fair enough.'

I look at Darren's parents, Sheila and Steve, in the row in front of us, sat next to Luke's wife. We smile and make pleasantries when we see each other, but I'm not a fan of her. I didn't like her before Luke died, and I certainly wouldn't make any effort to get to know her now.

They're such a dysfunctional family, Steve never praises his sons for anything, it's always Sheila telling everyone how proud of her boys she is, but Steve, I'm not even convinced he wanted kids. There's no father and son bond there with either of them, they didn't go anywhere when they were younger and not because they couldn't afford it, because they never made the effort.

Darren doesn't like to talk about his childhood much, nor his feelings either. The two go hand in hand.

As Luke's friend stands up on the podium to say a few words, I glance at Luke's coffin. It's a veneered wood choice, something he actually wanted. He didn't even want the fuss of a service and hoped he could get away with a cheap direct cremation.

Darren's been living in his own world recently; not that he's unaffected or immune to his brother's death, he is grieving in his own way, but throughout the illness and the final few weeks, he's been distant and withdrawn. I've made the effort for both of us and at least Luke got to see Lauren before he passed away. Kieran hates anything medical and bodily; he can't even watch hospital dramas on the television without feeling sick. He too made the effort recently which took courage for him. It's the first time the kids have had to deal with death.

This is the quietest I've ever known Darren to be. I'm not complaining, but he's not touched any alcohol in over a week. I pray he can make it two weeks, then three, then one month then six, who knows. I'm hopeful but not convinced.

Darren is looking at his brother's casket in the middle of the church, his eyes glancing at the flowers whilst everyone else is facing forward. I place my hand on his leg to show him that I care.

'I can't do this. I'm sorry.' Darren says, standing up and leaving. His mother turns to look at us, 'I need to get some air. Excuse me. I have to get out of here.'

'I'm going outside with your dad.' I say to Kieran, 'you stay there with your nan and grandad. We'll be back in a minute.'

CHAPTER THIRTEEN

I get up out of my seat too and a few turning heads, but I rush outside to be with Darren. He's standing by the corner of the church.

'They can't afford all this. How did they pay for it all?' He says, wiping his eyes. He's been crying. 'None of this should be happening, none of it. Lauren should be here.'

'I know. It's like we're living in a nightmare.' I reply, comforting him. 'She wouldn't even know he's died, either. I just want her back.'

'Do you think Luke told her something?' Darren asks, 'you were there at the hospital, the day she went missing. Was she at any time on her own with him?'

'I don't think so, but let's be realistic.' I explain rationally, 'what could he possibly have said to her, whilst he is on his death bed, which would make our seventeen-year-old daughter run away. They barely knew each other.'

'Nothing is impossible, is it?' He says, 'I'm covering all angles here. It all happened on the same day, didn't it? Everything about that day isn't clear. Something about that day can't be right.'

I frown, I don't know what to say. I've gone over it and over it with him, the police, the papers, the neighbours, family, friends. I've repeated myself that much it comes out of my mouth like a well rehearsed play.

'We saw your brother at the hospital in the late afternoon. Earlier in the day she went with me to get the roses, she even picked the colours. It was a lovely day; she was taking the morning off studying; we went to the shops.' I continue, remembering it like it was yesterday. 'It was just the both of us doing our normal everyday things. She was tired, I know that much. I think the stress of the exams was taking its toll on her, but I don't think Luke had anything to do with it.'

I can tell by the look on his face he disagrees.

'You're looking for someone to blame, aren't you?' I say, because I know exactly what he is doing. 'This hasn't got anything to do with Luke. Something happened that made her quite clearly want to walk out of that door. We don't know who, what or why, but we will. I promise you, there will be a day or a time when we know everything.'

'The truth always comes out in the end, doesn't it.' Darren agrees, 'I can't stop focussing on it. I'll always remember the last words I said to her. It was goodnight and take it easy.'

'We should go back inside.' I say, holding his hand again. 'Everyone will be wondering where we are, I think they're about to play the last song. I know today has been tough for you too.'

'I never got to tell her how proud I was,' Darren cries. 'Why? Why did she do this and put us through this hell. If she was struggling with her mental health, or studies, we'd support her. She must know that.'

We walk back into the church; Kieran is on his phone again. He notices us walking back to our place and he quickly rushes the phone back in his pocket.

'Who's that you're messaging?' Darren whispers. 'Is that your sister?'

'No, it's nothing.' Kieran replies. 'Just a mate from school.'

'Give it to me.' Darren demands, 'let me see. You were looking a bit sneaky there with it.'

'No, Dad.' Kieran snaps. 'It's private. I'm not a kid.'

I close my eyes knowing this is the worst thing Kieran could have replied with, making it look even more suspicious. I don't want a scene; I don't want the fuss or embarrassment of what Darren is capable of.

CHAPTER THIRTEEN

'Just do it.' I whisper to Kieran. 'Listen to your dad, will you.'

Kieran pulls me a look of disgust, and hands Darren his mobile phone after unlocking it. Darren scrolls through the messages.

'We'll talk about that later at home.' He says, handing the phone back. 'Now isn't the time or place.'

We all stand up for the final song, all looking at the vicar. I know during this time; the coffin will be placed behind the curtain and I'm trying to contain all my emotions for Darren's sake.

Throughout all of this turmoil, grief and stress, I'm the one who's expected to pick up all the pieces, the one who keeps carrying on, carrying on. Cooking dinner, going shopping, doing all the washing. Kieran is lazy, but a typical teenager and Darren is battling his own demons.

My demons won't get a look in.

Chapter Fourteen

Tuesday, 6 June 2023
Brenda

My spiritual thoughts are urging me to do things that I would normally leave well alone. Where I was previously unsure about the persistent thoughts and signs in my head, and what everything meant, I'm now certain that I have a purpose when it comes to missing Lauren. I have a calling spiritually to find her.

The signs are far too strong for me to ignore them any longer. I still need to interpret some of the meanings better, I admit, but I'm making slow progress. I'm going to try the tarot cards again another time. That's where I feel my real connection to my Gran spiritually. Holding her very own cards, channelling her strength and energy. I know she was with me last night; she was guiding these thoughts. I miss her.

A fleeting thought about a missing girl in my local newspaper has now developed into something much more personal. Lauren being sighted not far from my own house, the girl's mother being in my locality, coupled with the voices in my mind, the tarot cards, the feelings and emotions that flooded me when I touched that keyring with Lauren's face on it. I can't

CHAPTER FOURTEEN

ignore everything, I have a duty, a sense of purpose to answer this girl's disappearance. I want to help because if I don't, I will never forgive myself. This is a calling in my head from my heritage, it's part of who I am. I don't know why I was so closed to these thoughts before. It's as though I'm becoming alive again with a new life, a new purpose. I believe I can really help, if only I could spend more time with them as a family.

'Bren, you are being unreasonable. You can't just intrude on this family's grief and loss. You should stay out of it.' Al says, while driving me to Southleigh Holiday Cottages. 'What on earth will they think of us? Imagine if someone tried knocking on our door with bad news. You'd be the first one telling them where to go, wouldn't you?'

I spent my whole childhood worrying and wondering what everyone thought of me. A child who was abandoned by her own mother, a gran who was the talk of the town with her clairvoyant readings, and neighbours who I know talked about us. I'm not as resilient as my gran, nor am I as outspoken, and never have I felt spirituality as close to my heart as missing Lauren.

'You don't have to say anything, in fact, you don't even need to be with me. You can wait for me in the car.' I reply. 'I know I've gone on about this for a long time, but I can't ignore it, and Al, I need you to support me. I have to speak to them both, I can't rest until I see them. I hope they're home.'

Al doesn't understand any of my spiritual beliefs, and I get how crazy he must think I am, but he is my husband, he knew my background before we even got married. If there's one person in the world, I expect to support me, now matter how crazy, it will be Al.

'Is this all because of that dream you had last night? It's

just a dream. God's sake, you really are turning into your grandmother.'

'It was so real, Al. I can't let this go. I heard her voice. It was like she was talking to me. There were plenty of things that could be interpreted, but I need to ask them, face to face. I need to know what they think when I tell them parts of what I saw.'

'I'll do this for you, but only this once, and Bren, if they kick off or ask you to never see them again, will you please listen to me and let it be?'

I nod and agree. I don't want to be insensitive to the family's feelings.

'Thank you.' I reply, 'I promise. If they tell me to go away, I'll never bother them again. I'll accept that we might never have answers and move on.'

'Great. I'm worried they'll end up calling the police on us, and they will send you off to a mental institute. Just joking.'

The dream last night to me was a definitive spiritual encounter. Never before have I had a dream where I felt as though it was actual reality. I remember the scents from the forest, the smell of the river, and the breeze blowing in my face. I felt a warm rush of love hit me. It was Lauren, she came to me and told me something that I have to tell her family. If I trust my senses, I think they will understand it more than me. It was so vivid and a calling. I hope I am delivering a spiritual message they can relate to.

Lauren and I walked hand in hand along some of the greenest of fields I had seen. She dipped her toes into a running river, and it was picturesque and serene. She was smiling and happy, looked similar age to the image in the newspaper. There was a sequence of locations. One minute we were in a forest, the next we were walking by a lake. There were moments when it was bright and sunny, then suddenly the weather and skies turned darker. Like daytime going into the evening.

Do I read something into that? If I was to interpret that as my gran would, I think it means that happier times went to darker times, but there's a reason she vanished which I tried to resolve.

'Why did you run away?' I asked her, my voice echoed far across the dreamlike forest. 'You are loved and missed by your dear family. Tell me why, Lauren?'

I remember feeling instantly cold. It felt like thunder was approaching.

'I'm trapped, like a black widow spider.' She replied, her voice soft, fearful. I sensed she was afraid. 'Black. Widow. Spider.'

She spoke slowly, and I remember feeling my heart beating in my chest so fast. I was scared, then excited, then worried again. I didn't know what it meant, and why she was saying that.

'Tell Mum, I'm sorry.' Lauren said, again slowly, handing me a necklace from her pocket with a small silver teardrop design hanging from the delicate chain. 'I never meant to hurt anyone.'

Then our surroundings changed to fields of rose bushes everywhere around us. Roses in all different colours in glowing sunshine. It was as if they were growing in seconds all around me, but then I became warm and happy again. It was so spectacular; I didn't want it to end.

I woke up covered in goosebumps, but it was the white feather on my pillow that made me cry. I know the spiritual signs, I know she was really with me, she had to have been. It was far too real, and of course, Al wouldn't understand.

'What are you going to say to them exactly?' Alan asks, breaking my trail of thought. 'What if they're not even home? What a wasted journey.'

'It's coming up for eight, in the evening. They'll be in, I'm sure. I'm going to be completely honest.' I sigh, 'I'm going to tell them that I come from a family of Romany Gypsy Spiritualists and I can't stop feeling some kind of spiritual connection to their missing daughter. I'm going to lay all my cards out on the table. Well, not literally, but you know what I mean.'

Al nods. I know what he must be thinking, but I don't want to hear the same old talk of how there's no significant proof of spirits. I feel what I feel, and I believe what I believe. I'm not hurting anyone, and this might end up showing him that there's something in it. If he was more open minded, he might have experiences of his own.

'I'll wait in the car. We're almost there.' He replies. 'There's no rush. Take your time. I expect we won't be there long.'

As we pull up in the site, Al drives slower to make way for the couples and children heading into the club house. They're all dressed up, likely for dinner and drinks.

'We should pop in there one night, shouldn't we?' Alan says, parking in the car park. 'We've both worked here now for how many years?'

'Oh, it's been a few, hasn't it.' I reply, reaching out to hold his hand. 'We can, but it's not like we really go out anymore, is it?'

'We should.' He replies. 'You know I love you, Bren, don't you?'

He doesn't say it often, but we've been married for almost forty years. We've had countless nights out, dinners, cinema

CHAPTER FOURTEEN

trips, theatre visits, that I now find it more comforting being at home, relaxing with my feet up. If there's anything we don't do enough of, is going on holiday.

'I love you too.' I reply. 'Don't think I don't know you well enough already.'

I smile at Al, because I knew he was about to ask how I am, how I'm feeling and that he's worried about me.

'I'm worried.' He says. 'I've never seen you this obsessed with it.'

'It's not obsession. It's a real connection.'

He looks at me, still concerned, but shows me a wry smile. I know what he's thinking and for once he has kept his mouth shut.

'I only want support. You don't have to like it, but I feel something strong, and you remember my grandmother don't you? How highly intuitive she was?'

Al nods.

'I'm not as polished as her in that respect. But it's like this hit me out of the blue. I can't let it go, but I accept that if I'm wrong, then I'm wrong. I have a need to help this family. Something spiritual is reaching out to me with Lauren, and if it wasn't all the same things Gran experienced, I'd stop being so focussed. I have to keep at it.'

'Just be careful.' Al replies. 'Not everyone shares your beliefs. You know that.'

I undo my seat belt and get out of the car. Al turns on the radio and fiddles with some switches.

As I walk closer to their holiday cottage, I'm now becoming nervous. I look around the site, which I know so very well, and I rarely get to see how lively it is at this hour. The sun is starting to set, and it has a busy feel to it. It's a warm evening, but I hope

I'm not delivering unsettling news. This will really show me if Lauren connected with me last night. I'm counting on them to understand. The Cooke's cottage is now in sight, and all I want is for them to listen. I want to explain about the necklace, the spider, the rose bushes, then hope they are willing to remain calm and open minded.

If all of this is meaningless, then I will walk away convinced that maybe, just maybe, I've become too invested, but that's my head talking. If there is a meaningful connection, which my heart truly believes there is, then I want to help, but to help, I will need to embark on a spiritual journey with them as a family to learn my craft and learn more about them too. If they'll allow.

I'm ready and knock on the door.

Chapter Fifteen

Tuesday, 6 June 2023
Brenda

Their shouting is getting louder and louder. I've knocked the door, but still neither Carol nor Darren has answered. I've tried listening to their argument, although it sounds too muffled. I'm getting concerned by their tones, it's some kind of verbal slanging match. What is happening?

I turn around to face Al who is unaware; I can see him bopping his head to whatever song he's listening to on the local radio station. I knock on the cottage door, one more time, only this time much harder to make more noise. Still nothing, other than the sound of a heated argument.

A cool breeze blows across the park making me shiver slightly with the chill, the red cloudy skies. I walk to the front of the cottage hoping to catch their attention if they can see me from the window. I spot Darren, he's standing and waving his arms around, pacing up and down. Carol is sat down on the sofa. She looks depressed with a vacant look on her face. Do I knock on the window, or should I leave?

Walking on this uneven land is playing havoc with my joints, but I slowly stumble back over a small steep towards the door.

I knock again, loud and clear and wait. Their arguing stops, which is a clear sign they've heard me. I strike the door again with my clenched fist, hard, loud and clear.

The door opens.

'Carol?' I say, a slight panic in my voice. 'Is everything alright? Are you ok?'

I give it away that I've heard their argument, but not clear enough to hear the specific details.

'Carol.' I say again. 'Do you need any help?'

'Please, we don't need any cleaning or extra towels' Carole replies, only peering through the door. 'Now is not a good time. Can you come back tomorrow?'

I turn around to face Al, he's still not paying attention and I'm left with a decision to make. I'm bemused by her assumption that I was here for work, I'm not even carrying any towels.

'I really wanted to explain myself about yesterday.' I explain. 'It's been on my mind an awful lot. You must think I'm mad. I mentioned The Empress, and some other things. You see, my love. I'm not here tonight as a cleaner; I need to talk to you.'

'Who the fuck are you talking to now?' Darren shouts from the background. I know he can't see me. 'We are good thanks. Shut the fucking door.'

'I'm so sorry, he's been drinking. It's been a long day.' Carol explains, red faced with embarrassment. 'He will sleep it off soon. I'm ok, nothing to worry about, but thank you. I'm really sorry.'

As Carol is about to close the door in my face, we maintain eye contact and she tightens her lips with a nod to signal a non-verbal goodbye. She looks exhausted.

'It's Lauren.' I gasp out loud. 'I'm here because of Lauren.'

CHAPTER FIFTEEN

'What about Lauren?' Darren says behind the door, this time showing his drunken aggression. He pulls the door open wide and stands tall behind Carol. 'What about my daughter? Lauren, Jenny, or whatever she calls herself now.'

My mouth drops because I feel slightly threatened by his tone. I should walk away, but I'm concerned for Carol's welfare. If there's any time I should show her my support, it is now. Is she safe?

'Can I please come inside; it's getting cold out here on the doorstep?' I politely ask now that I have both of their attention. 'I'm freezing. May I?'

I've managed to break their argument at least. Carol looks tense, her body language is awkward. Her eyes now looking downwards towards the floor. I'm not even sure how to explain what I need to say. As I'm talking to them, watching their expressions, I'm also thinking of my Gran and what she would have done in the same situation.

'Of course.' Darren mutters under his breath. 'Be my fucking guess. Come on in. Do you want a drink? Vodka, Rum, or a nice glass of wine?'

I step inside the cottage and immediately my eyes are drawn to the broken wine glasses on the kitchen worktops. There's a smell of burnt food in the air, and an open vodka bottle near the kitchen sink. I head into the lounge where I sit down on the sofa, and both of them are standing in front of me.

'What about Lauren?' Carol asks me. I notice her hands shaking. 'Have you seen her?'

I smile and my eyes start to feel watery as my emotions shift. I should stop seeing crying as a sign of weakness, but I can't help it. I'm nervous, but I know what I need to do. I need to behave like my Gran.

What's the worst that can happen?

'I don't exactly know how to say this.'

Darren shrugs his shoulders while Carol sits on the chair opposite me.

'I'm quite sensitive. Well, so my grandmother used to tell me anyway. I feel things. Things that sometimes can't be explained directly with words or specifics. But I can interpret signs.'

'What in gods name are you banging on about lady?' Darren interrupts me. 'What is it you're feeling because you ain't making much sense to me. Is she you, Carol?'

'We put out some flyers today around the harbour and near some shops and restaurants.' Carol says. 'We were both hoping that would spur people to contact us, but as of yet. Nothing. There was one woman who thought she saw Lauren about a year ago in some charity race.'

'I'm a spiritualist.' I drop the bombshell and their face drops. 'You could say that I am also a psychic, maybe, but I don't feel like I'm a psychic. I'm not that advanced or gifted, but I feel things that I can't explain emotionally, and l needed to see you because of a dream I had. It left me shaken.'

'Pack your fucking bags. I don't give a shit who you are, but how dare you come up here and stand in front of us with that bag of bullshit.' Darren says, walking towards me. 'Get out of our fucking house. I will call the police, or security, whatever the fuck it takes.'

'Darren, stop.' Carol stands up, rolls up her sleeve and spots the bruise across her wrists. I look at Darren. 'Can you just calm down and stop swearing with every other word that comes out of your mouth. Please? She's trying to speak. Let her finish.'

Darren takes a few steps backwards and is pacing up and

CHAPTER FIFTEEN

down near the kitchen. At least he's away from me. If he becomes violent, I look around the room to see what I could defend myself with.

I'm not strong enough to pick the lounge table, but I'm in close vicinity to the television set. I'm aware I have my mobile phone in my pocket and I will call the police if I need to.

'At least hear her out. I'm sorry I've forgotten your name?' Asks Carol, who's red faced with embarrassment. 'What was it again?'

'It's Brenda.' I reply. 'Or Bren, for short. I'm not bothered either way. I know this might seem strange, but I had to do this. I had to bring myself here and tell you what happened. I know it's weird, but please give me a chance.'

'This is the problem with small villages.' Darren interrupts, pouring himself another drink. 'Nut jobs everywhere you look. I knew coming all the way out here was a bad idea. I said we should have stayed at home. I knew it would be like this. A bad fucking idea. I told you so. There's no way our daughter would put up with all this shit round here. Let's go back home.'

I carry on talking as he's taking a sip of his vodka and shaking his head. I can read the room, I know I only have one chance and it's either going to be meaningful or downright nonsense.

'Lauren came to me in a dream.' I explain. Darren laughs, Carol is looking at me like I'm crazy. 'I know it might sound strange, but I wouldn't expect anything less. No one believed my Gran when she experienced signs. But Lauren was showing me rose bushes, and she handed me a tear drop necklace. It was silver and very smooth.'

Carol immediately placed her hand to her neck. I spot more bruising. Darren for a few seconds continued to gulp down the rest of his vodka.

'Does that mean anything to you both?'

Carol stares at me, I'm not sure if its with joy or anger. Her eyes aren't blinking and she has broken her dark stare.

'Everyone knew about the necklace, didn't they?' She says, looking towards Darren. 'The papers reported it didn't they. I'm sure they did.'

I'm not sure what she's talking about, but Carol seems shaken.

'What do you mean?'

Carol stands up, while Darren is still smiling and shaking his head in disbelief.

'It was the necklace we gave her for her sixteenth birthday.' Darren snaps. 'She was wearing it when she left.'

My immediate thoughts were on what Carol stated about the papers. I've been focussed on this case so much, that I am confident no one has mentioned the necklace. She wasn't even wearing it in the pictures.

'It's not in any of the local newspapers that I've read.' I defend myself. 'I remember when she first went missing, and I've seen the re-released story with the same picture. It doesn't mention any necklace. This is the first time I've heard about it.'

I start to doubt myself, but I've been that obsessive, I trust my instincts. I've definitely not read anything anywhere about the necklace.

'Was it a teardrop one?' I ask. 'Silver?'

'Yes.' Carol says, walking over to my direction. 'We bought her a bunch of roses and gave her a silver teardrop necklace. It was one she'd seen walking past a jeweller in Plymouth town centre.'

I'm stunned, but more assured that I am mastering my

skills. I feel emotional again because of their reaction and their acknowledgment of the necklace affirms that Lauren did reach out to me.

How? Does that mean she's dead.

I didn't even want to think about it, my head now flooded with other questions.

'Black Widow. That was something else she told me.' I explain further. 'Does that mean anything to you?'

Carol shakes her head.

'Lauren hated spiders.' Carol replies, pulling down her sleeve to cover the bruising now. 'No, that means nothing to us really. I mean, who likes spiders anyway.'

'Can you please leave now?' Darren asks. Slamming down his glass on the worktop. 'I think it's best you left us both alone. Don't you?'

I stand up, aware I've outstayed my welcome. Carol is rubbing her eyes and trying to mask her tears. I walk past her and catch another glance. I've upset her, I can tell.

'I'm sorry if I've upset you. I didn't mean to do that, but I felt that strong. I needed to know about the necklace.'

'You haven't seen her in person, have you?' Darren asks. 'Have you?'

'No.' I shake my head. 'Not in person.'

I walk to the door and Carol follows me.

'I'll let you out,' she says, looking flustered. 'We will make sure we leave this all clean and tidy by the time we go on Friday.'

We both walk to the back door. Darren is out of earshot as he has moved further into the lounge.

'That was her necklace.' Carol whispers. 'Are you sure you didn't read about it in the paper?'

'It's not in the papers.' I assure her. 'When you met me

yesterday and I touched your keyring. I felt something. I can't seem to let it go. I'm sorry to have upset you.'

Carol places her hand on mine. Her bruise now visible again and she has caught my eyes fixed on it.

'He loves his family.' She says. 'He doesn't mean what he says. He's drunk. Lauren walking out of our lives has taken its toll on us both. He will calm down in the morning.'

I shake my head. I don't know what else to say or do.

'I'm sorry, but thanks for your time.' I reply. 'I better get back to my husband, he'll be wondering where I've been.'

Carol pulls out a leaflet from her back pocket. It's folded and looks creased, but she hands it to me.

'My number is on there, at the bottom.' She whispers. 'Let me know if you have anything else. Send me a text.'

I take the flyer, I don't unfold it, but I feel a sense of warmth from her. Is this her way of asking me to contact her again away from Darren. It wasn't the rejection I was expecting.

'Do you think Lauren is dead?' Carol whispers. 'Is that what you think?'

I take a deep breath.

'I'm not sure. I'm being honest.' I reply. 'My gran always said I had the gift, and when I saw Lauren in the paper again. It awakened something, feelings I can't express. I can't imagine what you have gone through as a family. But I don't know if she's dead. I only know what I saw in my dream. The necklace, the roses, and the spider.'

'You best go now.'

We don't say our goodbyes and I silently leave while Carol shuts the door behind me.

I fear for her, but I can tell she wants me to reach out. I look up at the darken sky and head walking back towards our car. I turn around and take one more look at their cottage and listen. There's no more arguing, everything seems quiet.

I'm desperate to check in the papers if they mentioned the necklace. It's the first thing I'm going to look at when I get back home.

Chapter Sixteen

Wednesday, 7 June 2023
Carol

Darren's drunken snoring had kept me awake for most of the night. He was tossing and turning, as he always does when he's been drinking for hours on end. I tried moaning at him, prodding him, but he was out for the count.

I wish he wouldn't drink as much as he does when he's having one of those days. He can go weeks without any, but then when he starts drinking again, he goes all in. It's never just the one, it's never just for happy hour, it's never really stopped either. He tries his best, but I've given up giving him advice.

I was hoping today we could get up and out early, maybe use this time away for a day trip to some other holiday parks in the area nearby. I thought it might be useful to spread our flyers a bit further afield. I keep checking my phone after everything we did yesterday, but no one has reached out. Not one text message, not one phone call. I thought we'd generate more interest than that and we're only here a couple more days. There must be more we can do.

After Brenda left yesterday evening, Darren went straight to bed whilst I sat up watching reality television. I think I

CHAPTER SIXTEEN

was watching something about a group of young, tanned and perfectly toned people trying to find love on an island, my eyes were fixated on the television, but my mind was focussed on everything Brenda had told us.

I don't remember falling asleep, but I remember waking up gasping for air, panicking and reliving the fear. I turned to look at Darren who was out for the count, then I felt resentful that he could even sleep. He never has restless nights; he never talks about how he is affected about our missing daughter. I'm sick of him constantly trying to be emotionally hard. There are some moments with tears when he lets his guard down, but it's rare.

I got out of bed early with no appetite for breakfast. The corner of my eyes sore from all the crying. I'm a mess. As much as I have tried over the past ten years to carry on as normal, some days I need a break. I can close my eyes and remember every detail of Lauren's face, even her last words to me.

Maybe coming out all this way was a bad idea?

I've had a few text messages from my Kieran asking how we are doing? I've replied that we are remaining hopeful, but no real change. I daren't tell him about Brenda, he'd kick off just like his father. He's been through enough of his own troubles. I hope for his sake he gets his head down at the builder's firm he works for and has a good career for himself. I never wanted either of my kids to have the same struggles as me. If Kieran isn't careful, he'll end up just like his father, getting into debt and making bad decisions. I wanted both of my kids to grow up happy, settled, and maybe have kids of their own. I burst into tears as I think more about my situation. I'm trapped with no way out.

'Morning.' Darren says, wiping his eyes, walking out of the

bedroom in just his boxers. His voice croaky. 'Did you sleep well?'

'Like a log.' I reply, not to bother getting into a discussion about it. 'Do you want me to cook you some breakfast?'

I hear the bathroom taps; he's cleaning his teeth.

'I had a text from Kieran this morning.' I shout through, 'he was only asking how we were getting on. I told him, no luck yet.'

Darren pops his head round the door. There's toothpaste all down his chin. He annoys me at home when he does that because it drops all over the carpet and it's not him scrubbing it away.

'Did you tell him about that weirdo woman who came round last night?' He asks. 'Psychic Brenda whatever she was called? He'd have a right laugh about that.'

'You were so mean to her. Do you remember anything that you said last night. You were quite aggressive and swearing at her.' I reply, smiling, but a little awkward about it. 'She was the cleaner in here, remember me telling you about her? And no, I didn't tell Kieran because he'll only come storming out here in a temper. Just like his father.'

Darren approaches me with his arms out.

'Come here,' he says, and I stand up. 'Let's have a hug. I'm sorry for what I said yesterday. Not to Brenda, but to you. I didn't mean any of it. If anyone else comes near either of us with all that crap, they can fuck off. You shouldn't have let her in.'

The smell of alcohol on his breath was still quite strong even though he had cleaned his teeth. I pulled my face away a little. Darren places his arms around me tightly and squeezes. He won't even be fully aware of what he told me or to Brenda. He knows that he's done wrong and says the same exact thing every morning. I was expecting an apology, but he never changes.

'Why don't we go back to bed for a little while.' He begins to kiss my neck. 'We can go out for breakfast later. We don't often get time alone like this, come on, come back to bed with me. Like the old days.'

'No, I can't. I don't really feel like it.' I quietly reply. His grip on me still firm, his hands all over my body. 'I'm not in the mood. I can't. I'm sorry, not today.'

Darren gently pushes me away; I sense the tension already.

'You're never in the fucking mood.' He snaps. 'We don't make time for each other anymore and I'm fed up with it. I think we've had sex like twice in the last year, haven't we? It's not healthy.'

I shrug my shoulders, head lowered. I wasn't keeping any kind of count on it. We've been together a long time, we've had two kids together, we've been through a lot. Is it really that important, right now?

'I feel neglected. Sometimes it's like we're just housemates.'

I'm sure I stopped breathing for a few seconds. He thinks that he's the one who is neglected?

'This isn't some kind of second honeymoon, is it?' I give as my annoyed response. 'We will spend time together, give me time. I promise. I don't feel sexy. I don't feel like I can enjoy sex while I'm here looking for our missing daughter.'

Darren storms off into the bedroom alone.

'You aren't the one going through the menopause.'

He doesn't reply.

'What shall we do today?' I shout through, minutes later, changing the subject, hoping he suggests the same idea I have in mind. 'Do you think you're in a fit enough state to drive?'

He comes back through to the living room, fully dressed in his dark jeans and polo shirt. Any mention of us having sex and I'll get up and go for a walk.

'I don't know about you.' He says, sitting down on the chair in the corner of the room. 'I plan on going to the pub when it opens.'

I sigh with disappointment. It's on the tip of my tongue, but I don't want to say it out loud. Does his daughter not mean anything to him? Does he even care? To avoid another argument, I don't bite.

'I searched online through some of the old news reports. While you were sleeping. I needed to be sure.' I say to change the subject. 'We were both wrong about Lauren's necklace. It isn't mentioned anywhere that I could find. Not in the local news, or that time it went national once. Nothing.'

Darren doesn't seem phased.

'Maybe you haven't checked everything, or everywhere good enough.' He replies. 'I know I must have mentioned it to someone. It was ten years ago. I'm sure we mentioned her necklace to at least somebody in that time?'

I nod, again to save another argument. I'm not in the right head space for a battle.

If Brenda knows about the necklace, which she was quite specific with its detail. It was silver, it was in a teardrop shape design, then what else does she know and how does she know it.

Was it really a dream?

'The one part that's been bugging me, and I wish I thought of it at the time.' I say to Darren, 'what if she's hiding something?'

CHAPTER SIXTEEN

'What?' He says, lowering the television. 'Hiding what exactly? Let's be real here. It's some old cleaner who read about us and had some weird fucking dream.'

'Hear me out.' I continue while I have his attention. 'What if she knows something about Lauren, and is maybe using the dream she had and all that psychic stuff as a ploy? We don't know who she knows, or who she talks to, but it was very specific.'

'Who care's what she thinks and says.' Darren says, firmly. 'Steer well clear of her, she's not right in the head. If she hasn't seen or spoken to Lauren, or even knows where she is, then what use is she to us. She'll fuck with your head.'

I don't say anything and we sit there in a moment of silence.

'Why don't we have a chill day today?' I suggest. 'Since we're here for two more days, I guess one day won't hurt. What time did you want to go to the pub?'

Darren rubs his hands together with excitement.

'Great idea.' He replies. 'How about for lunch. That nice one down near the harbour again. I really liked it there yesterday.'

'How about, you go to the pub. Enjoy the weather and the cold beer. You have been working really hard lately, so you deserve a bit of a break.' I say. 'I will visit some of the shops and businesses that we didn't manage to fit in yesterday. I want to cover as many areas as possible. Maybe, Lauren if she is here, then she might have worked for someone, or still be working for someone close by.'

'You don't have to do it alone. We can always go now, and then head to the pub after?'

'No. You go to the pub, and I'll do it alone. I will phone you if I need you. I don't mind. Go on, you might even make some friends.'

Darren smiles and we seem to have agreed today to go our separate ways this morning.

What I haven't told him is that I have decided that I will speak to Brenda. Although she my number, I don't have hers, but she works here so I don't think it will be too challenging getting hold of her. I can ask down at reception for her to call me. They'll contact her on my behalf, I'm sure they'll help me if I ask nice enough.

'Are you sure you don't want me to help you at all?' Darren asks. 'I don't mind if you want me to?'

I know he's only being polite.

'No, it's a going to be a warm day today, and I know how much you hate walking around in the sun.'

Darren comes over and kisses my forehead.

'I love you.' He says. 'I'm sorry about arguing yesterday. And, sorry about wanting to sleep with you this morning. I was insensitive.'

'I know.' I reply. 'I love you too. You aren't wrong. We don't have much of a sex life anymore. It's not either of our fault, but life sometimes gets in the way doesn't it.'

I close my eyes and smile. I'm not even sure of my emotions anymore. I'm living an existence rather than a life. I don't really go anywhere, we don't have holidays, I'm not even sure what happiness is anymore. How can I feel sexual when my mind is constantly focussed on our loss.

We are the couple who's daughter vanished, and everyone must think we are bad parents.

Chapter Seventeen

Wednesday, 7 June 2023
Brenda

As usual, Al has told me to keep my nose out of their business, but I think he's getting used to me ignoring his advice lately. Carol's phone call came completely out of the blue. After agreeing to take her call from Southleigh's receptionist, she sounded afraid of something, or someone, and she was talking really fast. I had wondered if she wanted to get away from that awful husband of hers. I didn't get good vibes from him; there's something not quite right. I'm concerned about all her bruises.

'Is there anywhere we can go that's not on the main waterfront?' She asked. 'It would be great if we could chat somewhere in private.'

'I know a small woodland patch down the road from me.' I replied, hesitant. 'I can always come to your cottage, is that any easier for you?'

'No.' Carol said sharply. 'Sorry, I don't want Darren to see us. I'd rather he didn't know, I don't want all the fuss. He's taken it very hard. We are both struggling with the loss again, being here, talking about Lauren, it's reminding us of the nightmare that we live in.'

'Meet me at Meadow Ridge. It should be on your phone map app if you have one.' I said. 'I'll be there soon. Take a left at the entrance and I'll be near the grassy verge where there's a bench. It's the first bench you come to.'

It's taken me about fifteen minutes to walk to the small woodland area close by, but why does she want to meet me in private?

I'm standing against a wooden gate, in exactly the same spot I'd advised, but she's nowhere to be seen. The bench is next to me, and I'm wondering if she's had second thoughts.

'Come on, Carol. Where are you?' I whisper, but the only sounds I hear are the birds in the trees, and the occasional footsteps from the curious squirrels running by. 'You should have been here by now.'

I've smiled at every dog walker that has passed by me, and now I have this feeling that she's not going to show up.

'Thanks for meeting me.' Carol says, startling me from behind. 'I found it eventually. Sorry I'm late, I took the wrong turning but realised my mistake.'

I place my arm on her shoulder and give it a gentle squeeze. In that moment of touch, I felt goosebumps, unease and queasy.

'Why the secrecy?' I ask, bluntly. 'Why do we have to make sure Darren doesn't know that you've met me?'

Carol turns her head to look away from me as we keep walking down the wooded path. It's quiet, peaceful and a gentle breeze is blowing. I'm silent and waiting for her response. I need to walk slowly because of my dodgy knee.

'He doesn't believe in anything like that.' Carol says, 'all stuff about psychics and spirits. He thinks it's all a load of nonsense.'

'He wouldn't be the first to think that.' I reply with a smile, trying to engage in eye contact. 'No doubt, he wouldn't be the last either. My husband thinks the same. Calls it a load of old bullshit.'

'So, is it true then?'

'Is what true?'

'Can you speak to dead people? Do you hear things?'

'Look, I'll be completely honest with you, as was my grandmother with me.' I reply, and finally Carol is looking right at me. I can see and sense her nervousness. 'I only know what I know, and I don't know what I don't know. It's as though it needs interpretation which is why I had to tell you. It's not for me to interpret, it's for you to know and what meaning it has to you. That's the only way I can describe it. It's not explicit, it's more implicit, but it seemed to have real meaning for you. It was her necklace.'

Carol smiles. For a moment she shakes her head but smiles at me again. It feels like she understands.

'I believe there is something after we die. As to what exactly, I'm not sure. We lose our physical existence, but I believe a part of us can still linger on in a non physical sense.' I continue. 'I think of it like different planes of existence. Earth is physical, but I do think we move on in this universe. Or maybe we just fade away into a part of something bigger that we don't even know of.'

'So how does it work for you. How do you know you're getting signs, or whatever you call them? Messages?' Carol asks. 'Sometimes I want to believe, but then I see things online, and I wonder if maybe it's just coincidences, or lucky guesses.'

'My Gran used to say that when she feels like she is communicating with someone, and by that, I mean someone in a non physical sense. She's interpreting or reading a sign, a message. I'm new to all this and have to use my own judgement.'

We stop talking for a moment as a dog walker approaches. I recognise it to be Gary from a few streets over from me and his beautiful Collie cross Jack Russell called Dinky. I smile and they both pass.

'Have you been doing it long?'

'My grandmother always said I had the family gift, but I shut it out. Until recently, then as more and more thoughts and feelings came into my head, and I decided not to ignore them any longer.'

'You were right about the necklace.' Carol says, now emotional. 'We gave Lauren a teardrop necklace in silver for her 16th birthday. She was wearing it when she vanished. I've not seen it anywhere in the house and believe me I've looked everywhere for it high and low.'

'I checked the newspaper articles, you know.' I reply. 'It didn't mention anything about the necklace. She wasn't wearing any jewellery in the photographs of her either.'

Carol stops to wipe her eyes.

'Is she dead?' She asks me. 'Do you know for sure that my little girl is dead?'

The moment she ended her sentence I felt my own breath stop. In that split second, I was over analysing what was going through my mind. I had a flashed image of the necklace again, the roses, and that feeling of immense sadness.

But does that mean she is dead?

'I don't know. I was letting you know what signs came to me as a message.' I say softly to comfort her. 'I felt so strongly about my dream, that it was some kind of connection with Lauren, but it doesn't mean people are dead when that

CHAPTER SEVENTEEN

happens.'

We are both interrupted by the sound of Carol's mobile phone ringing. She pulls it out of her pocket and doesn't answer.

'That's Darren, he'll be wondering where I am.' She says. 'He's back at the pub; I'm meant to be joining him for lunch.'

Her body language was tense when she spoke about him. I can't forget the bruising I saw, and the way he seems so aggressive.

'Is he always very aggressive?' I ask, polite and calmly not to unsettle her. 'Just, yesterday when I was there, things seemed very tense. Are you ok?'

'You seem like a very nice, kind lady.' Carol replies, avoiding my question. 'I better go and get back to Darren before he starts worrying about me. I'm ok, thank you.'

'You have my number if you need to talk.' I say, sensing that she wants to leave. 'You can call me any time. I can't imagine what you've been through as a family.'

Carol starts crying. I spot another bench a few yards ahead, and suggest we sit down for a few more minutes. I don't want to draw any attention to us, since it might encourage her to run away from me.

There's no one else around thankfully, and we sit on the bench. Carol composes herself. I need to think fast, I have no idea when I might see or even speak to her again.

'I believe that there is something out there wanting us to connect with each other.' I tell Carol, and I'm not lying either. 'Something spiritually was reaching out to me when Lauren went missing. My stomach tenses when I think about it. I know we aren't in any way connected, but I've been saying it for years. I can't help but think about Lauren when I always hear about sightings, or reminders in the press about her disappearance.'

Carol is sat, listening to me, still holding on to her mobile phone.

'That necklace is a sign for both of us. So, if you want to get up and never speak to me again. That is fine.' I explain, but I have to say it, and she might be quite shocked. 'I believe I'm meant to help you. I feel it, I sense it. You might think it's weird, but it's not just about the necklace. Here you are in my location, we've been brought together and look, we are speaking to each other, we've made a connection.'

'I don't even really know why I am here.' Carol says. 'I'm always lost, confused, and I never know what to do anymore.'

'We can build on those connections. If not now, another time.'

'I'm sorry about Darren' Carol replies. 'He's only ever like that in drink. I know he'll regret it today. Knocking on our door, when to us, this is our lives. It's our missing daughter and it never feels any easier.'

'I want to help. Let me help.'

Carol nods and holds my hand. I feel a chill in the air.

'This kinda thing has never happened to me before. I'm not sure how you can help unless you know where Lauren is, or how I might find her. What you told us about the necklace, do you know where she is, did Lauren speak to you directly?'

I can feel the goosebumps on my arms.

'Are you saying what I think you're saying?' I'm not sure I understand what she means. 'That I have spoken to Lauren directly about the necklace, and she sent me to you? Why on earth would she do that?'

'How could you know about the teardrop? It's not like it's a guess about a necklace, you were actually very specific about the design, the metal, everything.' Carol says. 'You've got my attention with that necklace detail, and I just want to know woman to woman what exactly is it that you know. What are you not telling me? Do you know what happened?'

'I'm sorry, I have no idea what happened or where Lauren is. I wanted to reach out and help spiritually.'

'This is all just too fucked up. It's fucked up. I have to go because Darren will be getting stressed.'

'I didn't want to offend you.' I reply. 'I'm being honest. Trust me, please.'

'You're not being honest with me, are you?' Carol shouts. Her mood now as aggressive as Darren was last night. 'You're fucking with my head. You're fucking with me, aren't you. What the fuck are you doing. I'm struggling to cope as it is.'

Sometimes telling people to calm down is the worst kind of advice you can give. I remember my gran telling me that when I was a young girl. I've seen her in the same situation, I know what she would have said. Here goes using some of her advice to me.

'Step out of the situation a second. You already know that I am right about the necklace. I mentioned roses too.' I continue, calmly and looking her dead in the eye. 'I'm offering my support to help you, even if you don't believe in spirituality. I can help you in other ways. Talk to me, give me some leaflets to hand out. I just want to offer support to you and your husband. Al, my husband can help out too.'

I wanted her to know that I am a kind, caring and thoughtful person.

However, Carol might feel about me, or my beliefs. I can support them both. I want her to concentrate on the necklace because that is my evidence that someone, somewhere, whether it is Lauren spiritually, or my grandmother guiding me down a path, it was accurate, meaningful, and I don't want her to back away. Carol should open her mind and embrace it.

'Can you tell me something more about Lauren?' Carol asks. 'Do you need anything to be able to do that?'

I smile, and I have a feeling of warmth again, despite the breeze. She's listening to me, she's back where I need her mentally. Open minded, but I'm not an expert. How I wish I'd listen more to my gran as a teenager. I had no idea how invested I'd get.

'Do you have anything of Lauren's on you, as odd as it sounds. If I have something of hers that I can channel in on?'

'I don't have anything on me. I don't carry anything except her picture on my keyring, but it's mine.'

'It's ok. Let me close my eyes and concentrate for a second. I need to clear my thoughts and mind. It may work, it may not.'

Carol sits still on the bench. I close my eyes and I try to concentrate on an image of Lauren in my mind. I try not to focus on the background noises from the birds, the wind blowing the leaves in the trees, and the sound of nature. Soon, as I think about my environment as layers, I've stripped back to the emptiness of a dark void. My own thoughts blank, but I can hear Carols deep breathing.

'I keep seeing a gold ring, it's like it's going higher and higher.' I explain. 'I know that gold is a sign of commitment and love.'

'Anything specific to Lauren that could tell me why or where she is.'

I shake my head, but I feel dizzy with the level of concentration. I focus on my breathing. Carol is still talking but all I see is darkness. Her words now muffled, my mind confused, the feeling of a rush of heat works its way up my body. I'm feeling flushed. I'm suffocating, hot and confused.

'Well, I should have fucking known you'd meet that cunt again.' I hear, that startles me. I take in a big deep breath and open my eyes. Darren is walking towards us. 'I've been fucking trying to ring you. You've not answered.'

Carol looks at me.

'I'm very sorry,' she whispers. 'I'm so sorry.'

Darren is stumbling, clearly drunk. Carol is nervous, her head looking down, her whole stance wilted. He grabs her forcefully by the arm.

'Stay away from us. Do you hear me.' He slurs. 'I mean it.'

I don't say anything, but I am nervous too for my own safety, there's no one else around to witness anything should he kick off.

'How did you find me?' Carol asks, 'what are you doing here?'

'We share our locations.' He says smugly. 'We set it up years ago. It's a click of a button on our phones. Remember?'

I watch on as Carol grabs his hand and together, they walk away from me. I'm looking at them both, their reaction to each other and I feel I'm being over analytical. Why is he drunk, is he an alcoholic? Why is she so nervous?

When I channel my thoughts about Lauren, I feel suffocated. Is that why she ran away? What kind of home life did she endure?

Chapter Eighteen

Ten Years Ago
Carol

The sky is a blanket of thick grey clouds that smother any trace of sunlight. I stand at the window, contemplating my life and all the choices I've made over the years.

I turn away from the window, the silence of the house closing in around me, making me feel lonely. Darren's absence today is a small mercy, but his presence lately more of a haunting than a comfort. My right-hand fingers rub over the thin band of gold on my left hand, and an involuntary shiver runs through me.

With a hesitant touch, I slip off my wedding ring. A tiny, metallic whisper as it leaves my skin. The sensation is alien, the nakedness of my finger unsettling. It's cold to the touch, lighter than I remember. I hold it up to the dim light, the band dull and full of scratches that symbolise all the years we've spent together.

I let the memories seep in of our wedding day. So much hope cradled in my heart, my hands trembling with joy as Darren slid this very ring onto my finger. We were two halves of a whole, or so I believed. His vows were tender, promising a fortress of love and protection around our family. How complete my world felt then, brimming with expectations of happiness and shared dreams. I'm not sure where all the disappointments started. It never used to be this way and it's not like I didn't know he was aggressive. Back then it was a trait I admired, I felt protected.

But all that remains now is fragment of a life I can hardly recognise. The weight of those broken promises weighs heavy on my mind, making it hard to breathe when I think of all the bruises.

I close my hand around the band, its edges biting into my palm. The physical pain is almost welcome, a distraction from the relentless tide of grief and guilt washing over me.

'Luke,' I whisper, 'how could two brothers be so different? You were the kind one, the thoughtful one.'

As the wind howls outside, a tear slips down my cheek, tracing a path that's become all too familiar. I quickly wipe it away with the back of my hand, angry at the show of weakness. Darren mustn't see. Mustn't know. I keep my feelings private these days.

The ring remains clenched in my fist, a symbol of a life I'm no longer sure I belong to, a life I might soon leave behind if I'm brave enough.

My fingers tremble as I dial Kerry's number. The phone feels like a lifeline, my connection to a world beyond this suffocating house. I glance at the darkened window, the clouds outside mirroring my turmoil and loss. I don't always feel this low; I somehow manage to keep going, but it's all becoming too much. I'm lost and exhausted in this trauma.

'Carol?' Kerry's voice crackles through. 'Is everything ok? Are you alone?'

'Kerry, I... I need to do it. Today.' I cry down the phone. My words are a hurried whisper, 'I'm strong enough to do it. It's now or never, really. I can do this.'

'Are you sure? I can come get you whenever you're ready,' she replies, her tone steady but laced with concern. 'I'm proud of you. Stay strong, and I'll be right over.'

'Darren's gone out, so it's the best time.' I reply. I'm gasping for air, each breath a battle. 'I'll pack my suitcase now. It won't take me long.'

'Okay, I'll be there. Text me when you're set, and I'll be on my way.' She explains. 'You're doing the right thing. Pack as quickly as you can and text me.'

'Thank you.'

The call ends with a click, leaving me in the confines of the silent room.

I turn to the wardrobe, pulling down the dusty suitcase from atop. It's a relic of happier times, a ghost of past holidays we had in the caravan in Cornwall. I throw it open with more force than necessary, the sound loud in the quiet room.

I pull and tug my clothes from their hangers, folded without care, stuffing them into the case. The fabric wrinkles under my frantic hands, but I can't stop. Each garment is a day of the life I'm fleeing, memories I'm desperate to forget.

A sweater, one Luke bought me for Christmas one year, it's my favourite. A dress, worn on an anniversary long forgotten. They're all part of a costume I wore, playing the part of Carol Cooke, Darren's wife. But that woman is fading, her edges blurring into something new. Something I'm afraid of.

I zip the suitcase shut, its teeth biting together like the finality of a prison door. There's no going back. Only forward. I feel energised, proud of myself, but not so strong, not yet.

CHAPTER EIGHTEEN

'Freedom, at last.' I say out loud in the empty room. 'I can't breath.'

The suitcase sits by the door, a silent testament to my decision. Darren's shadow looms over me even in his absence, but not for much longer. Soon, I'll step out of it and into the unknown.

My hands tremble as I pause, a single thought crashing through my mind, a vision of Kieran's face. He's Darren's son too, and if I leave, a shiver runs down my spine. Darren's temper, which is known for unleashing a fit of rage, could it find a new target?

'Kieran,' I say out loud, his name a sharp pang in my chest. Would he understand? Or would he hate me for abandoning him? The guilt, a living thing, twists inside me, wrapping around my heart like cold fingers. My boy, caught in the crossfire of a war he never asked for. I don't know if I can go through with it.

A car door slams shut outside. He's home early. Panic surges, hot and immediate, and my breath is short bursts. It's him, it's Darren. What's he doing back so soon?

'Shit!' I shout in urgency. 'For fucks sake. Why is he home so soon?'

My movements are frantic now, hands grabbing clothes, shoving them back into the darkness of the wardrobe. The gold band on my finger, an unyielding shackle that I had almost left behind. With shaking fingers, I slide it back onto my finger, feeling the weight of it, the burden of vows turned sour. Everything almost as it was a moment ago.

The suitcase is heavy as my guilt when I hoist it up, muscles straining, breaths coming short and fast. I shove it back at the top of the wardrobe, dust and hair disturbed by my desperation.

They settle slowly, like the silence that follows a scream.

'Carol?' Darren shouts. His voice is a low rumble, the calm before the storm. I freeze, wedding ring secure, clothes hidden, evidence erased. But my heart, my heart betrays me, racing as fast as it can.

'In here,' I manage to say, my voice steadier than I feel. 'Just in the other room.'

'Everything alright?' He asks. 'Why is the front door left open?'

'Fine,' I lie, raising my voice slightly. 'I must have forgot to close it?'

I hear the bang of the front door closing shut behind him, once a sound that used to signal safety, now a warning siren.

'Carol, what room are you in?' He shouts through the house. 'What are you up to?'

'I'm in the kitchen.' I say, forcing a smile, keeping my hands busy, wiping at an already spotless counter. 'You're back early, what's the issue?'

'Traffic was light, plus I'm fucking starving.' He replies, leaning against the sideboard, arms folded. The room shrinks, walls closing in, air thick with unspoken questions. 'Are you sure you're, ok? You seem off.'

'I'm fine' I nod, swallowing the knot of fear in my throat. 'Everything is good. Just a little upset still about Luke that is all, and I've been thinking about Lauren a lot, naturally.'

The phone vibrates in my pocket, a jarring buzz against my thigh. I ignore it, but Darren's eyes flicker, hawk-like, and he's stares right at me.

'Who's that?' He asks, casual, but there's a tone. 'What do they want?'

'Nobody. It's probably just work stuff.' I say, nervously. My fingers twitch to silence the phone, betraying me. 'Nothing important.'

'Work? Now?' He snaps. 'You don't go back for weeks. They've let you have time off under the circumstances. What the hell, tell them to fuck off.'

'It's Kerry,' I blurt, the name slipping out before I can stop it. 'She's... she's been covering for me. With everything going on. I've been helping her with some stuff.'

'Kerry?' He repeats. 'Kerry? Well, it sure must be important if she keeps calling you like that?'

'Probably just checking in. Checking I'm ok too.' I shrug, trying to seem indifferent, but the lie tastes bitter on my tongue. 'People are worried about us, Darren. It's normal.'

The phone keeps buzzing; Darren's gaze hardens, and I know he doesn't believe me. He steps closer, and I fight the urge to flee. But there's nowhere to run, no place to hide, especially when the threat lives inside your walls, shares your bed and suffocates you with constant questioning.

'Let it ring,' he says. 'We've got things to talk about, haven't we?'

'Sure,' I reply, 'Things to talk about?'

The phone falls silent, but the tension remains, a taut wire stretched between us, ready to snap. I clutch the phone, a lifeline that now feels like a lead weight. My thumb hovers, trembling. I type as fast as my fingers allow, desperate. **Will call you later – C.**

The message sent, my breaths come short and sharp. I can't leave, not yet. Kieran's face flashes in my mind, young and vulnerable. Darren's shadow looms over him in my thoughts, dark and threatening. I hope Kerry doesn't turn up unannounced, she might get the hint with my message and lack of response.

What if Darren turns on Kieran? I can't risk it. Not now. Not after everything.

'You don't seem yourself?' Darren replies. 'You seem nervous and tense. I can tell you aren't happy about something. What have I done now?'

'I told you I was fine.' I say too quickly. 'I'm exhausted with all this worry, and I'm tired. What is it that you wanted to talk about?'

I am absolutely guilty and he can tell it, just waiting for me to admit it. For the lies. For the secrets. For Kieran. I tuck the phone away, a silent betrayal in my pocket.

The room feels colder, the air thicker. I'm trapped in this house, in this life. But Kieran, he still has a chance. If only I can keep him safe.

'Kieran's taking it hard. He needs us,' I whisper, more to myself than to Darren. 'We haven't really thought about the impact of everything on him.'

'Us?' His laugh is a bark, sharp and bitter. 'Don't kid yourself.'

Darren turns away, and I let out the breath I didn't know I was holding.

I look at the phone again, the screen dark. Later, Kerry. I promise. I'll find a way.

For Kieran. For me. For the ghost of the family that we used to be.

Chapter Nineteen

Wednesday, 7 June 2023
Brenda

The rain has come out of nowhere to our surprise. We can hear the pelting of the hail stones hitting against our window. Al and I finished our evening dinner about an hour ago, a nice pasta dish with some strong cheese and garlic bread, and now we've settled down to watch our favourite quiz show in bed together.

I know he'll end up falling asleep before the credits even roll, I can tell by his eyes that he's falling asleep already. Every time he does this; he suggests we watch something in bed together and I'm the one then left awake with no one to talk to. I just as well have stayed downstairs and put on a nice old fashioned romance film.

'Are you falling asleep before it's even started?'

Al turns to face me. Smiles. I can tell on his face he is trying to fight it.

'I'm only chilling. I'll be ok.' He replies. 'I'll make it all the way to the end, if not, here's the remote. You can be in charge if you like, but don't switch it to those bloody shopping channels. You'll end up buying all that crap through the night.'

I can't deny it, it is a favourite hobby of mine, watching the shopping channels late at night thinking that I need yet another calming mood candle, or some overpriced facial skin cream to ease my wrinkles. I've bought tons over the years, but I gave up. You can't fight nature; it'll have its way with you.

Although it's been on my mind most of the day, I don't really like to talk about it much because it took a long time to come to terms with the death of my grandparents after the accident. It's almost thirty-three years to the day it happened. June 10th nineteen-ninety was the day life become even tougher for me. Al hasn't mentioned it once, he surely couldn't have forgotten, but then I remember he always likes me to mention it first. He has some odd traits when it comes to communication, typical man of his generation.

'Do you know it's nearly that time of year again isn't it. June tenth. I always hate that day. It's like a sweeping storm that comes and goes. I get mixed emotions all day about it.' I say. 'It never gets easier no matter how much time passes. I miss them so much. It doesn't feel all that long ago, but my goodness, how time has flown by and life has changed.'

Al rubs my hand to comfort me.

'You were robbed of so much extra time with them, and all that bastard got was three years and his driving license removed.' Al reminds me. 'If only he hadn't been drink driving that night. There's no comfort in it, I know when I say this, but others die much young at times, some of diseases. You're always the one to tell me that life is fragile.'

He's right. I always tell him.

'You remember what your gran always used to say?' He continues, still stroking my hand. 'When your time is up, it's up. That's what she'd say if she was right here with you now. I miss them both too, you know. They were a funny old pair.'

Al is right, that's exactly what she'd say. I'm not upset anymore when I think about the effect of their loss on my life. It was the day I felt like an orphan.

I already had a mother who abandoned me, a father who died due to suicide, and the only two people who I felt loved me were killed in a tragic fatal accident that night. A drunk driver who took a wrong turn, too fast and hit them head on. The only comfort I have is that it was quick, so I know they didn't suffer at least.

Over time, sad memories have turned into happy memories, and I will forever be grateful for the way they brought me up. It may have been difficult, at times very different and unconventional, but I know they loved me, and I loved them. I learned my grandmother wasn't a witch, but a kind, caring, spiritual woman.

I always feel saddened that they missed out on so many years of us all having time together and making memories. I miss them both dearly, but the shock will forever have an impact on me. I wouldn't wish that news on anyone.

'They were a right old chalk and cheese pair your grandparents, weren't they?' Al interrupts my thoughts. 'Always bickering, but nothing all that serious. I don't think one could have coped without the other. Like two peas in a pod.'

I laughed because it's true.

'In a way it's nice that they went together. I get some comfort in that.' I reply. 'Gran would have been lost without him. She'd have no one to blame for anything that went wrong in the house.'

Al and I both laugh a little.

I hope they're looking down on me now and proud of how I

continued to live the rest of my life. I have a few minor regrets at times when I think of all the times I rebelled against their strict behaviours, but we were still a family. I will always miss them. I didn't realise until much later that she shaped the woman that I am today, she made me who I am, with or without my birth mother. She was the one who stuck around and made it count.

It's quite muggy and warm in this room now, which reminds me that I need to change our winter duvet for our thinner summer one. I've got my feet hanging out of the end of the duvet to help me cool down, something I used to do when I was going through the menopause too. That reminds me that I still need to buy a fan for the bedroom to make it more comfortable. I should have ordered one I saw on the shopping channel the other night. I swear the weather gets hotter and hotter every Summer. It must be global warming. That, or I manage to forget every year how warm it gets.

'I do hope Carol's ok, you know. I bet she's going out of her mind.' I say to Al, who's in bed next to me engrossed in the adverts on the television. 'Their marriage isn't very healthy. I think he's a bit of a control freak. He's quite scary should you ever get to meet him. We should pop in together next time, say hello. What do you think?'

Al pauses the television; that's still a magic function I can't believe exists. When I was a child, nothing was online, nothing could be halted. Now I look at the remote control and there are more buttons on it than what our car has.

'Are you still talking about that bloody family, again?' Al groans, 'We will probably never know where that poor girl went. Give it up. There shouldn't be a next time. I don't want to meet any of them.'

CHAPTER NINETEEN

I roll my eyes, but I know I can't leave them alone. I'm too invested.

'Carol isn't anything like I thought she'd be.' I explain, certain I can hear the sound of thunder. 'I was expecting someone who was strong, independent, a fighter. I don't know. I just think that there's something inside holding her back. I wonder if it's him.'

'Yes, it probably is him.' Al replies, un-pausing the television. 'I can fast forward to the start now. I wonder if anyone will win the million tonight on it? When was the last time we watched someone get all those questions right to the end?'

I stare at the TV, but I'm not interested. I see the screen of my mobile phone flash. I turn over to my bedside cabinet and read the message.

'Oh, my goodness, Al.' I gasp. 'It's Carol. She needs help. Look. What do we do?'

I pass Al the phone, he holds it to his face, then pulls it back to read the screen more easily. I'm ready for his moaning and groaning, but he'll come around to my way of thinking in the end. He always does.

'Why have you given her your number?' He says, 'what the hell does she want. We're about to watch our programme, it's getting late. Last thing we want is some stranger coming over and talking to us about all her bloody problems and issues.'

I let him vent, and as he's talking, I'm scrolling further down the messages. She has nowhere to go, and no one to help her. I can't not be charitable or help. I wasn't brought up that way to ignore those in need.

'She sounds like she is quite emotional.'
'Doesn't she have family she can visit instead of you, Bren?'
'I know, but I've already said it's ok now.'

'So, what does she need your help for, then?'

'She has nowhere to go and wants to talk.'

Al starts huffing and puffing, I'm flustered and shocked at the same time.

'She's at the holiday park, there's plenty of places she can go.' Says Al.

'I've already given her my address now. She wants to get a taxi.'

'I bet she was hinting for us to pick her up.'

I rush out of bed, grab my dressing gown from the back of the door and leave Al sat there moaning to himself.

'You don't mind if I stay up here, do you?' He asks, 'I'm not really in the mood for talking. I can't believe you did that. Why?'

'Because we are decent, caring people, Al.' I reply, doing up my belt. 'She's on her own, and she needs help. What would my Gran do, hey? She'd have done the exact same thing. Please, don't worry. I feel comfortable to let her in for a chat and a biscuit, or something.'

'You don't know what kind of trouble you're bringing into our home, Bren.' He continues. Huffing and puffing under his breath. 'Be careful. Don't let her take you for granted.'

'She needs someone to talk to, that is all.' I say, knowing more about her situation that he does, as he is not aware of the meeting we had earlier. 'I'm concerned for her. I'll make sure she knows where she can get help. Try not to worry.'

I give him a kiss on the forehead and leave the bedroom, closing the door behind me. I know he'll be asleep soon.

Looking down at my phone, I see she's said she will be about fifteen to twenty minutes. She's waiting for a taxi by the holiday park club house. I walk downstairs, put on the lights and I'm nervous. I hope Darren doesn't follow her like last time.

I feel uneasy about this and a little sick to my stomach.

Chapter Twenty

Wednesday, 7 June 2023
Carol

The lights are on, but still no answer at the door. I knock again, only this time louder. I start to see the silhouette of Brenda walking towards the door. Shaking and nervous, my emotions are running high and I have this overwhelming sense of fear. I feel like Darren's watching me, even now. I look around, but I'm alone.

'Hi, love. How was the taxi ride?' Brenda says, her smile beaming to greet me. 'Come on inside, I've just put the kettle on this second if you fancy a brew?'

I turn around, again, nothing and no one is behind me. The taxi left a minute ago and there's a gentle breeze blowing my hair into my face. I glance at the moon, the first few stars are visible, then I turn again to face Brenda.

'I've left him. I've walked out on him and I don't know what else to do.'

As soon as I watched her expression switch from that of happiness to a genuine look of concern, her arms open wide, I couldn't stop the tears. She hugged me and pulled me in closer. This made me even more emotional.

CHAPTER TWENTY

'I'm so sorry. I really am.' I explain. 'We had this argument from earlier. He'd been drinking again.'

'Stop.' Brenda says. 'Get inside, close the door behind you and we'll talk. You'll have to excuse the dressing gown; I was in bed.'

I close the front door and follow Brenda to the kitchen. Her house was charming, an old county cottage feel with plush red carpet, matching wallpaper and wooden banisters. It was dark, not very modern, but clean and tidy.

'How is your leg?' I ask watching her struggle to walk. 'Did you fall?'

'No, it's my arthritis, again. Can get like that some days. Usually worse on a colder night, but I am ok. Don't you worry about me. Sit your ass down over there.'

'Thanks.'

'A bit of rest will do it good.'

I walk to the bench; it was something I am sure my own mother used to own from the seventies. I haven't seen a table and bench set like this in years. It was hard and cold, but I sat down as comfortably as I could.

'Do you take milk and sugar?' Brenda asks, pouring the water into the teacup. 'I have sweeteners if you prefer?'

'Milk, one sugar.' I reply. 'Thanks again for this. I didn't know what else to do or where to go. You were the first person I could think of because you are nearby.'

Brenda walks slowly with the cup of tea in her hand.

'I should go, shouldn't I really. I feel like I am intruding.'

'No, don't be daft. Stay.'

Brenda is now seated opposite me. She places her hand on mine and leans forward a little. I get goosebumps.

'Look, I had a word with Al. He's upstairs and probably asleep by now the lazy git. But you can stay for as long as you want tonight. I have some spare blankets if you needed a sofa to sleep on, and the downstairs loo is in that door right over there, looks like it would be a cupboard under the stairs.'

'Thank you, you are so kind. Considering you don't even know me that well. That's very hospitable of you.' I say, placing a hand on my heart. 'I really felt like we had a connection earlier. In the woods. I don't know what it is, and I struggle to explain it, but maybe our paths were meant to cross.'

'Have you been drinking too?' Brenda asks. 'Is that alcohol I can smell on your breath. Seems strong?'

I am now panicking because I don't want her to kick me out of her house. I need to be here tonight; I need a roof over my head. I can't go back to that cottage, not now.

'I'm sorry. I had a couple of drinks, but not a lot.' I explain, showing emotion and holding back the tears as I think about Darren. 'I'm not drunk, I swear. It was just a couple of vodkas. He was very insisting I joined him. He doesn't like to drink alone.'

I see her eyes looking right into mine. That looks of disapproval. I should go, and thank her for her time, but if she is going to lecture me tonight, then I have to leave. I'm not in any fit state to listen to the rights and wrongs of alcohol.

'Is everything ok?' I ask. 'You're not saying anything, are you disappointed?'

I brace myself, pull in a deep breath and prepare myself that I will have to leave.

'Do you think you're up for another one?' She says, and my face must say it all. 'I have an unopened bottle of rum from Christmas if you fancy it.'

I wasn't expecting that from her. I smile and relax a little.

CHAPTER TWENTY

'I thought you were going to ask em to leave then.' I reply. 'Go on, then. Just a large one. I'll make it last.'

'Yeah, fuck the tea.' Brenda says. I'm sure it's the first time I've heard her swear. 'I'll go grab the rum from the cupboard. Do you want some cola in it?'

I nod and watch her get up to her feet. I try to control my breathing because I'm panicking, nervous, unsure of what to do or say really. I'm here because I know she would take me in. It's not that I want to take advantage of her, but there is something unusual about her. She does know things, but I'm not sure how.

'What were you arguing over? If you don't mind me asking?' Brenda asks, placing down the bottle on table, followed shortly after by two small glasses. 'Was it about me? He wasn't happy that you met me, was he?'

'A combination of things.' I pause for a moment. 'It's really mostly about me. He likes to know everything that I do and where I go. He's always been like it since we met. But the drinking started after his brother died.'

'Is he an alcoholic?' Brenda asks. 'Sorry, I shouldn't have said that. Will you forgive me, love?'

'He's not an alcoholic. He has his moments, and they are rare, but it's also coming up for ten years since his brother died.'

'Oh, I'm so sorry.' Brenda interrupts. 'You don't have to tell me anymore.'

Brenda pours the rum into the glasses and tops both up with a little cola from a can.

'It's ok. He's a typical man if you know what I mean. Doesn't like to talk about his feelings, but it comes out in other ways.'

Brenda nods and agrees. I sense she was about to say

something but I continued.

'The day we were told about Luke's terminal diagnosis, it's as though as a family our whole world stopped. We thought it might be cancer but was always told it was likely treatable. It wasn't until oncology had their meetings with further specialists and unfortunately, Luke was clinically unwell for treatment. He had too many infections and chemotherapy would have shortened his lifespan.'

'Life can be so cruel.' Brenda replies. 'There's nothing anyone can say to make that pain feel better.'

'We all watched him deteriorate.' I say, crying in the memory of it all. 'By the end of it, I barely recognised him. We had the funeral and planned it all as a family whilst he was still alive. It's sad, odd, surreal conversations that you never believe would be part of your life. You hear it, see it, in others, but I wouldn't wish that trauma on anyone. The worst part was knowing he only had six months left to live.'

Brenda holds my hand. I sip on the rum and cola, and she doesn't say anything more. I remember how difficult the funeral was for us as a family, how we kept an empty seat there for Lauren. Darren was tense and blamed all of us, one by one for her disappearance, including himself.

'Luke was an incredibly kind, caring, young man.' I continue. 'He's five years younger that Darren. They were like chalk and cheese. I still miss him. We all do.'

'If he's as beautiful a soul as you imply, then you will always have your memories to comfort you.'

She comes across like a mother figure to me. It's odd how I feel a connection to her, but I barely know her at the same time. I don't get a sense that she would judge me. She sees the good in people, and it's been a long time since anyway actually asked me about how I feel. I've spent so many years looking after our son, Kieran, that my own emotions in all this have become lost. I've kept everything bottled up inside. Struggling to cope at times.

'Do you think Darren will have calmed down in the morning? Is it over for good, or one of those in the heat of the moment things? We've all been there. At my age now, Al and I barely even talk, let alone argue.' Brenda says lightening the mood. 'You've been through a lot together it seems. The passing of Luke, as well as Lauren going missing. It's a lot on a young family, but you've stayed together through all of it. I hope you can work it out between you. I really do.'

'We've never had a row like this. I'll be honest with you. I think it's over. I told him for the first time that I am not even sure I love him anymore.'

Brenda looked surprised.

'I think I am better off without him. He's only been interested in going to the pub since we got here.'

'There's a lot of think's in those replies.' Brenda interrupts, and that makes me think about what I just said. 'You don't seem convinced that you've left him for good. I have noticed the bruises too. Does he hurt you, or is that from something else?'

I pull my sleeves down, unsure of what to reply.

'He loves me. I know that he really does love me. But I need more out of my life now. We've spent ten years looking for Lauren, we don't talk any more. Apart from visiting places where she might have been seen, we do very little as a family now.' I explain, 'we're broken. Our lives feel like it's drifting in different directions. I don't even know what I want to be honest. I can't reason with him when he's drunk, he's angry all of the time and I forgive him constantly because of Lauren. We've never gotten over it. Our relationship is a mess.'

'Well, I have a perfectly good sofa you can sleep on, and maybe in the morning when you've both sobered up, you'll see sense.' Brenda says. 'It's not my place to tell you what to do, but you've been through a lot together. No one else can understand that apart from each other. If he is violent in any way, then that is unacceptable and you should see help, but it's your life. No one can tell you how to live it, not even Darren.'

'I blame myself for Lauren going missing.' I explain. 'Every day I wake up with the same guilt, the same unanswered questions. Did we grieve so much over Luke that we ignored any problems she might have been going through?'

'You shouldn't blame yourself.' Brenda replies, sipping on her rum. 'At least you've had the chance to be a good mother, good parents. You have a son, a daughter who I am sure loves you. When I had those dreams, those feelings, it's with love, not anger. She loves you; you are her mother.'

As soon as I heard Brenda say those words I break down in tears. They're streaming heavily down my face, and as her mother, I wish I could see her to say how sorry I am. I miss her every single day.

'I'll never have that opportunity.' Brenda says, handing me some tissues she got from another cupboard in her country cottage kitchen. 'I know what it's like to have that guilt burdening you every day. There are some things I've never even told Al.'

I'm intrigued, confused and unsure of what she means.

'What are you saying?' I ask, politely, wiping my eyes and blowing my nose. 'What have you got to feel guilty about. Surely it can't be that bad?'

CHAPTER TWENTY

I watch as Brenda knocked back the last of her glass of rum. She reached out and held my hand again. I can see she's teary too and in this weird moment, I sense that she's done something terrible. I don't say a word, but I look at her, waiting for her to finish her sentence.

'I've lived with guilt for many years now.' Brenda blurts out, but quietly. 'Please, I've never told anyone in my life until now. No one knows, not even Al.'

'That's ok.' I reply, giving her a sense that all is alright. 'Whatever it is, I'm sure it's not that bad, surely.'

'No, you don't understand.' Brenda continues. 'I always wanted to be a mother, but when it actually happened, it wasn't the right time. I put my career first and had a secret termination without telling anyone. Since then, I had never been able to get pregnant again. I always thought it was some kind of cruel punishment for what I did.'

'No. No, don't be silly.' I reassure Brenda, 'you made the right decision that was right for you at that time. Don't be so hard on yourself. If getting pregnant again wasn't meant to be, it wasn't meant to be. I wouldn't read anything into it.'

This time I hold Brenda's hand as she starts to sob into her own tissue. I never would have thought she was the type of woman to hide secrets from her husband. She fascinates me.

I wonder what other secrets she is hiding.

Chapter Twenty-One

Wednesday, 7 June 2023
Brenda

My head is killing me, but I'm too far gone. We've drank the whole bottle of rum and are both now in the living room listening to some music quietly whilst Al is still sleeping upstairs. I'm surprised he hasn't come down the stairs moaning since it's almost midnight and I should have been in bed hours ago.

'You know what, I just had a thought.' Carol, slurs, slowly drinking the last of her rum and cola. 'If all that stuff about the afterlife is true, then why can't we see dinosaur ghosts?'

I feel the frown on my head growing, my eyes widening and an overwhelming urge not to laugh. I don't remember how we have got to this point of being emotionally upset, sharing some personal insight into each others lives, and I genuinely feel like I'm bonding and connecting with her on many levels, but what kind of weird question is that?

'Interesting question. I'm not really sure of the answer.' I reply, raising my glass. 'I've never seen the ghost of a snake, or a monkey, or even a mouse. Doesn't that speak volumes. What about you?'

'So, what are you saying?' Carol asks, 'are you saying they

don't exist? I haven't seen any ghosts, not that I've been looking.'

I paused for a moment, her tone was more aggressive, her expression fiercer than the sombre mood she was in earlier. It's as if a form of Darren's personality is rubbing off on her.

'No, not at all.'

'You are, Bren. Be honest.'

'No. I know that ghosts exist. I've seen ghosts. I prefer to call them spirits.'

Is she mocking me?

I'm silent and look directly into her eyes. I'm trying to read her mood, but I'm so tired. I don't know if she's playing with me or trying to start an argument.

'What's going on Bren. Cat got your tongue?'

'I'm a little drunk. I can feel my head spinning.' I explain, politely. 'You know why I don't think we see ghosts of dinosaurs, bats, snakes, mice and whatever else.'

'Oh, why?' Carol interrupts. 'It's interesting stuff. And go you for being drunk. It doesn't hurt to let your hair down once in a while. I'm sure the spirits don't mind.'

'As humans, we don't connect with them, do we? As physical beings, our connections and love are mostly for other individuals, human beings, and of course, our pets.'

Carol nods.

'Amen to that,' she says. 'I always thought death was final, but you are opening my eyes to a few things.'

'I'm no expert, but it could be because of intellect, intelligence, how open minded you are. My gran always said it was about perception, and how sensitive we are to their world.'

'Maybe.' Carol says, lowering head. 'I've never seen Lauren, does that mean she's still alive. Wouldn't she come to me if she was dead, as a ghost? She's my daughter, why would she tell you about spiders, roses and a necklace and not come to me?'

I don't really know what to say. I'm not an expert, but I believe in what I believe.

'You're her mother. I am certainly sure that if she has passed over, that she would be with you and around you all the time. Her spirit is eternally connected to you. Just because we don't see them, doesn't mean they're not there.'

Carol is starting to look tearful. Her hands are shaking, and her mood has shifted to a darker tone. There's a chill in the air too, and a cold draught is coming in from the door. I'm sure I've not left any windows open.

'Do you feel how cold it's gotten now?' I ask Carol, changing the subject from death. 'Do you fancy some tarot. I have my grandmother's old cards. How about some reading before bed and see what the cards say for you?'

'Yeah, it's getting cold, but I don't know.' Carol hesitates, 'isn't it getting late now for tarot?'

'I can keep it short if you want. Go on.' I reply, 'just the once while we have been so honest with each other. I remember my grans quick three card method. It doesn't need to be a full reading.'

Carol nods and agrees. I head over to get my grandmothers box and I shuffle the cards. We both agreed to have no more rum.

'Now Carol, I need you to repeat after me.' I say, shuffling the tarot cards. They're rough round the edges and starting to deteriorate, but I can be super careful. 'My spirit guide, if you are here, please surround me with light. I need your guidance and direct me.'

CHAPTER TWENTY-ONE

Carol closes her eyes and repeats the statement slowly. I was expecting her to laugh as not to take it seriously, but she is sat in front of me with her eyes tight shut and waiting for my next line.

'Please guide me to an answer through the cards.' I say, 'fill the room with love.'

Carol opens her eyes after repeating those words, and I lay all of the cards down on the floor, face down. There is still a draft coming in behind me and I am convinced this is something spiritual. They're reaching out.

'Hold my hands, please?' I demand of Carol and already grab them. She doesn't let go. 'Say out loud your question.'

'Why?' Carol asks. 'Why did she abandon me. I'm her mother?'

I sigh and feel a sense of grief. That heavy look of loss and stillness in her expression. A family that has been torn apart by the mystery of her disappearance and clinging on to the hope that she will walk back into their lives. My stomach feels heavy, nauseous and I'm shaking with nerves and fear. I'm scared of what the cards will reveal in this tense atmosphere.

'Why?' Carol shouts louder.

I turn around expecting to see Al behind me, complaining of the noise. The room is still cold, and I can smell the alcohol on her breath.

I keep shuffling the tarot cards and I place them face down in neat rows, and we both sit looking at them all.

'All you have to do is pick three.' I say to break the silence. 'One at a time.'

Carol places one hand on her chest, and with the other, slowly reaches out with a finger and places it firmly down on one of the cards. I pick it up, look at the card myself and show it to her.

'The Tower. Of all the cards, I can't believe it.'

Carol looks lost.

'What does that mean?' She asks, bewildered. 'I've got no idea.'

'It's upright, at least. It's all about loss.' I explain. 'How can I explain this from memory. It's like when your tower has come burning down, or a more modern way of looking at it is like a plane crash. Everything is fine one minute, and then out of nowhere it's not.'

Carol nods.

'That's pretty accurate isn't it. I just watched you shuffle and by sheer coincidence that is the first card. How fucking weird is that?'

I don't reply, but I nod back. I watch on as she places her finger over another card.

'I want that one. I don't know why, but I feel drawn to it. I should have picked it first, but I can't stop looking at that one.' Carol says. 'I hope this one is more positive.'

I pick up the card, and again reveal it to her, holding it closer to her so she can see it. The card is worn and a little faded. I'm not pleased to see it, and Carol can tell by the look on my face.

'What is it?' She asks, 'please, tell me. How bad?'

'It's the Seven of Swords.' I say, showing her. 'The Seven of Swords. It's also in the upright position.'

I shake my head trying to think of a positive spin on it, but I can't think of one. I'm going to have to be honest.

'It means dishonesty, deceit, cheating and manipulation is at play.'

'They know don't they. They know.' Carol says, tears starting to roll down her cheek. Her hands trembling as she

CHAPTER TWENTY-ONE

talks. 'They all know, don't they?'

I'm not sure what she means, but I go on.

'It means you really need to look closely at those around you.' I reply, convinced this card is about Darren. His controlling manipulative ways. 'You need to open your eyes to any kind of manipulative behaviours. Stay guarded and grounded. Remember too that this was the card you were drawn to the most. Think about it.'

I hope from that explanation she can see the positive and remain strong.

'One last card. What are you picking, then we can look at all three together and see if there's a theme to the question you asked out loud.'

Carol wipes her eyes with her sleeve. Hesitates, but hovers her finger over the final card. I pick it up and for the final time, evaluate it.

'Are you ok to continue? You seem upset.'

Carol nods.

'The final card is Judgement. And this one is upright too.'

'Could it get any worse.' Carol interrupts. 'I mean, really, is this really happening?'

'It means having some kind of reflection on past actions or choices, my love.' I explain. 'I don't think this is a bad one. It's upright, it's definitely about the past, and thinking about what you could have done to make things better.'

Carol looks broken. She's emotional and I'm intrigued. I didn't think she would take this as seriously as she did. It makes me wonder what is going on in that head of hers.

'I didn't mean to upset you.'

Carol shakes her head.

'It's ok, it's not you.' She replies. 'It's weird. I'm not sure what to say, but it's true and I don't know how to take it all in.'

'Would you like a tissue?' I ask, 'is there anything you'd like to share with me? That's the beauty of tarot, and sometimes other forms of spiritual messaging. It means something to the person asking the questions, not me as the messenger.'

Carol wipes her eyes again with her sleeve, and I notice how wet it is. But my eyes wander back to her face.

'Can I tell you something?' Carol asks. 'Please don't judge me. I've never told anyone, but this has really shocked me because it's so accurate. I know what those cards all mean. I know what they're trying to say. Do you?'

'I think I do.' I reply, looking vague, but her intensity surprised me. 'If I was looking at all three together. The Tower, the Seven of Swords, Judgment, then it has something to do with a secret in your past that might have shaped the outcomes of today. Reflecting on it and making sure that you learn from past mistakes.'

Carol places both hands over her face and the outburst of tears continue. I sit here, confused and surprised by the reaction. It wasn't what I was expecting at all from her.

'I was having an affair with Luke. Darren's brother. Before he became ill, before he died.' Carol announced. 'Is this message from Luke? Is it revenge.'

My mouth is wide open with the sheer surprise of this revelation. I can feel my heart beating heavy in my chest.

'I need to tell Darren. I need to tell him don't I. If he understands, then he might forgive me. I'm sorry, I'm really sorry I should get back to him.'

It's not my place to judge. It's only my place to send the message. She asked the question, but I have no firm answer. The reading is hers, and hers alone.

CHAPTER TWENTY-ONE

'You've been drinking, you're very upset. Don't you think you should sleep it off here tonight and I'll get Al to drop you round in the morning.'

Carol shakes her head, then nods again.

'Think about this logically. You've just left him, he's probably upset, or even angry.' I say. 'Tomorrow is a whole new day, and maybe think about having an adult, open and honest conversation with each other. This is your marriage, and many people have secrets, but don't make any stupid decisions. Not tonight.'

Carol thanks me and I assured her she was fine to sleep on the sofa tonight. I don't know how I will ever sleep tonight with that knowledge, but it only makes me have more questions about their relationship. Some, that I might never get an opportunity to ask. It's none of my business.

If she admits an affair to Darren, I fear he could be extremely violent.

Chapter Twenty-Two

Thursday, 8 June 2023
Carol

If it wasn't for those damn tarot cards, I might never have admitted my affair with Luke to Brenda. Actually, no. If it wasn't for the amount of alcohol I drank last night, combined with those fucking tarot cards, then I might not have blurted it out. I'm not proud of cheating on Darren with his brother Luke, and there's not a day goes by now where I don't regret it. So much of my life is complicated and there's no escaping the regret, hurt, anger, guilt and sadness.

I know I need to go back and see Darren. I'm dreading it. I've had two cups of coffee, a few interesting chats with Brenda this morning about her cleaning job at Southleigh Cottages, and now my stomach is in knots at the thought of returning back to that cottage. The last time I spoke to Darren, he was angry, I've run out of posters of Lauren, and the whole trip hasn't gone to plan.

'Can we pull over for a minute? I feel sick. I think it was all that rum from last night playing havoc with my stomach.' I ask. Alan is driving, I can smell the country air from farmers spreading manure, but I am shaking head to toe with what feels like a lump in my throat. 'Please, just at the next lay-by or something? I feel light headed.'

Alan pulled over at the next lay-by, and I jump out of the car, standing on a grassy verge while looking out at the farmer's fields. I know we are only a mere few minutes away from the holiday park, but I can't stop shaking. The wet grass is touching my ankles, and the dark grey overcast sky will likely rain again soon. I can't describe in words how I feel, yet my stomach and head are reacting to what is soon to become a reality. I must face Darren.

'How are you feeling?' Brenda asks. 'I'm sure you'll be ok; you've had arguments before, and always made it up, haven't you?'

'Yes, but this time it's different. It's all a mess, Bren. I don't know what to do.'

'Has he messaged you yet?' She asks, 'sometimes that can be a good way to beak the ice. Do you remember what you told me, last night?'

I cover my eyes with my hands with the shame of it. Sleeping with my husband's brother, all for what – a bit of attention because my husband works long hours. I tried to blame Darren, I then blamed Luke, but it is my own fault. All of this mess is my fault and I don't know how to repair it.

'I'm sorry about last night, I shouldn't have said anything.'

'It's none of my business, and you can trust me. I'm not going to tell a soul, I promise.' Brenda replies. 'I don't want to sound patronising because everyone's marriage is different. You'll not be the first nor the last to have made mistakes but do what is right for you. None of us are perfect, love.'

I smile at her sincerity, but she has no idea what it's like to be me. I turn away from her, see Alan still sat in the car and I place a hand on my stomach. I feel uneasy, queasy and restless.

'It is really over between you?' Brenda asks. 'Are you serious about telling him?'

'It's really over I say.' My voice cracking with the emotion. 'He hasn't even messaged me to see where I am. It's not like him. He's normally persistent or will turn up somewhere when you least expect him.'

I drop to my knees, and sob. Brenda places a hand on my shoulder.

'The one person he trusted was Luke.' I cry, 'I'm such a terrible wife. Terrible mother, what have I done. I've destroyed my family, haven't I?'

'Oh, love. You ain't half been through the mill.' She says. 'We better get back in the car, so, let's focus on one thing at a time.'

'Can you come in with me?' I ask, 'when we are at the cottage. I don't think I can face him on my own.'

I get back on my feet, hold Brenda's hand and she guides me back to the car. There's a lump in my throat, an uneasy feeling in my stomach and the complications of my marriage now exposed.

I don't know what to do next.

We must have driven for another five minutes. Every minute the dread of facing Darren worsened to the point where I am now shaking with fear.

'Here we are,' Alan says, undoing his seat belt. 'I'll wait in the car. If you need me, Bren can give me a call.'

'Thank you for your hospitality.' I reply, tearful and nervous. Aware I'm breathing heavier. 'And, to you Brenda for last night. I know we haven't known each other long but thank you for your kind words. And, for listening. I know I have to move

CHAPTER TWENTY-TWO

forwards with my life, whatever is thrown at me, I need to rise above it.'

We get out of the car and I look around the site; my sickness has eased, but now replaced with this weird feeling of disconnect with my surroundings. I know I have the inner strength to do this. I know it has to be done.

I knock on the cottage door twice and there was no answer. Brenda is standing behind me, wearing a flowery dress and a knitted cardigan.

'Does he normally stay in bed this late in the day?' Brenda asks, smiling. 'Making the most of his break away. Has he still not texted you?'

I shake my head and pull at the door handle to check if it's locked. It opened first time.

'Darren?' I shout through, looking at the cans of beer and vodka bottles. The cottage is a tip. Plates and cups all smashed on the floor. 'Darren, it's me. I'm back, what are you up to?'

Brenda follows behind me, her jaw dropping and her eyes widened at the mess.

'Oh, my goodness,' she gasps. 'This is going to take some cleaning up this is. Do you need me to help before they see it. You might get charged extra.'

'Darren?' I shout, 'Oi, where are you? Darren?'

Brenda is still talking, but she's wandered into the living room area.

'Oh, there's a note here.' She says, walking closer to the table and picking it up. 'It says, I'm sorry for everything. I'm sorry. Love Darren.'

'That's not like him.' I say, looking shocked. 'He must have smashed the place up in a drunken mess. It didn't look like this when I left. He needs to get help, counselling maybe. We can't go on like this.'

'I'll get the dust ban and brush to start clearing some of this mess up.' Brenda replies, continuing on through back into the kitchen. 'We'll have it looking clan and proper in no time before he gets back. I bet he's in the bar. Shall I ask Al to go and find him?'

I stop and look at Brenda going through the broom cupboard in the kitchen. I still have that feeling of disconnect and wonder why I ever came here in the first place. There had been other sightings of Lauren in other locations but coming to Salcombe felt the right thing to do. I had a feeling that I had to come here and I couldn't shake it off. I feel tense at the thought of facing Darren on my own.

'He's probably out for the count, sleeping it off.'

'What? He wouldn't wake up with you calling out his name. Not a murmur, or nothing?'

'Not if he's been drinking all night. He has a habit of passing out; he'll be in a deep sleep.'

Brenda bends down to bag up the broken plates, she holds on to the cupboard door to lower herself slightly with her bad knee. I turn around and leave her there as I head up the stairs. I walk straight into the main bedroom and there he is, slumped over the bed, face down and the stench of vomit makes my stomach churn.

'I found him, he's out for the count, just like I said he would be.' I shout down the stairs. 'He's been sick, I'm going to have to clean all this up, we're meant to be leaving in the morning.'

Brenda's reply sounded muffled; I wasn't sure what she was shouting back at me.

'Darren, wake up.' I say, prodding his shoulder, but he doesn't stir. 'Darren, we need to talk, wake up.'

I walk around the bed and lower myself to feel the back of his head. He's stone cold. My heart beats faster, and I scream as loud as I can. His vomit is on the floor, his hands are various shades of blue and I don't know what to do next. I'm gasping for air and the room is closing in on me. I hear footsteps coming up the stairs.

Brenda rushes into the bedroom, holding a cup of tea.

'What's happened? I heard you scream' She asks. 'Is he ok? I thought you might like this cuppa?'

I struggle to find the words with my heart still pounding in my chest. I have an awareness that I keep shaking my head and I can't stop trembling. I'm gasping for air in the anxiety and panic of it all.

'He's dead, Brenda.' I manage to say, as she's walking closer towards his body. 'He's dead? He's, I can't believe it, dead.'

Brenda drops the cup of tea to the floor; it splashes all over the carpet as she rushes to feel his pulse.

'Call the ambulance, my love.' She shouts at me. 'Call them now. Call them. Call them.'

I place my hands in my pocket and reach for my phone. It's not there. I start patting my pockets, front and back furiously. Nothing.

'I must have dropped it when we pulled over, or it's fallen out of my pocket in the car.' I say, crying now. 'I don't have my phone. I can't find it Bren. What do we do? What do we do now?'

Brenda doesn't reply but starts fumbling in her cardigan pocket. She pulls out her phone and starts pushing in her unlock password. I watch as she shakes with the shock of seeing Darren dead on the bed. I start to walk back towards the bedroom window and I turn to look outside. I see the clouds, the sun starting to break through and I can't stop staring into the nothingness of the horizon. That feeling of disconnect growing as my thoughts turn to our son. How am I going to tell him his father has died, like we've not been through enough already.

'Ambulance please, there's a man dead at Southleigh Cottages.'

I close my eyes and raise my head as she repeats herself, telling the emergency services the cottage number.

'I can't find a pulse. He's covered in vomit. He'd been drinking. His name is.'

'His name is Darren Cooke.' I interrupt, 'My husband. My husband is Darren Cooke.'

I continue to look out of the window amidst a sensation of what feels like time has slowed down. I watch the children playing in the park, the old couple walking their dog and the families chatting to each other on the grass banks.

My husband is dead and Brenda is now telling the emergency services what happened before we walked in. I can't unsee the position he was lying in, the blue hands of his and the vomit all down the side of the bed, and floor. That image haunting my mind.

'The ambulance and the police, they're on their way, my love.' Brenda says, placing a hand on mine and joining me to look out of the window. 'We need to go downstairs; I need to tell Al what's happened. I won't ask you if you're ok, I know that's a silly question but think about if there's anything else I can help. Anyone we need to call.'

I don't say a word, I can't even bring myself to speak, but I don't look at Darren as we slowly leave the room. Brenda doesn't even close the door behind her.

'I'm so sorry.' Brenda says. 'I don't know what else to say. This is tragic, it really is.'

'The note.' I gasp. 'He's killed himself hasn't he, He did this on purpose. That's what he's sorry for isn't it? He couldn't cope and decided to end it. How selfish of him, even now. To put his family through this after everything we've been through together.'

Brenda closes her eyes, takes a deep breath and opens them again.

'You're in shock. We both are.'

It's as though my body has become twice as heavy, the realisation of the situation hitting my core and now a wave of emotion hits my senses hard and fast. The tears of mine, now a release of anger, regret, hurt and pain. I don't know what's happening.

I follow Brenda down the stairs and I'm lost in the emotion and anxiety of it all.

What am I going to tell Kieran?

Chapter Twenty-Three

Ten Years Ago
Darren

The house has become more of a tomb to me since Lauren disappeared. Carol and I are barely talking and I'm losing my mind. I'm meant to be the man of the house, strong minded, showing my family and all those around us how great I am at keeping everything together. It couldn't be more wrong; I've failed everyone and myself.

It's silent and suffocating. I fucking hate it. I can't go to work, I can't eat, all I want to do is drink myself into a state of unconsciousness and switch off from the world. I wake up most mornings now and dread getting out of bed. I hate having to open my eyes and be reminded of my loss.

My little girl is out there, she left us. I can't take the worry and the pain any longer; it's all my fault. My younger brother died of cancer; I was never there for him when he needed me. We drifted apart over the years, went through stages of talking to each other, then falling out, and repeated the same cycle over the years. We were brought up in a competitive environment. I don't think Dad ever wanted to us to get on. He never praised us for anything. He wasn't interested in anything we did either.

CHAPTER TWENTY-THREE

We brought ourselves us whilst mum was always out working too. A pair of latchkey kids.

I'm sat here now in the dim light, watching the shadows cling to the walls like the ghosts from my past. Making this decision was easy, I'd thought it about all day, and the more I kept thinking about how to do it, the more it felt real. I could picture it, it felt peaceful. There's only one way out of this misery I face.

My heart is beating like crazy the more I look at the bottle of pills on the side. I think about Carol's face, twisted in hurt each time I tried to cage her, it haunts me. I'm poison. A toxic shroud over my own family that I've destroyed over the years.

I can't breathe. The bottle of sleeping pills is now empty, betrayal against my wife's trust, I've swallowed them all. It's getting hard to think, to stay awake. Each blink is a battle. I slump in the chair, my head lolling back. This is it, the escape from the monster I've become.

But then she's there. The front door creaks open and I'm not sure if its an apparition or my mind playing tricks on me. Carol's voice cuts through the fog in my brain. 'Darren? Why are you sitting in the dark?' She asks me. Her steps are cautious as if she senses something is wrong. 'Are you ok? Darren? Darren, answer me.'

'Carol.' I murmur. 'I'm sorry.'

My tongue is thick, heavy like my heart. It's too late for words, please let me go. You'll all be better off without me. I'd hate for Kieran to grow up like me and follow in the footsteps of a monster, he needs to break the cycle. A son I will be proud of.

Carol flicks on the light. I hear her gasp, see her freeze, the room suddenly becomes too bright. There's a sharp intake of breath, then a scream, raw and frightened.

'Darren. What have you done?' She asks, now running around me. 'No. How could you. How could you be so stupid? What have you done?'

My eyelids droop: I fight to lift them, to see her one last time. To tell her how much she means to me and how sorry I am. But the darkness is slowly pulling me away from her as I'm struggling to stay awake, my vision is blurred.

'Stay with me, Darren. Stay with me.' I hear and vaguely see Carol's shaking hands fumble with her phone. Her voice is a desperate tremor as she dials. 'Please send help. It's an emergency. I think my husband is dying, he needs help now. Now.'

Carol stammers into the receiver, her tone shattered by fear. I'm not afraid of anything anymore, I'm happy. I have an overwhelming sense of joy that I'm leaving them. They will move on with their lives, of course they will. Maybe my death will bring Lauren back to her mother and they can both rebuild their lives without me.

'Help, I need an ambulance. Please, it's urgent, hurry. My husband has taken an overdose.' She shouts. 'He's taken a load of pills and drank a load of alcohol; I can smell it on his breath. I'm not sure what it is, fuck, I can't even think straight.'

I only made it to half a bottle of vodka. There's still another half I'd have drank if only I had the strength. The hardest part was trying not to vomit against the bitter taste of my concoction of pills.

'It's vodka. I don't know how many pills though.' She continues. 'Please help me. It's sleeping tablets, I can't remember their name, it's too long. But there were over twenty left in the bottle. He's had them all.'

CHAPTER TWENTY-THREE

Her touch is feather-light on my cheek, a stark contrast to the weight pressing down on my chest. I want to tell her not to worry, that this is for the best. But the words are lost, swallowed up by the void that's claiming me. My last anchor to the world is the sound of Carol's voice, cracking as she fights to keep me here, to keep us from splintering even further apart. I hear her confirm our address.

Everything around me is blurry but I see her holding the phone to her ear. Carol's pacing up and down. As I watch in confusion, I remember a time when I last threatened to leave her. It was the Christmas party at the hotel where she cleaned. I was convinced she would leave me for another guy. I thought she was already having an affair, and every time I saw her smiling and leaving her workplace talking to him. I hated it. The jealousy consumed me, but I'm fragile and not the rock she thought I was. I'm broken.

'Stay home,' I had demanded, my words wrapped in a threat like barbed wire. 'Or we're done. Me. The kids. I'll leave you and take them with me. Making sure you'll never see them again, everything in your life. Gone.'

She had stayed, likely suffocated by the fear of losing everything, but I meant it too. I felt guilty for a few days afterwards and then we never spoke of it again. She hasn't been to a Christmas party since. I've never cheated on her, not once.

The wail of sirens jolts me out of my daydream. Red and blue lights flash through the curtains, painting the walls with fleeting promises of help. I don't want to be saved; I don't want help. Why did Carol come home early, what happened. How the fuck did she know?

'Mrs Cooke?' I hear the paramedic's voice loud and clear. 'We need to move him now. The ambulance is ready, we'll get him stabilised, do some tests and pump his stomach, as quickly as we can, please. Can you move aside?'

I see Carol nod, I can tell she's crying and nervous, watching them as they lift me onto a stretcher. I hear them talking to me, but I don't answer. All I want to do is close my eyes and go to sleep, never to wake up. It seems peaceful and I'm relaxed.

The night air bites my skin, sharp and sudden. I don't need to see anything to know that our neighbours will be crowded by their windows, peering behind twitching curtains. Whispering on their concrete doorsteps, judging us, always judging me.

Katie from next doorsteps forward, her eyes soft with pity I don't want.

'Carol, love, I'll look after Kieran if you like?' I hear her voice. 'You go with him, and don't worry about your lad. We'll take care of anything you need. Be strong, thinking of you all.'

'He's at his friends house.' Carol replies, still sobbing. 'Thanks though. I appreciate the offer. He doesn't even know yet. What am I going to tell him? I hope he pulls through.'

Carol's hand on my arm is warm, a stark contrast to the chill that has settled in my bones. I'm at peace with myself and assured that I made the right decision to die.

As the ambulance doors burst open, the street becomes a theatre, and I, unwillingly, its star. I'm lifted inside on the stretcher and greeted by further paramedics. It's cold and unwelcoming. I hear the engine humming, a lullaby for the life I'm leaving behind with every mile we take, hopefully.

I am better off dead.

Chapter Twenty-Four

Thursday, 8 June 2023
Brenda

Giving my statement to the police felt such a cold experience. There was no emotion or feeling coming from the officers as I reminded them that Carol was here to find her missing daughter, and that the deceased was her husband, not some random bloke she didn't know. When I told them Carol had slept at mine all night, I noticed they raised their eyebrows. Why wouldn't they believe me?

The officers spoke about her as if there was no connection between them. Al reminded me they're only doing their job; it's not about emotions; it's about facts and evidence he said. I know he's right, but he wasn't there to see the ordeal and how distraught she was. I'm still shaking myself and don't know how I kept my cool. Incidents like that make me realise how sometimes you find an inner strength to keep on going.

The police cordoned off the cottage and they placed an officer outside guarding the building until forensics are finished gathering all that they need. Al and I helped Carol collect a few of her belongings and some clothes whilst the site placed her in another nearby cottage. She should have come back to ours, but she wanted to be close to Darren. It's her choice, but I'm not happy about it.

'We shouldn't have left her Al, should we. Should we take her some dinner?' I say, whilst Al is reading the newspaper at the kitchen table. 'I'm worried about her.'

'You offered and she didn't want it, Bren. We can't force her.' He replies, 'she said her son was coming straight there. After what she's been through today, I doubt she can eat anyway. We've offered her a place to stay if she needs it, but it's all on her.'

I stop and take a breath, open the kitchen window to let more air in as I feel claustrophobic. I can't remember the last time I saw a dead body. I get a chill up my spine every time I think about his face.

'How selfish of him to kill himself, and like that too.' I say out loud, angry what he's put that poor woman through already. 'How fucking dare he.'

Al drops his paper, walks over beside me and starts massaging my shoulders.

'It's not like you to swear.' He says, patting my back now. 'You've been a great support to her, and we barely know her. Why don't you go and sit down in the other room, and I'll bring you in a cup of tea? You put your feet up, I demand it.'

I smile and hold his hand, before hugging him. As soon as I placed my head near his chest, my tears came thick and fast.

'Oh, it was so bad, Al.' I explain. 'You should have seen the state of him, it was like something out of a movie.'

Al holds me tight and kisses my head.

'I love you.' He says. 'Now, go and sit down and I'll be in soon. We should have an early night too. You need to get some rest.'

CHAPTER TWENTY-FOUR

I let go of my husband.

'I love you too. I really do.' I reply, walking away from him to head into the room. 'I'm drained. Absolutely knackered after all that talking to the police today.'

I sit down in the living room and look at my phone, there's no reply from Carol to a message I sent earlier.

'Anyone have any idea how he did it?' Al asks, handing me the cup of tea. 'Did he just choke on his own vomit, or something?'

'No idea, but it looked strange. He did write a note too, so there must be more to it.' I reply, but my voice still shaky with emotion. 'They've really been through hell and back that family. Carol deserves a medal to cope with a missing daughter, bringing up their son with little support from their alcoholic father, and now this on top of that. What is she going to do?'

'I know it's still quite raw, and that you are more sensitive than me.' Al explains, 'but, she has her own family, her own network of friends, her son is still around. I mean, he's on his way, or with her already by now isn't he. We have to let her deal with this herself, in her own way, with her own friends and family.'

'I know, Al. I know.' I reply, 'I worry that's all. I can't help who I am, where I come from.'

'What I'm trying to say without upsetting you, is, be there when she needs you.' He replies, showing me a look of concern. 'Let her have her private space.'

I barely touched my dinner. We only had a couple of microwave meals for quickness, but as I sit here and close my eyes. I keep seeing the image of Darren in my mind. I'll never forget the coldness of his hands, that amount of vomit all over the floor, but it's the note I am focusing on. Why is he sorry and what for?

I look at my phone again, tempted to send another message, but I decide to phone her to check in.

'Carol, thanks for answering. I'm worried about you my love. Is Kieran there yet, is he with you?'

Carol is sobbing, not a word is spoken by her.

'Carol, I know it's hard, but I care. Al and I are here if you need us, will you be ok tonight. The offer is still there if you want to sleep here.'

'Thank you.' She says, through the crying. 'My boy is on his way; his work mates are bringing him out. He's in a state as you can imagine.'

'I can't imagine what you're going through, but you are very strong, remember that, and that you have people who care. We care.'

'I'll be ok here tonight because I need to see Kieran, we need to understand why he did this. I must explain it to him, and try and make it all make sense, if you get me.'

'Have the police left you alone now?' I ask, hoping. 'Are they still guarding the cottage?'

'Yeah, they've left me alone. I gave them my statement about how we argued, and he was aggressive. I showed them my bruises, they know his past anyway. I went over it and over it and over it.'

'You sound tired, are you sure I can't help in any way?'

'No but thank you. I'm good. They have removed his body now, but they're knocking around the site looking for any witnesses.'

'Witnesses to what?' I gasp, 'what more do they need, he was on his own, he was full of booze, he left you a note.'

'It looks like suicide, but they don't know until they've done some toxicology tests on him. Maybe something happened while I was at yours, I don't know. But I think it's suicide, he once said he'd kill himself if I ever leave him. That was years ago, but now. Now, I don't know what to think.'

I close my eyes and listen to her crying down the phone. Al is next to me, looking at me, concerned, but offering me some biscuits.

'Text me when Kieran gets there, will you?' I beg, 'please, let me know so that I know you're ok and you're not alone.'

'I will,' Carol says, sounding certain. 'I promise. And thank you, to both of you for your support. It means a lot to me. I'm sorry for everything, I really am. I didn't mean to get you involved in any of this.'

'It's fine.' I reassure her, not that Al would agree with me. 'I think we were meant to cross paths. You take good care of yourself, I mean it, and make sure you stay in touch.'

I hang up the phone, place a hand on my chest as I spare a thought for Carol and her son. I take the biscuit from Al, and he doesn't say a word. He sits in the chair beside me, now with his paper again, and the room is silent.

I'm so lucky to have had the life I have lived, the events of today have really put things into perspective. I may have been abandoned by my mother, and lost both of my grandparents, but I have a kind, caring husband. We are not super rich, but not poor either. We get by on what we have, but more importantly is that we have each other. We've rarely had massive arguments, and he's been by my side through it all.

'We should go and visit your brother in Bristol, one day soon, shouldn't we?' I say to Al to break the silence. 'He's family, and we don't see him enough, nor our nieces and nephews. We're out of touch.'

'He has his life, and we have ours, it's just how it is.' Al replies, giving the exact response I expected. 'How about we plan a little trip after the Summer?'

'That'll be good.'

'I'll phone him tomorrow, see if September or October is any good for him.'

'Thanks, Al.'

We sit back in the silence, but I close my eyes and concentrate on the image in my mind. Darren's body on the bed, the vomit on the floor, the note saying he was sorry. What are you sorry for? I ask in my mind. What did you do?

There are lines and shapes, colours that fade, but as I channel my mind and mental thoughts. I repeat the question again, and again. Then in a flash, I see roses, red ones, and I feel warm and cosy. An energy is coming through to me that signifies warmth and love. This can't be Darren.

'Who is there?' I ask out loud in the room. 'Come forward, show me, speak to me. Feel my energy.'

'You really have turned into your grandmother, haven't you?' Al says, standing up. 'I'll leave you alone if you're going to be trying to speak to any ghosts.'

Al takes his paper with him. I smile because I know he doesn't really believe in life after death, but he's respectful enough to let me try and follow in my gran's footsteps. I don't want to repeat time and time again, that I know what I feel, know what I know and have seen, experienced things first hand. I should believe, and no matter how much I try to convince him. I blame that he isn't open minded enough to allow different energies into his life.

'Lauren is that you. Can you give me a sign.' I ask quietly, closing my eyes and visualising the roses again. 'Are you there?'

CHAPTER TWENTY-FOUR

I try to relax my thoughts to allow whoever is showing me the roses through. Then I see her, it is Lauren, exactly the same features as she was in the paper. She's holding up a piece of paper and ripping it up into shreds. I still don't know if it's Lauren allowing me to see her, or if it's some other spirit showing me Lauren. I feel as though it is Lauren, but I'm afraid of that. Does this mean that Lauren is dead?

I suddenly remembered my grandmother's words.

'You'll be surprised how many people who don't believe in what I do, want readings from me.' She said, as I was walking with her to a friend of a friend who wanted to know what her future had in store. 'They have to do their part too, you know. I can tell them until I'm blue in the face that they will have great jobs, more money. But they still have to make it happen and risk the opportunities that come their way.'

Sometimes, she said a lot of things to me that never made sense, but they make sense to me now. I think about her all the time, and she once told me that she always knew she'd never grow old and frail.

'I don't know what will kill me,' she said to Al and me once when we were talking about growing old together. 'But I don't think I'll see old bones. I know that. I don't know how, but I just know it will be quick.'

She was right though, they were killed instantly in that car accident, but at the time I thought being in their seventies was old, however now I'm getting closer and closer to her age, it doesn't feel that old.

'Gran.' I ask, 'Is this you coming through?'

I close my eyes and rest. I listen to the silence, visualise the roses, and think about my gran, trying to build a sense of connection with the images in my minds eye and her.'

I don't feel it. This isn't her. It wasn't the same feeling I had when I remember hearing her words, this isn't the same feeling I had when I had that dream of the spider, roses and of Lauren. I don't feel a connection with her, nor Lauren the more I concentrate because I feel nauseous.

I have a growing sense of negative energy now that is making me shake with worry. I don't know what it is, or who it is, but I feel strange. It's as though there's a disconnect between what I am thinking and what I am feeling. The feeling of intensity is growing, like the time I met Darren and he was arguing with Carol. Like the time I saw him turn up in the woods and practically drag her out of there.

This energy is strong and I can't shake it off. I think it's Darren.

'Darren, if you can hear me. Give me a sign.'

The living room door thuds itself shut with an almighty bang that had me jump out of my skin.

'Al was that you?' I shout, 'Al?'

Al comes rushing in.

'Did you hear that?' I say, shaking and tearful. 'I think I channelled him. I think his spirit was with me.'

'It was the bloody wind, Bren.' He says, 'look, the window was open out there, it was the wind. Don't be worrying yourself.'

I look at the open window and the curtains blowing, but it was at the exact moment. I asked. With the feelings I felt, I know it was strong.

'Something's not right, Al.' I say, and I feel it, it's strong and I know I am right. 'I know you don't want to hear it, but I saw a vision of Lauren in my mind, and she was ripping up paper. I'm sure it's the note. Then I felt the same way I felt when I met Darren and he was kicking off.'

'What are you trying to say?' Al asks, 'it doesn't make any sense to me?'

'I think now I can't un-think this, is what I'm trying to explain.' I say, trying to make sense of it, but feeling nervous. 'I think Darren knows what happened to Lauren.'

Saying it out loud made it feel right to me. My gut instinct, my intuition, my gift that I'm still learning all makes this feel probable.

'You know what this means, don't you?'

'I'm listening, Bren, but I think the trauma of what has happened is playing with your brain. Please, take some rest. Work surely won't be expecting you in tomorrow, are they?'

'They're both dead. I think Lauren is dead too.'

I've connected with this and I feel a sense of authority when I say it out loud. It's right, and I know I am right.

'You can't know that or prove that Bren.' Al says, closing the window that he believes caused the door to slam. 'We can't go around telling people these things. Please don't say that to Carol. She won't appreciate hearing that.'

'I'm not that cruel.' I reply, 'but I am going to prove it. You just watch me. If the police can't locate her, then the best I can do for that poor woman is find her daughter myself.'

Al is speechless for once; I can see it in his facial expression that he's uneasy.

'I'm not going to be persuaded otherwise.' I continue. 'I feel a sense of responsibility with this missing girl. I've been around the parents, and the whole lack of support they're getting from the police. I'm going to find Lauren so Carol can have some peace.'

Al turns around and walks up the stairs while I head back

into the living room. I want to do this for Carol, People may laugh, people may think I am crazy, but I am going to find out what happened to her.

Chapter Twenty-Five

Friday, 9 June 2023
Brenda

Carol called me first thing this morning to ask for help moving out of the cottage. Kieran arrived late last night, but she couldn't face it alone. She explained that Kieran is too angry to talk and isn't really supporting her because he's very angry about his father killing himself.

In some strange way by fate, I am now connected to her unfortunate circumstances, but I wanted to help them both. I need to know she is going to be strong enough to deal with this. I think she's in shock and not really taking it all in. I remember how that felt when my grandparents died; you have to keep on living, but you still need time out to process everything in your own time.

Al dropped me off this morning to the site, and to my surprise has not mentioned a word of my spiritual beliefs today. We sat down for breakfast as we normally do together and talked about the shock of it all, which is the reason why Southleigh Cottages have allowed us both a week off work to mentally recover. Special leave with full pay too, which is nice of them, since we weren't expecting that generosity.

There was an initial awkward moment with Carol and I, when I arrived, but she gave me a huge hug. I didn't know what to say to her, there's no way I can make any of this better or ease her pain. I was standing there with a sad look on my face, it was very emotional.

'The police came and knocked our door this morning, telling us that Darren's death is unexplained, but no suspicious circumstances. It appears to be a suicide, but they'll know more when the toxicology comes through in about a week or so.' Carol said, as I sit on the sofa in this smaller cottage, holding my glass of water. 'They found a bottle of pills, I'm not sure what they were. I said he hadn't taken any drugs in years, but he must have had them on him for a reason. I've never seen them before.'

'You said he has been struggling with dealing with everything around Lauren being missing on and off for years, didn't you.' I say to make sense of it, 'sometimes men just bottle everything up and it comes out in other ways. Alcoholism, running away, struggling with their mental health. Men don't talk about things that affect their emotions. Al is the same, he just won't do anything deep. All I get is that he's ok, nothing else. But I know deep down. I know when he needs space.'

'Darren was like that too wasn't he Kieran?' Carol explains, 'I can't believe I'm talking about him in past tense now, but there were times he was like a closed book for someone with such a big mouth.'

Carol stops to take a moment, wipes her eyes dry with a tissue. I turn my thoughts to Al, who I know would have gone back home by now, but he's going to pick me up later.

'I can't believe how much I have cried. I go through stages of being so angry with him. Why did he do this, why now, why me. Why didn't he get help?'

I don't say anything, but I look towards Kieran and give a small smile of concern, but that I want to show I care too.

'Because Dad is a fucking cunt, mum.' Kieran says, 'he didn't care about any of us, never really did. Always shouting at us, always moaning, always down the fucking pub, mate.'

I am absolutely shocked and appalled by the tone of language used and I try to conceal my expression of distaste.

'He never bothered to ask me how I felt when Lauren fucked off out of it all,' Kieran continues. 'He's always been fucking selfish.'

'Mind your language, son.' Carol says. 'He was your father, he loved you, and he dealt with things in his own way. He wanted the best for you both, he really did.'

Kieran huffs but doesn't say a word. He looks at me with a look of disbelief.

'Look at the weather out there now.' I interrupt to distract the conversation. 'All those dark clouds.'

'I can't bring myself to look at his body, mum.' Kieran says, holding his head in his hands. 'I can't do this. I can't cope with all this. Why did he do it mum, why?'

Carol comforts her son, who is now drying his hands in his joggers.

'This emotion comes over in waves, doesn't it.' Carol says. 'One minute I'm ok, then the next I am balling my eyes out uncontrollably. I love him and hate him all at the same time, but I can't change a thing. What's done is done. It hurts, but we have to keep going. We have to keep carrying on.'

'For fuck's sake, mum, he's barely been dead a day.' Kieran chips in. 'I don't know how I feel, what I feel. I wasn't expecting this. I wish I could have said more to him, done more with him.

I don't know anything about planning a fucking funeral.'

'Brenda and I are just going to go over to the other cottage and start packing up my things. I know you said you can't go in there, and won't go in there, but are you alright here on your own until we're back?'

'I'll be sound, mum. I'll phone Liam at work again and update him, tell him I'm not coming back for a while. You go, and I'll drive us back home after.'

I stand up, straighten myself, place my water on the table and head out of the back door. Carol follows, and she's still wearing the same clothes from yesterday, must have slept in them too.

'I'm sorry about Kieran. He and his father didn't have the best relationship.' Carol explains, 'after Lauren left, and Luke's death, Darren completely changed personality. I don't whether he blames us, or himself.'

'That's ok, don't worry about it.' I reassure her, 'at least he didn't get to see him in the way we did, and you've been a great mother to them both. I can see that you both have a close relationship.'

'I've always been the peacemaker. Darren didn't even visit Kieran when he was in prison a few years back. He was ok when he got released, but it's like tiptoeing on eggshells when you're in a room with Darren. We're always afraid of saying the wrong thing, doing the wrong thing, it's been tough at times.'

As we stand in front of the cottage where Darren died, I close my eyes and take a breath to prepare myself mentally for going back inside. I'm trying to get in the zone spiritually, but I'm struggling with the distraction of Carol. Mentally, I can't take myself into that tuned in space. It's like a radio signal that's dim, I need to slowly concentrate and fine tune it until I can pick up everything when it feels right.

'They took him late last night.' Carol said, 'the two who stood guard left this morning. The guy at reception said that I don't have to worry about cleaning anything, they will do it all, which is very kind of them.'

'I am so sorry for your loss.' I reply. 'Really, Carol, I have no idea what to do or say, but you are incredibly brave and strong. This must be horrendously difficult for you.'

'I don't have a choice.' Carol says as we walk inside, 'I remember how I felt when Luke passed away all those years ago. But, back then, I went through those emotions on my own and in secret because I had no choice then either. No one knew about our affair.'

I stopped dead in my tracks because I hadn't realised.

'You loved him?' I ask because I thought it was just the odd one-night stand now and then. 'That must have been incredibly difficult to go through alone. Did he love you too?'

'I absolutely most certainly loved him.' Carol admitted. 'He was like a kinder, softer version of Darren. He felt like something that was just for me. I had security with Darren, but Luke made me feel loved and wanted. I Loved Darren too, but it was a different kind of love. We'd been together a long time; they were very different.'

Looking around the cottage, I see the difference since forensics have been in. There's more mess scattered here than yesterday. Cushions are overturned on the floor, everything is out from the cupboards, but because of the heat build up, there's a putrid musty smell that's accumulated through all the windows and doors being closed. I've left the door open to get some air through the property.

'Would you have left Darren for Luke if he hadn't have passed away?' I ask, feeling a sense of caution around it. 'Sorry to ask, but I feel a real sincerity around you every time you talk about Luke. Your eyes sparkle, and it's clear you loved him very much.'

'I think I would have, but we never discussed it.' Carol replies, and I sense the edge to her tone, she wasn't happy that I asked. 'It's a different kind of love. Remember that Darren is the father of my kids, the man I married, the man I shared my life with.'

I don't reply, but I can tell she was in love with Luke, and I'm not getting the same feelings about Darren. Her body language is different, she seems cautious and guarded.

'Can I ask you something too since we're alone?' Carol asks, and we sit on the sofa together. I notice that Darren's sorry note is still on the table. 'Can you sense him here, is he with us?'

'Who, Darren?' I reply, knowing that's exactly what she meant, but I was taken by surprise that question. 'It's difficult because he's only just passed and I know he was here before hand. It's all still so raw, but spirits will never leave you. I'm sure there will be times when you can feel him near you, sense him around. Maybe even smell him.'

I say that to comfort her, but in reality, I am getting the same negative energy in this cottage as I did the first time. It seems to follow us in here like a bad smell. I'm not comfortable, I feel very strange and uncomfortable.

'Can I hold that note to see if I can get a reading from it?' I ask, politely, 'I feel drawn to it, and if you are comfortable, I can try and get a sense of how I feel holding it. Considering this is the last thing he wrote?'

Carol nods, as I stand to grab it from the table. I hold it so carefully so as not to damage it in anyway and I'm fascinated by the angry scrawl of writing. I can see the depth of the pen marks and the full stop that looked like it was pressed so hard into the paper it caused a small hole. If he was that sorry about something, would he have been so angry?

'I'm not going to lie; I'm not an expert at this.' I explain, knowing that I've said this before when we were drinking together only the other evening. 'But I've watched my gran do this enough times, and I know I can mentally switch off to allow pure natural thoughts and energy come through. I might be a little rough around the edges.'

'Thank you for doing this. There's no harm in trying, is there.' Carol says, smiling. 'I am sorry to have dragged you into our messy, confused, strange life. I'm very sorry.'

I sigh and close my eyes whilst I hold the paper with both hands. I try to shut off the noises from outside and I concentrate hard on the darkness I see. I always seem to see stripes, and different shades of colours as my eyes react to the sudden darkness and the hard concentration on it. I can hear Carol crying on the sofa.

I see the vision of Lauren again ripping up pieces of paper, did she mean this piece of paper? I didn't connect the two, but the ripping won't stop. I see her ripping it into tiny little pieces, then I sense anger. That must be Darren. I feel like there's a fist banging down hard next to me. Like I want to rip up that piece of paper and smash the table up. I won't do such a thing, but it's how I feel. I don't hear voices, but then there's a sense of calm. I see fields that are very green, and then sunflowers everywhere.

'I don't know if this means anything to you, but I'll give it my best try.' I explain. 'I get a sense from holding this, that it should be torn up and destroyed, there's anger over this note.

But I then got a sense of calmness, and I saw a field filled with sunflowers. It's like it's gone from one extreme to another. The sunflowers seem to be the stronger sense that I have, like everything is fine now, here's a sunflower.'

I turn to face Carol and her jaw is open wide. She's staring right at me, eyes full of tears and her whole body is shaking. I don't think she's aware that she keeps shaking her head.

'No, it can't be.' She says. 'You're making this up aren't you. He told you didn't he. Someone must have told you. No, he couldn't have, No one knew. Not one person knew. How did you know?'

'Are you ok?' I ask, Carol is clearly distraught and looking shocked by what I had said. 'No one has told me anything directly. I'm describing what I saw in my mind and how I felt when I concentrated. I'm only the messenger, did any of that mean anything to you?'

Carol stands up and starts walking around the living room. I'm not sure how to react or respond.

'It's Luke.' She says, whilst holding the note herself. 'One of the last things he said to me when I visited him in hospital was about a dream that he had of us running through fields of sunflowers. I know it's only a dream, but it was so vivid for him. Then he died the next day. I never told anyone, no one.'

Carol sits back down on the sofa crying into her hands.

'If it's any comfort to you, then that shows me that he is with you, and with you at this difficult time. He's showing you that everything is going to be alright, and that you'll get through it. Just like you did when he passed away.' I say, 'I didn't mean to make you more upset. I'm so sorry.'

Carol wipes her eyes, stands up and to my surprise starts ripping the note to shreds. Piece by piece like little bits of confetti the note is ripped all over the lounge. I stand there and watch, my thoughts now contemplating the dread of going upstairs to help pack up her and Darren's clothes.

Carol comes closer towards me with her arms out. I'm still in awe of my own abilities that are showing improvement. I can't explain how I thought of sunflowers, but they were there. His spirit must have projected them to me.

'I'm sorry too.' She says, giving me a hug. 'My head is fucked, but I needed to hear this. Why don't you stay at mine for dinner tonight, both you and Al. I could use the company.'

I didn't know what to say. I wasn't comfortable with this, but I didn't want to let her down either.

'Sure.' I replied, nodding. 'If, you're sure.'

'I insist.'

Together we made our way up the stairs and I am almost certain that Al will not want to stay for dinner, but I'll let him know that I will have to. He'll moan about having to pick me up from Plymouth instead, but he'll still do it.

He'll understand given the circumstances.

Chapter Twenty-Six

Friday, 9 June 2023
Carol

Kieran helps carry in our bags in from the car, whilst I've gone on ahead and opened the front door. I'm overcome with emotion because I am standing here facing the reality of my life as a widow, outside our house without my husband.

Some of the neighbours have come out to say hello, a few have waved and gone back inside, but I nod to accept their acknowledgment. I stand and stare at my house, coming to terms with reality. The last couple of days have been dramatic, stressful, intense, emotional and draining. I'm dreading being out in public with all those people staring at me again. Not only am I the mother with a missing daughter, but I'm now the mother with a missing daughter and a dead husband in their eyes.

It really is just me and my son from now on; I must keep moving forward and find an inner strength to keep on living.

'Carol, I'm so sorry. I heard about the news because it's made the local papers. I don't know what to say.' Liz says, walking towards me with a Plymouth Local News in her hand. 'What a shock this must be. If there's anything you need, you let me know.'

I nod and dry my eyes. Brenda is stood one side of me, Kieran now the other.

'Who the fuck told the press, you bastards.' Kieran shouts. 'Who did this. Who the fuck did this. We don't need any of this you bunch of cunts.'

'Kieran, please don't do this. Not now. Get in the house, please. There's no time for kicking off. People actually care about us; they're not talking about us. It's different this time.' I shout to calm him down. He has a bad enough reputation around St Budeaux anyway and a temper like his dad. 'Liz is only trying to help; she doesn't need you shouting on at her. Nor does anyone else, get inside and shut up.'

'I'm really sorry Liz,' I say. 'He's dealing with it in his own way. Please forgive him, he's stressed. And thanks for the offer of help too. I know where you are if I need you. Appreciate it.'

Liz stands there looking solemn. We've known each other for about fifteen years, she'll not take Kieran's actions personally. She's seen and heard far worse around here.

Brenda is looking at the street and I can tell she's not impressed. It's a world away from the luxury cottages of Salcombe, but St Budeaux has been my home for many years. It might not be the best street in the neighbourhood, but here it's a real community of friends who will help each other out. It's not about what we have or haven't got, but it's about how we treat people. We look after our own.

'None of us have a lot of money round here, Brenda,' I say, breaking her trail of thought. 'We might be what some call of low social economic background, which is a tarted-up way of saying poor as piss, but we help each other help when we need it. Everyone knows where they stand.'

Brenda smiles, nods and walks inside after Kieran holds the door open for the both of us. I follow on in behind her and I can still smell Darren in the home. I close my eyes and take in the scent of his jackets hanging up in the hallway.

How did it ever come to this?

It's a weird feeling that I am on my own now. No more arguments, no heavy handedness, no more explaining what I'm doing and where I'm going. No more shouting and screaming at each other. But with that comes no more security, no more stability, no more structure and a loss of routine. I feel like I just exist. The only way I can describe it is as though, everything that has happened, happened to someone else. Not me, I'm numb to it. I know it is my loss, but that overwhelming feeling of sadness is so heavy that it's beyond the point of tears. It's there, it's in me, I feel it, I can't express it.

A huge part of my life has died, and my emotions are all over the place. I'm merely two feet walking forward and trying to function without sinking into some kind of depression. I have to get through this, I know I will have to keep on living, but my head is in overdrive. I might have to get more sleeping tablets from the doctor. That really helped after Lauren because I couldn't switch off from the misery of losing her, and I don't want to be that person again after Darren. It's not healthy.

Kieran puts the bags away so I take the opportunity to speak to Brenda about her gift.

'Al didn't mind you staying for a few hours extra then?' I ask Brenda as I see her texting someone. 'Thank you for being you. And, for coming back to the house. I can show you Lauren's room later. I'm keen to know what you think, what you feel and if you sense anything.'

I can't believe the support that Brenda has offered considering she was the woman cleaning our cottage on Monday, and now we've developed this friendship through weird circumstances. She's kind to us, which is rare. I'm not used to strangers being so friendly, but I'm fascinated by her so-called psychic abilities. I never believed in psychics, but I am open minded.

With Brenda telling me things about the fields of sunflowers in those visions, I don't know what to believe anymore. Could it be a complete coincidence that she guessed, or is there more to it? I have this need to keep her close to me, to understand if she has an ability to really understand everything that has gone so wrong in my life. Right now, I'm leaning towards her being able to know everything.

'He said he's pick me up about seven, if that's alright with you, my love?' Brenda asked. 'I've sent him the address, and I told him if it's any earlier, I'd message. Are you sure you don't mind me being around. Wouldn't you rather have some peace and quiet, you and Kieran to process everything that has happened?'

'Mum, if Brenda is here until seven, do you mind if I go and see Chantelle. She'll be worried about me.' Kieran asks, 'Only if you don't mind. If you'd rather I stayed with you, then I can?'

If I'm being honest the only thing that I want right now is to be alone. Completely and utterly alone with no one talking to me. I have Brenda here because she fascinates me, and I want Kieran to be himself, and to do whatever he needs to cope. If that means going to see his girlfriend down the road, then so be it.

'I don't mind. I'm sure she'll be worried for you.' I reply, 'I don't know why you don't move out of that flat of yours and get a place together? You've been seeing her for a couple of years now.'

'I'll pop back in later on.' Kieran says, not answering my question. 'If you need me, text me.'

Kieran leaves the house and I'm now alone with Brenda in the kitchen.

'Hard to believe I was standing here a couple days ago, shouting for Darren to get a move on.' I say, still feeling emotional. 'If these walls could talk, they'd tell you a few stories. I know it sounds all doom and gloom, but despite all the misery, there were mostly happier times here. Our lives were so different ten years ago, believe me.'

I watch Brenda's curiosity. She doesn't ask any more questions, but she's giving me a warm smile.

'Can I get you a drink?'

'A tea would be great, if it's no trouble?'

'It's the least I owe you for putting me up the other night.' I reply. 'You know what really bothers me, something that I think I will feel guilty about for the rest of my life?'

'What's that, love?' Brenda replies. 'I know this will be difficult for some time, but you are strong. Strong minded and you'll pull through this as a family. You did before.'

'I wonder if things would have been different if I hadn't have walked out on him the other night.' I say, wiping my eyes. 'It is all my fault. I caused all of this, left Kieran without a father, without a sister. Where did it all go wrong?'

Brenda looks uncomfortable as I start to cry, she comes over to comfort me, but I understand this isn't her house and we barely know each other.

'Thank you, for everything.' I say, 'you are one of the kindest people I have ever met. Thank you.'

I dry my eyes once again and put the kettle on before grabbing two mugs from the cupboard. There looking right at me, staring me in the face is Darren's favourite coffee mug. I pause for a moment and remember some of those days he used to sit in the garden, drinking his coffee, putting the world to rights.

'This was his favourite mug. Lauren bought it for him one Father's Day.' I say and hold the mug up to show Brenda. 'It says to the Best Dad in the World. He treated her like a princess, shame about the way he treated me at times, hey.'

He absolutely adored Lauren, she really was his little girl, his world. I miss that time period when our lives felt normal and complete. The kids had everything they wanted, we made ends meet, we struggled financially, had pretty much everything on credit or buy now pay later, but it worked. We were one little happy family.

Everything changed when Luke was diagnosed with terminal cancer; I had to watch his wife suffer and care for him when all I wanted to do was be there right by his side up until the end. It hurt to walk away, knowing I'd never see him again. He went downhill physically quite rapidly. He slept a lot, was on oral morphine for most of the pain, but I did get to tell him how much I loved him one last time. We held each others' hands and our dream of running away was ruined by that deadly awful disease. He was taken far too soon.

'Here you go.' I say, handing Brenda her tea. 'How does it feel being in the house, any strange vibes?'

Brenda takes the mug and places it on the work top. She looks around the kitchen. It's half the size of her house.

'Not at the minute.' She replies, now sipping her tea, 'It's too soon. I'm concentrating on supporting you for now. Is there anything you would like me to do to help, even if it's a bit of cleaning, I don't mind. How about I cook you a big dinner that you can have over two days to save you having to cook?'

'I want to cook; I'll need to keep busy.' I explain. 'If I learned anything about myself after Lauren went missing, is that I need to keep on being busy otherwise I'll end up sitting in bed for days on end, not washing or bothering with the outside world. I don't want that again. I don't want to be that person again.'

I can't stop myself from crying as I remember that period of my life. Brenda keeps looking out of the kitchen window and rarely making eye contact with me. She places her mobile phone down on the side next to her mug and starts to walk towards the window.

'Would you like to see Laurens room?' I ask, aiming to focus her thoughts on Lauren. 'Everything in there is exactly as she left it. Nothing's changed. Sometimes I sit on the bed and I can still feel her there, it gives me comfort. Darren thought it was strange, but now. Now I feel emotionally drained. I don't know what to think anymore.'

'Of course, I'd love to.' Brenda replies. 'I might need some time to really think about Lauren. I can't guarantee anything.'

'You were spot on about the sunflowers. You also knew about her necklace.' I reply, which I am confident that if she tries hard enough, she might get some kind of spiritual message about Lauren. 'You can take all the time that you need. Let's go upstairs.'

I lead the way and Brenda follows behind me. I catch her looking at the mirror in the hallway, I see her slightly investigate the living room, but as I approach Laurens bedroom, I stop outside the door.

'Please let me know what happened to our little girl.' I beg. 'I live with this guilt every single day. I miss her and I love her. It's as though she's vanished into thin air.'

Brenda places a hand on the door handle but doesn't open it. She closes her eyes and I watch on tenterhooks. She's so unpredictable that I have no idea what kind of surreal message could come out of her mouth. It's chilling.

I'm glad that Kieran isn't here to see this because, like his dad, he'd fly off the handle and kick her out of the house. He would say it's all nonsense, she's crazy, she's playing tricks on me.

I trust Brenda, there's something mesmerising and sincere about her that's drawing me in. She's told me things over the last few days that I don't think she could have known.

Does she really have the ability to know everything?

Chapter Twenty-Seven

Friday, 9 June 2023
Brenda

The metal door handle leading to Lauren's room is icy cold to touch; I get a chill that causes me to shiver. One of those moments when you hear people say that someone must have walked over your grave. I have an instant feeling of coldness. I'm nervous too and in awe that I'm about to see Lauren's bedroom. I hold my hand tight on the handle, giving it a strong grip as my emotions are wild.

When I think about the time when I first saw her face in the local newspaper and the goosebumps I had then, it's like that now. What was a mere black and white image and a connection I couldn't explain, followed by the chance meeting of her mother that has led me here to her personal space.

I'm cautious about the signs, the way that I feel. I'm conscious that Carol is close to me, so I don't want to give too much away in case I'm not accurate enough. I keep my eyes tightly closed, and there's a sense of sadness and disappointment. There's tension, and I have a feeling of needing to run away, it's so strong. These feelings connect me to Lauren; I'm assured this is her.

CHAPTER TWENTY-SEVEN

'May those in the light, guide me on this journey.' I whisper, 'Surround me with your energy as I interpret your messages.'

I remember those words from my gran, every Sunday as she used to do her readings for friends. What I don't want to happen is my overwhelming shock of Darren's suicide tainting my channelling of Lauren. Will my nerves interfere with the spiritual messages?

Carol is standing next to me, and I can feel her intense anxiety while she stares at me. I know she's desperate to know what happened to Lauren, and I want to help in any way that I can.

I open the door and then my eyes. Taking in the instant view and making sense of my first impressions. The room is smaller than I expected, there's a bed up against the far end wall, a window to the right and a wardrobe against the wall. The colour scheme is soft pink and greys with a number of plush toys sitting on top of the wardrobe.

'It's just as she left it.' Carol says, barging in and standing next to the wardrobe. She opens the window to let some air in, and immediately I'm uncomfortable. 'Sometimes I sleep in here, so I can still feel close to her in some way.'

'I'm being honest with you. I don't feel comfortable; it's a strong sense of dislike about something.' I explain, closing my eyes, taking in a deep breath and understand my gut feelings. 'Has anything changed in here, have you moved some things around?'

Carol's expression changes. There's a moment of awkward silence.

'I feel all boxed in. Like I want more space around me.' I say how I am feeling, 'I sense that the bed might have been coming off that wall horizontally, and the wardrobe next to it. Giving me this big square area here?'

Carol places a hand on her chest, then one hand on her hair. She looks uncomfortable with me. I'm not offending in any way.

'You're exactly right.' She says, now fidgeting some more. 'I forgot about that, it was so long ago. It's all her belongings, but, yes, the bed was kinda in the same place, but not so pushed against this wall. The wardrobe was right here next to it. I hated it that way.'

I glance up at all the soft toys, see that some are clearly older than others by the raggedness of some.

'She loved them very much. Most of them were from when she was very young.' Carol explains, grabbing a grey bunny rabbit plush toy with a red ribbon around its neck. 'This was her favourite. All those times she broke up with her childhood boyfriends, she'd be sat in here cuddling this one. She would only be about ten, if that.'

Carol hands me the bunny and again I have that cold shiver. I'm feeling how soft it is, rubbing my hands all through the fake fur, but I don't associate this item with sadness.

'Give me a moment, will you, my love?' I ask. 'I'd like to concentrate and get a sense of how this room makes me feel right now. Can I have five mins alone. I'm sorry to ask.'

'I'll be outside if you need me.' Carol says, walking away and out of the door. 'Don't be sorry. You take all the time you need.'

As she closes the door, I walk towards the bedroom window. I'm draw to the shed and the garden looks well kept which surprised me. I'm glad Carol has given me a few minutes to myself because I found her very distracting. I don't associate the soft toys with anything negative, but I can't get enough from them. Nothing is happening. I seem to want to keep staring at the shed.

CHAPTER TWENTY-SEVEN

I place the toy on the bed and close my eyes because I'm not getting any readings from the room itself. I felt more from the door handle, I also remember the keyring with her face on it, and that triggered me to think about the Empress tarot cards. I know that was my grans voice, I'd never forget those tones.

'Gran.' I say out loud, feeling a little daft. 'I don't know how you did it. I don't know how you were so accurate for so many people.'

I stand in the centre of the room, my eyes wide open as I am breathing in the fresh air from the window, but it feels empty. Like I don't belong here, as though no spirit is willing to show me anything. My presence in this room means nothing; the sun is shining bright now and it's causing the shadows from the blinds to be visible on the soft pink rug. I don't think there's any more I can do in this room.

I slowly place my hand over the door handle again and feel it's coldness. No shiver this time, no mixed emotions, but I turn around to look at the room one more time because I might never be here again. One thing that really stood out was the cleanliness, the lack of posters, or anything that showed Lauren was into music, or gaming, or magazines, everything looked straight out of a catalogue.

I pull hard on the door handle, but it doesn't open. The door is stuck or locked. I rattle the metal handle again, only harder, but it's not budging so I let go.

'Is everything ok?' Carol asks, opening the door and walking inside. 'I thought I heard you struggling?'

'It wouldn't open.' I say, catching my breath, as I hurt my hand. 'I pulled on it, but it wouldn't budge. Was it locked from the outside?'

'There are no locks on any of the doors.' Carol replies, 'Maybe it was just stuck for some reason. How odd.'

I wonder if we were holding the door at the same time, maybe, but it didn't seem logical. Was she holding it the whole time?

I can't help but feel like I am intruding on her time. A period where Carol is maybe making more of an effort for me and being polite, when she might want to be on her own to grieve for her husband. I'm disappointed that being in Lauren's room didn't give me a sense of her belonging in this house. Maybe it's me, or I should have brought my tarot cards.

We're both startled by the sudden thudding of the front door. The doorbell rang twice, followed by further aggressive knocking.

'I'm not sure I'm really up for visitors; I'll ask them to come back another time.' Carol says walking down the stairs. 'Unless Kieran has forgotten his key.'

I look around the hallway and spot the wedding photo of Carol and Darren, instantly see how young they both were. Then to the side of them, separate photos of Kieran and Lauren, both in their school uniforms. They look happy kids, they're smiles are wide, but there's a sadness in their eyes. I look again to confirm my thoughts that if you don't look at the smiling mouth, both of their eyes look empty and emotionless.

'Go away, please just fuck off.' Carol shouts and slams the door shut. 'I don't want any of you lot back here.'

I had been so engrossed in the photos I hadn't even realised the commotion that was going on downstairs. If these are the kind of objects I am drawn to, then maybe my attention should be there and not on the bedroom. I wonder if she'll let me take them down and hold them?

'Is everything alright, my love?' I shout. 'Are you ok?'

I head down the stairs as fast as my poor legs would allow

me, and see Carol on her knees in the hallway, crying heavily into her hands.

'I can't take any more of that lot.' She cries, 'I want them to go away. I want them to leave me alone.'

She's sobbing and sobbing, but I place my hand out to hold her, and she gets back to her feet.

'It's the press. The local newspaper crew.' Carol explains, 'They wanted me to talk about Darren, and Lauren, and how fucking inconsiderate is that. He only died yesterday. He's not even been gone a day. I hate them.'

Carol cries as she walks away from me into the kitchen, she opens the back door.

'I need some fresh air.' she says. 'I feel like I'm struggling to breathe in this damn house. It's been nothing but a nightmare ever since I moved in here. Nothing has gone well for us. That lot have been no help to me whatsoever. Didn't find Lauren, did they?'

I don't say a word for a minute or two, but I let her get it off her chest.

'They must have gone. They haven't knocked again.' I reply, heading into the kitchen. 'Do you want me to check for you. I'll give them what for.'

Carol opens the back door and stands out in the garden. Rather than go and check the local press have left, I follow her outside.

'You have a beautiful little back garden.' I compliment her efforts, 'I assume all these pretty flowers are your doing, and not Darren's.'

I make her smile.

'No, he's definitely, not the gardening type.' She replies, 'never really ever stepped foot out here.'

I glance at some of her bruises.

'Was he always abusive?'

Carol closes her eyes and nods to confirm. As she starts to cry again, I walk in closer to comfort her. I look at her and wish I could be more help.

'He loved us, but there were times I didn't know when it would stop.' She explains, 'I felt sorry for him because of his brother, and guilty for what I was doing behind his back. If I ever left him, I knew it would drive him over the edge, and it did, didn't it?'

I squint my eyes as a short, sharp pain went through my head. It shocked me, scared me.

'Are you ok, do you need to sit down?' Carol asks, noticing I'm clearly surprised. 'What's going on?'

'It's the back of my head; I just had a real sharp pain hit me right there.' I explain, showing her the back of my head. 'Came out of nowhere?'

Carol points the way to the garden furniture in the corner and we take a seat together. I take it slowly and wonder if I need a painkiller.

'Thought I was going to fall down.' I say, trying to make light of the situation. 'That, really, bloody well hurt my head.'

'Can I ask you a question too, and be really honest with me?' Carol asks, placing her hand out to hold mine. 'Being here, right now, do you have any real sense of Lauren and what happened at all. Do you know why she ran away?'

I don't answer immediately because I like to think about my response to be really certain. I turn to my right side, look at the ivy growing up the fence and see it clear as day. The blackest of spiders, sat there tucked in its web. I've not seen one in years, but I know a fake widow when I see one.

'Oh my god, shall I kill it.' Carol snaps, standing up, noticing it too. 'I'll take my shoe off.'

'No, no, please don't.' I say to calm her down. 'It's a fake widow; they move on anyway after a few days. Please don't harm him. He's only sat there doing his job. He won't hurt us, it's not dangerous.'

I've convinced her to leave the spider alone and further up the garden near the run-down old shed are rows of red, oranges and creamy white roses in bushes.

'Wow.' I say looking at all the roses, 'they really are striking. I could never get mine at home to grow like that.'

'Come up with me and take a look?' Carol asks, 'every year they seem to be at their best around this time. It's a south facing garden, so they love all the sunlight. I planted them after Lauren left, she loved the sun too. They remind me of her, everything does.'

I get up out of my seat and together we walk closer to the roses. The closer I walk to them the more I feel danger, and anxiety. Carol is holding my arm, smiling at me and leading me to the bushes. I have the nausea back and the uneasiness.

The spider, the roses, the bedroom, my pounding head and that need to run away returns. It's strong, sickly and I'm shaking. A dark, sense of uncertainty causes me to stand still in my place. I remove Carols arm and look straight at her. It's the only logical explanation and I am absolutely certain of my feelings.

'She's dead. She's crossed over.' I say, with my own eyes watering with the emotion. 'I think she got hit over the back of the head. She's dead. I'm so sorry, but that is genuinely how I feel. I can't shake it off.'

Carol stands in front of me looking distraught, but she

wanted me to tell her the truth.

I'm sorry.

Chapter Twenty-Eight

Friday, 9 June 2023
Carol

The sun was shining down on us, but the dark black cloud of my dysfunctional and depressing life overshadows the weather. I wasn't expecting Brenda to say those words to me, I am shocked and surprised by her directness considering she wanted to look at the roses. I'm in no fit mental state to deal with anything else. Hearing somebody say that out loud shook me to the core, who does she think she is?

'How fucking dare you stand there and say that to my face.' I shout at Brenda, her expression shows she's shocked by the confrontation. 'How could you tell me that she's dead. What evidence do you have. You're lying to me, aren't you? Making it all up in that head of yours.'

It's like a red rag to a bull telling me that. Something in my mind has snapped and the anger I'm feeling is intensifying by the minute. Brenda doesn't even have any kids, so she doesn't know how it feels to lose a daughter. The child I gave birth to, mothered and loved. My own flesh and blood.

The two of us, still alone, standing in my garden. I'm looking at her face and all I want to do is punch her in the mouth. I daren't, but the feeling is strong.

'It wasn't intentional to offend you. How insulting you are of me now.' Brenda shrieks, 'not in all my life has anyone been this rude to me. I tried my best. I helped you when you needed support. I let you sleep in my home.'

Brenda turns to walk away from me, muttering to herself. I watch her limp a little as she struggles with her knee. It's with all my might not to run up behind her and kick her to the floor.

'I'm sorry, my love. I'm really sorry.' She says, walking further and further away. 'I got carried away. I am telling you what I'm feeling, the honest truth. It got too intense. I shouldn't have come here really. I knew I shouldn't have, so I'll give Al a call in a minute to pick me up. It's been nice meeting you.'

Brenda starts crying which triggers some guilt. I'm going through an intense wave of mixed emotions and feelings that are difficult to explain to anyone, let alone deal with. I've shocked her with my temper. She's clearly not had the arguments in her life that I've had to deal with. Defending myself day in and day out with my movements, explaining that I haven't been chatting up other men, Darren throwing my dinner in the bin if I dare to be a few minutes late home from work. Times when I'd have to show him all the messages on my phone, and other times when he'd keep my bank cards to control our money. Brenda hasn't had my life. I wouldn't wish it on anyone.

'Ok, I'm so sorry. I'm really sorry.' I say, 'I didn't mean it, really, I snapped. You don't know me, or what I've been through as a mother, a wife, the challenges, the scrutinising, the failure. Please, I am sorry. Please stay and understand how hard it would be for any parent to hear that news. I snapped,

CHAPTER TWENTY-EIGHT

that is all.'

'I'm making this worse for you aren't I.' Brenda says, 'I'll text Al, he can come and pick me up sooner. I'll leave you in peace. I shouldn't have come back to your house. Not so soon.'

'I'm not like you. I didn't go to some fancy school. In this area, what you see is hat you get.' I explain, 'we stick up for ourselves. No one else will do it for us. Do you know what the police said to me when I reported her missing. They said, well since you live in an inner-city slum, sadly it doesn't get the coverage of the middle classes. What a joke. They made me feel really small, like no one cares. And they don't you know. They don't give a damn.'

'I care, Carol. You know what an impact this has had on me. I wanted to help, maybe I went too far.' Brenda replies, fumbling about with her phone. 'I should go now. Al said he is on his way.'

'No, please don't go.' I beg, wanting her to change her mind. 'This isn't a game to me, it's my life. I've lost them both, lets talk about this. If you think Lauren is dead, then who killed her?'

'I don't know. I can't answer that.' Brenda says, hesitating, 'Honestly, spiritualism for me is about how I feel, we went over this. I see things, tell you what I get a sense of and see if it has any meaning to the recipient. It's not meant to cause any offence, and now I am embarrassed for myself. I was out of order and you are angry with me. I'm sorry.'

'I'm confused, that's all. I don't understand how you can say that's she's dead if you don't know how, or by who, or even where she is?' I say, but more calmly and controlled. 'If you went to the police with that information, they wouldn't take it very seriously. Would they? I'm her mother and they still wouldn't, not even from me.'

'No, but I was answering your question. You asked me if I had any real sense of Lauren being here and what happened at all?' Brenda defends herself, 'I thought you wanted to know exactly what was going on in my head. I felt things I've not experienced before. It's strange to me too.'

'Your exact words were that she's crossed over.' I say, trying to keep myself calm, but the more I hear her words in my head, my eyes bulging with anger. 'Do you think Darren killed her, is that it?'

Brenda doesn't say another word. I can see she is shaking, but I'm struggling not to completely flip. Holding in all these feelings, emotions, whilst I think she is standing there judging me as a mother, judging us as a family. We don't know her.

'I've seen you looking at all my bruises. I remember the conversations we had about Darren the other night. I know what you're implying.' I say, 'you just want me to say it don't you? You want me to say that Darren killed his little girl, don't you? But he didn't. He loved her, he really fucking loved her. Treated her better than he did me.'

I start to cry and Brenda is seated at the table. The awkwardness and fear are evident on those beady eyes of hers. I don't want to be this upset. I don't want to be this angry, but she is pushing all the wrong buttons.

'Darren was clearly very aggressive and abusive towards you. You told me how guilty you felt about Luke, you loved him so dearly.' Brenda says, her shaking now less obvious. 'I never suggested Darren killed Lauren. I wasn't putting two and two together to make five, believe me. I thought I was genuinely helping. You have been very brave to live with a man like that, I can't imagine how difficult it was for you. And now you have to mourn him, it must be tough.'

'It is.' I cry, the emotional release making me feel better. 'He's the man that I loved, the man that I loathed. I don't even know why I stayed with him all these years. I should have left him a long time ago, but Luke.'

I pause and struggle to continue because I miss him so much. He knew how to treat a woman.

'Luke went and fucking got cancer didn't he.' I say. 'Nothing in my life has ever gone well. Nothing. It's a fucking mess; a joke. I'm a joke.'

Brenda slowly gets off the chair and walks back inside the house. I follow her in and close the backdoor. Now in the kitchen, I wonder if she has ever felt the same feelings as me.

'Have you ever had an affair, or been tempted?'

Brenda remains calm, and nods very slightly. She's looking directly into my eyes with a serious look of discontent.

'Not an affair, but I was tempted once in my life.' She explains, 'we all have feelings, all want to be loved, touched, have a great time. But I couldn't do it. It was a very long time ago now; this was when I was in my forties. Well over twenty years ago, but nothing came of it, because I stopped anything going further.'

'Who was it?'

'Just someone I worked with once, a few drinks out in town and we kissed. Nothing more ever again. I didn't even speak to him after that and I blamed myself entirely. I felt like I betrayed Al, but nothing really happened. Nothing serious enough to end our marriage.'

Brenda squints her eyes and touches her head.

'There it is again. I feel it.' Brenda says, patting the back of her head. 'I sense a bang to the head, like a thud, or a sharp quick blow. I don't sense that it's my pain, it's not physical to me, it's a sense of what has happened to someone else. Lauren. When I close my eyes I can see a flash of the Empress tarot card again too, and it's upside down, so the woman is not on her thrown. That card normally represents motherhood, do you remember?'

I can feel my heartbeat in my neck, my breathing speeding up and the palpitations in my chest. Panicked, I take a knife from the drawer. A long, sharp butcher knife that I use for cutting up meat.

'You know, don't you?' I say, waving the knife at Brenda, her eyes bulging with fear. 'You know everything, you always did, didn't you.'

Brenda is panicked, the colour in her face drained with shock.

'Touch that phone of yours and I'll slit my wrists. I'm warning you; I will do it.' I state, hoping that she listens and places it back down. I don't have much time to think about what I'm doing, but enough is enough. 'Put it down. Now. If you don't drop it. I don't know what I will do.'

Brenda fumbles and drops the phone to the floor; she kicks it under the kitchen table and holds up her hands as if I'm pointing a gun at her. She is shaking profusely and struggling to stand. I hadn't planned for any of this.

'I don't know anything.' She cries, 'I know nothing. I don't know what you mean.'

'All this time you've pushing me and asking all the questions. All this time you knew. Don't lie to me.' I shout, still waving the knife. 'How did you know that she is dead. How did you know my little precious girl is dead.'

I can't stop crying and I'm being driven by my adrenaline, but I've connected all the dots and realised she's been playing me for a fool.

'Please, let's talk calmly?' Brenda begs of me, lowering her hands. 'Please put down the knife and sit with me. Let's talk this out. Why don't you throw the knife in the garden.'

'No. No. Stop talking to me like that.' I shout. 'You answer the fucking question. How. Did. You. Know. So, how did you know.'

'I always had a gut feeling, my love. There, I've said it. Is that what you wanted to hear?' Brenda admits. 'I always thought I knew, I just didn't know how to find out, and I knew if I went around making accusations that no one would believe me.'

Brenda goes to step forward and I lunge at her with the knife. She stops in her tracks and puts her hands back up in the air.

'I'm telling you. I will do it. I will fucking do it if you don't take two steps back.' I shout. I watch her eyes lower to the phone. 'Don't you dare touch that phone. It's just you and me.'

Brenda is looking at me, holding out her arms and now smiling. I don't know who is the weirdest out of the two of us, her or me.

'Why don't you admit it to me.' Brenda taunts me. 'Tell me, admit what you have done.'

I hold out the knife and go to cut my wrist, my hands are shaking and she's still there, standing still and staring at me. Showing me more of her fake concern.

'Don't do it. You don't need to kill yourself.' Brenda screams, 'If you cut your wrist, it will be painful. A slow painful death. Please, my love. Please just drop the knife. Think of Kieran, your son, he loves you. What would he go through if you did that to yourself?'

I move the knife away from my wrist and I line it up with Brenda's head. I'm fucking angry with her, angry with myself.

I'm angry with Darren too because if he was anything of a caring husband none of this might have happened. None of it.

Brenda and I are locked in eye contact, she's fixated on the knife and I'm going to tell her outright. It's the first time these words have ever come out of my mouth.

'I killed her.' I admit it, shaking and trembling with tears streaming down my cheeks. 'I killed Lauren. I didn't mean to, but I did. And don't you bring Kieran into any of this, that boy would probably be better off without me. He doesn't deserve a mother like me. I've let everyone down.'

'And where is Lauren?' Brenda asks. 'Well done, you brave thing. Well done you for telling me, that must be a weight off your mind. What have you done with her body? Where is she, my love?'

I'm crying now with the relief. It does feels like a weight off my mind. I've never told a single person and lived with this secret for ten years. All this time eating away at me, convinced that someone will find out, or worse, find her.

'She's out there.' I point to the kitchen door with my knife. 'Under the rose bushes.'

Brenda doesn't move, nor say another word. I see her glance down again at her phone on the floor, but since she's remaining standing in the one spot, I don't have to shut her up.

'Why did you do it?' Brenda asks, still calm, but tearful herself. 'What drove you as her mother, to kill her. And under the rose bushes, all this time. Why?'

Brenda is crying heavy, the colour now back in her cheeks as they are flushed with redness. I'm not losing sight of her position and now that I've admitted it, I'm going to have to kill her too. I have to, this news can't get out.

She fucking pushed me to this.

Chapter Twenty-Nine

Ten Years Ago
Carol

Today was one of the hardest days of my life, I felt like it was the final goodbye. Luke has been a huge part of my life, listened to my troubles and supported me through my difficult times with Darren. Visiting him is the easy part, it's turning around, saying goodbye and wondering if I'll ever see his face again that's the struggle.

For the whole journey back home, Lauren hasn't been herself; she's snappy, talking to me through gritted teeth and no matter how hard I push to ask her what is wrong, I don't get a clear response. She seemed upbeat when we went shopping, but something's changed her mood.

'Nothing. It's nothing, Mum.' She says, I don't believe her. 'I'm having an off day.'

'It's ok to be upset about Luke, he is your uncle.' I explain, 'we all have to come to terms with it, he's accepted his fate, planned the funeral and he doesn't want any misery. He would rather we celebrated his life. He said we've had enough misery to last a lifetime these last few months.'

'Mum, can you please shut up.' She demands. 'It's not that,

leave me alone. I already said I didn't want to talk about it.'

'It's your exams isn't it. I know it's a stressful time for you. I'm here if you need to talk about it.' I try to probe further; she's looking at me in disgust. 'Have an off day. Let's watch a movie together later, after I've done your dad's fish and chips. Some mother and daughter time; I could even treat you to some wine. You'd like that wouldn't you?'

Lauren remained silent, the breeze now turning into something stronger. My mind in overdrive because I was taken by surprise, unsure how to manipulate the situation.

We've unpacked the car, and she reluctantly agreed to carry some of the rose bushes into the back garden after I had to ask for her help multiple times. I've been digging and planting flowers all Summer. I'm sick of it looking like a dumping ground out here. We might live in an area of poverty, but nothing says we can't make it look more beautiful.

The sun was setting, casting a warm glow over the garden, and there was a nice gentle breeze bringing with it the familiar scent of lavender. I stood there, watching my daughter Lauren approach me with a mixture of confusion and anger on her face.

'Mum, what did you tell Luke?' She asks me, her voice broke through the peaceful silence. 'At the hospice. To Luke. Do you remember in the last few minutes. I'd gone outside for some water, but I don't think you realised I had come back. You told him something that I don't think I was meant to hear?'

I looked away, unable to meet her accusing glance. I look around the garden, staring up at the neighbour's windows hoping no one can see us.

'It's not what you think, Lauren.' I defend myself, concerned about what she heard. 'He's been a part of the family longer than you've been born. It's all innocent.'

'Then what is it?' She replies, her tone was sharp, cutting through the air like a knife, begging for the truth. 'Why don't tell me what you think I heard, then? Explain it to me, so I understand it better.'

'I, I, erm, I promised to look after you,' I finally admitted, my voice barely above a whisper. 'And, that I love him. And I love him because he's family, Lauren. There's no harm in that. He was worried about you. He was talking to me about your exams. Nothing more.'

'Look after me, for him?' She questioned me again. Her words were like daggers. 'Why would you say that. It doesn't make sense. He has kids of his own, doesn't he. There's more to this, isn't there? I heard it, but it meant more than my exams.'

'Lauren, Luke is a dying man, I was being kind.' I reply, 'Don't be so daft in thinking there's any more to it. It's not what you think.'

'Why would you say what you said, then?' She pressed on, her eyes showing her emotion. 'You're lying. You're lying to all of us. Does Dad know about any of this?'

'Lauren, please. Be logical about this.' I pleaded with her, hoping she would drop this line of questioning. But she stepped closer, her hands clenched in fists by her side reminding me of Darren. 'Please, calm down, it's been a difficult day enough already.'

'Why don't you admit it right now, admit that you're lying?' She accused me, her voice rising in anger. 'What have you done, Mum? You've destroyed this family.'

Tears welled up in my eyes as I tried to find the right words to explain everything. But before I could speak, Lauren's next question stopped me in my tracks.

'Is Luke, my real Dad?' She asked, stern faced. 'He is, isn't he? I can't believe it. I don't even know what to say, or how I feel. Yes, I do. I feel, disgusted. You're sick.'

I couldn't bring myself to look at her as I answered softly, 'Yes.'

The tension in the air was intense as she processed my admission. I reached out to touch her arm, but she pulled away from me with yet another look of disgust on her face. A look she's learnt all too well growing up around Darren.

'I'm going to tell Dad.' She declared coldly. The weight of those words crushed me as I watched her storm away, leaving me alone with my guilt and regret. 'You lying fucking bitch of a mother. I hate you. I really fucking hate you for this.'

I followed her, trying to explain the complicated truth behind her paternity. But she wasn't ready to hear it, consumed by rage and betrayal. And as the words spilled out of my mouth, I saw her whole world shatter before my eyes.

'You're Luke's daughter,' I finally admitted, the words barely audible. 'It's true.'

I saw the anger in those eyes, another trait she's learned from Darren.

'It was just once, a mistake. It meant nothing, I swear it.' I pleaded, hoping she would understand and forgive me. 'Darren will always be your dad; he brought you up. He loves you so much. You're his world and nothing is going to change that.'

'Fuck you, you told him you loved him.' Lauren replied. 'And, even now you're stood there talking to me like I'm a child. All you're interested in is yourself. I don't care who my dad is, it's a shame I have to have you as my mother.'

And in that moment, I feared I had lost my daughter forever. The weight of my actions hung heavily on my shoulders as I watched her walk further away from me.

'Stop.' I interrupt her sharply, unable to stand another evasion. 'Lauren, I swear it was just once. But yes, I loved him. I've always loved him.'

My words hang in the air between us, heavy and undeniable.

'It's complicated. Really, bloody complicated.'

I watch Lauren, stumble back, the weight of my confession hitting her like a ton of bricks. Her mother's secret lover is her father's brother, and her real father confined to a hospice bed - our entire lives have been a tangled web of deceit. I have feared this day happening since the day she was born. No one was ever meant to find out.

'Lauren, please try to listen to me. I can explain.' I defend myself, but I can't deny how I feel. 'This will really hurt your father. His brother is dying, he's not dealing with it too well. You've seen how much he's drinking again; you've heard him snap at us all.'

I don't expect her to understand my lifetime of lies. How can she forgive me for something so unforgivable? I somehow need her to understand my point of view. I can't have this exposed, I fear what Darren will do to me.

'What is there to understand, Mum?' She snaps, 'that you chose to keep this from me? From Dad, too?'

I hope she can see the guilt weighing heavily on my shoulders, etched deeply into my face. I know that it's too late for apologies, too late for excuses. The damage has been done, and it's irreparable. When he gets home from work, our whole world will change forever. He might even kill me.

'Lauren.' I whisper, but there are no more words left to say. 'I'm so sorry.'

The world that she thought she knew crumbles around her.

We're both holding back the tears, staring into each other's eyes. I want to comfort her, to hold her, to make it all better, but the truth was hard and I am shaking with my nerves. She can barely even bring herself to look at me.

As my heart races in my chest, I watch Lauren rush towards the back door.

'I need to tell Dad; he deserves to know the truth.' She says, 'he doesn't deserve you. Fuck you.'

'Lauren, stop.' I demand, 'Listen to me. Please don't tell your dad. I am begging you. He will kill me. You know he will. Then what do you think will happen?'

I chase after her as I panic about Darren learning the truth. I should be the one to tell him. I grab onto the back of her neck because my fingers could only reach the chain as she ran, and I tug hard at the teardrop necklace I bought her for her sixteenth birthday. It was a gift from the both of us, now tainted with lies.

'Let go.' She gasps, trying to fight against my grip. 'I can't breathe.'

The chain snaps, sending both of us tumbling to the ground. Lauren breathes hard and fast for more air as I scramble to my feet, fear propelling me further forward.

'Please, stop.' Her voice sounds far away, almost unreal. But I can't stop - not now. 'Mum, no.'

I grab the only garden tool that was near my feet, the huge metal shovel. As Lauren goes to stand up, and turn from me, flinching. I hit the back of her head. I hear the clang, the crack, the snap.

'Lauren?' My voice echoes through the garden, only silence answering back. My hands are trembling as I hold onto the shovel, weighted down by what I've done. I look down at her lifeless body – my sweet daughter.

'Oh God, what have I done?'

Tears blur my vision, but there's no time to grieve. There's only one thing left to do, one last effort to protect what's left of my family.

I dig. The soil is stubborn and unyielding as I force it to hide yet another secret. Shovel after shovel, I dig a grave in the only place that could conceal her body. I see the rose bushes and I know what I need to do. I have no time to prepare a response, a reasoning for Lauren not being around, I'll have to deal with everything as it comes.

'Forgive me,' I whisper into the air, but Lauren doesn't answer. She can't.

The rose bushes will grow over her final resting place, their roots intertwining with my guilt. It's my burden to bear alone – the cost of keeping a secret for too long.

I plant the roses carefully, their thorns piercing my skin. In the stillness that follows, I stand over her grave and feel the weight of grief crushing me.

'Goodbye, my love,' I manage to say through tears. Concerned what the neighbours might have seen or heard, but everyone argues around here. It's that kind of area. 'I'm so sorry. For everything.'

I'll look after those roses for the rest of my life.

Chapter Thirty

Friday, 9 June 2023
Brenda

Never had I expected today to be as eventful as this. As much as I would like to think that I can predict a little part of the future or have a sense of reading situations; today, I failed.

I'm helpless and my phone is lying on the kitchen floor, it still has the power on because every time I glance, I can see the screen still lit. I'm relieved but because I'm not able to speak or get to it, I have no idea if what I think has happened, really is happening.

I don't know how to remain calm in her presence, since Carols mood and behaviour is volatile, unpredictable and my life is at risk. I'm hoping I'm not the only person who heard her confession, but can they save me. At least if I die here, stabbed by the knife on her kitchen floor, I know that someone out there might know the truth. Hopefully, they will hear everything.

I hear the loud sirens and her eyes are still bulging from the shock or adrenaline, or whatever is going on in that mind of hers. The police are getting closer and closer.

'Who called the fucking police?' Carol shouts, 'what are they doing here?'

CHAPTER THIRTY

'Maybe it's the neighbours, they might have heard you?'

'They wouldn't dare. Not to this family.'

'Why don't you put down the knife, it might make things easier?' I suggest, noticing the vein bulging on the side of her neck. 'Let's just talk, my love. It doesn't need to get nasty.'

As I watched her run forward, the knife coming right at me, I'm not even sure if I have been stabbed. In that split second, I could picture my husband and the love that I have for him. We've been part of each others lives for so long that being without each other doesn't seem natural. I love him, and he loves me.

I might never have given him a child, but we've been through our ups and downs. The death of my grandparents, our change of jobs, times when we struggled for money and scrimped and saved, and other times when I found the menopause difficult and life seemed hard because my emotions were all over the place, trying somehow to find my place and purpose on this earth.

Carol's right arm is tight around my neck and the knife in her left hand is pointing into my side. I can feel the sharp edge to it already piercing through my top, and it's hurting me. There's nothing I think I can say or do to ease this fear and my thoughts are alive with flashes of the roses. I can't believe I'm in the same situation as Lauren. I look down and there's no blood. All those years and she's been under the roses all along. Under everyone's nose. I'm angry with her but not surprised.

The sirens have stopped and the door is knocking. No one speaks or says a word. I don't know whether to scream or not. I have a split second to make a choice and I choose not to say anything either.

'Don't fucking move.' Carol whispers into my ear. 'Or else,

you'll die.'

I shake my head as fast as my breathing. My heart rate has doubled and I don't know how much I can stand much longer before falling down. My knees are in so much pain.

'Carol? Mrs Cooke?' I hear a friendly female voice talk through the letterbox. 'Hi Mrs Cooke, it's the police. I am officer, Harriet Edwards. Will you please open the door so we can talk?'

I don't see them clearly enough, but shadows wander past the window frames. I hear the footsteps very faintly, but I'm more concerned about the knife that's still pointed and held firmly into my side.

Not once has Carol realised that it was me who dialled the police as soon as her back was turned to the kitchen drawer. I knew I was in danger, I knew something was wrong. I could sense it coming. She was tense and angry, the atmosphere felt dark and claustrophobic. It could be a quick-thinking action that saves my life or one that ends it right here and now. I had to take the risk and respond fast.

'No. I have a knife. Don't come in or I will kill her.' Carol shouts back. 'Who called you, was it the neighbours. Fucking nosey bitches. I mean what I say. They all know I mean what I say.'

Whilst they spoke, I wondered if they had called my husband. Does he know how much danger I'm in? I'm worried about him.

'Can I talk to her? Brenda are you able to speak? She says, 'Brenda are you hurt in any way?'

I don't answer her because Carol has not cleared it for me to respond. I am not adding fuel to the fire. My life is literally in her hands.

CHAPTER THIRTY

'She's ok.' Carol shouts, walking us forward a little further. 'Look, I have a knife. It's up against her side, and I will use it if I have to? I said I meant it.'

'Carol, I hear you, and I want to listen to you. But I need to know Brenda is safe, can I hear Brenda talk please?' Officer Edwards asks, 'Brenda, can you talk to me?'

'Go on.' Carol whispers. 'Tell her that you're ok.'

'Hi, Officer Edwards.' I say, nervously and the emotion evident in my voice. Fearing Carol might kill me. 'I'm not hurt. I'm ok.'

'Carol. Please drop the knife and let Brenda go.' Officer Edwards pleas, 'Whatever is going on, we can talk about this together, just you and I if you open the door for me, please. Let me inside. We can chat.'

I can feel Carol starting to crack. She's cornered, we both know there are police officers crawling around the property, likely armed and can see her every move. At least that's what I am hoping for. Also, that one of them will shoot her before she stabs me. If they don't resolve this in sixty seconds, I'm dead. I know it.

'Come on, Carol.' I hear, 'let's talk, woman to woman. I know life can be hard, and times can be tough. No one else needs to be hurt, do they? What's your story. I know you had a missing daughter, and I know that you've recently lost your husband. Darren.'

Carol's crying; I can feel the dampness of her tears on the back of my neck. I'm not strong enough to overpower her, if I try, I'm done for. My arthritic knees wouldn't allow me to escape. Some days I can barely walk at a normal pace, let alone run for my life out the door.

'It's all my fault. No one will understand.' Carol cries,

walking slightly closer to the door. 'I didn't mean to. I loved her. I didn't mean to do it. It was an accident at first. An accident. You won't understand.'

I glance towards the window and hope that there's an officer lining up the shot. I'm concerned that if Carol keeps moving forward enough, we'll be out of sight and I'll be in more danger. They have to save me.

'Carol. There is a way out of this situation. You can drop the knife and walk outside. We can talk about it and get you some help.' Officer Edwards continues, 'all I want to make sure of is that you are both safe. Drop the knife now and think about your son. You have a son called Kieran, don't you? What would he say if he was here. He'd be concerned about his mum, wouldn't he?'

I'm relieved they've not mentioned my mobile phone. It led them here and I am anxious that they don't say a word about it to her.

'I love him. I love my little boy, so much.' Carol cries, the knife pushing more and more into my side, enough to scratch me. I feel it. 'My little girl; it just happened. I killed her, and it's killing me. It's killing me too. I can't stop feeling this guilt. I hate myself every day for what I did. I didn't deserve to be a mother. I was fucking useless.'

Carol screams and the more downhill she is becoming mentally; I fear that I am soon to be dead. I want it all to stop. I want everyone to stop talking and take the shot.

'Carol. Drop the knife. Now.' Officer Edwards says more firmly. 'You can end this by letting Brenda go and coming outside. You son will be waiting for you. Your son that I'm sure love's you very much, that you will see again. Come outside.'

'No.' Carol snaps. She's unsteady on her feet. I think about

CHAPTER THIRTY

chancing it to the front door. I can see it's only a few meters away. 'You're playing games with me.' I'm not playing games. I just told you I killed her and you haven't even asked any questions.'

'How did you kill her?' Officer Edwards asks, still firm. 'Do you want me to ask you questions, would that help? If we talked about it some more. I can understand why you killed her if you let me know how, and how that makes you feel.'

'She caught me.' Carol replies, a lower tone, but her breathing has calmed. 'She overheard me telling Luke. Luke is Darren's brother. We were having an affair you see. Anyway, long story short is that he died. He died and, on his deathbed, Lauren caught me telling him how much I loved him and how much I'd take care of his little girl. She heard everything.

Carol takes a deep breath and sobs.

'She wasn't meant to hear all that or know about us. She confronted me in the garden when we got home. I grabbed her by her necklace, but it broke. It snapped in my hand with the weight.' Carol keeps going, talking slower and slower. 'She was purple, as I was choking her with this necklace, but when it snapped, she was about to get up and run. I picked up the shovel by the shed and I hit her. She went down and never got back up. I panicked. It wasn't meant to be like that at all. She wasn't meant to know.'

The sharp pain in my side alerts me that I've been stabbed slightly. I wince in pain and try not to scream. I don't think it's gone deep, but I am alarmed and shocked that Lauren was not Darren's own daughter? Did he know?

'You are describing it like it's an accident that got out of hand.' Officer Edwards says calmly, even though I am crying myself in the knowledge of how poor Lauren was murdered.

'Talking about it, lessens the pain. You lost your daughter and you were still her mother. No one can ever change or take that away from you.'

I hold my breath because I don't know what is going to happen next. How can this end.

'Carol.' Officer Edwards, asks. 'One more time, I am asking you to drop the knife, and let Brenda walk free. You don't have to make that guilt you're feeling any worse. Do the right thing.'

'No. No.' Carol says, but not loud enough for anyone other than me to hear. 'I can't. I can't do that. I can't do this. I don't think I can.'

I scream loudly as Carol pushes the knife further into my side. As the front door opens with an almighty bang, I see the firearms police take a shot. I hit the floor and start to crawl a little and Carol hits the floor behind with a thud.

A swarm of officers run at us, and I see Carol being handcuffed. I turn to notice they tasered her and she's still alive.

Still on the floor, I realise I am bleeding and the pain is becoming worse. An officer is telling Carol her rights, and a medical team are all over my wound. Officer Edwards walks closer and bends down to my level. She's fully uniformed, about five-foot-two-inches and slender.

'Are you ok?' She asks. 'Are you well enough to give us a statement? We heard everything thanks to your phone. What you did there was outstanding, very smart and very clever in the moment. That call saved your life.'

I cry with relief that I'm still alive and the emotion of the officer saving my life.

'Is Al alright?' I ask, as I am helped up on my feet by the paramedic. 'My husband?'

'He's been made aware of the situation.' Officer Edwards,

CHAPTER THIRTY

confirms. 'He knows that you're safe. He knows everything.'

'He's not going to be happy with me.' I reply. 'I'm going to hear all about it when I get home.'

'Well let's get you to the hospital first' She says, 'let the medical teams give you the once over just to be sure.'

'Thank you, my love.' I say holding her hand. 'I really mean it. Thank you for everything.'

I look behind me and Carol is still handcuffed and on the floor. I don't know if they are going to sedate her, or what is going on, but she looks crazy and out of control.

I'm in complete and utter shock.

'Edwards.' I hear down the radio. 'She's confessed to the murder of her daughter, and there's more.'

'More?' Officer Edwards replies through her radio, walking me to the ambulance with a medic supporting the other side of me. Pushing in on my wound. 'What do you mean, more?'

'She has admitted to poisoning her husband in the caravan by spiking his vodka with some toxic bleach concoction.' He replies. 'We've just charged her with double murder. Once she's been to the hospital, we're bringing her in.'

I close my eyes and imagine all the roses blooming and starting over again. It's awful and cruel how another person on this earth can inflict so much hurt and pain. I had my gut instinct that she had done it. I couldn't fully be sure, but the closer I got, the more I was beginning to understand the signs. The messages and spiritual meanings when I was around her. Everything was pointing in her direction.

I open my eyes and look up at the sky. I feel relieved it's over and I really want to see my husband again.

The love of my life.

Chapter Thirty-One

Two Days Ago
Darren

The bottle of vodka is cold in my hand. I'm pleased there's even more in the fridge and it feels wrong as I stare across the room at Carol. The tension between us has been brewing all day, my mind flooded with thoughts and feelings I'd forgotten about. Memories that make me wonder. Doubts that awaken the monster inside me.

'Say it, Carol,' I spit out, my voice like gravel. My head throbs with each beat of my heart. Vodka burns all the way down my throat. 'You know something don't you? I've always felt that you've been hiding something from me.'

I walk towards her and she flinches. Her eyes, now a dull reflection of her former self, shift away from mine. She doesn't look me in the eye, she fears me.

'Darren, please,' she begs. 'Don't do this, not again.'

'It's about Lauren,' I ask sternly. 'You know something. You've always known, haven't you? Leaving me in the dark.'

'I don't know what you mean, or even what you're implying.' She explains and of course she knows. 'What do you think I know? I don't know any more than you know?'

CHAPTER THIRTY-ONE

'You've not done all the normal things a mother would do when their daughter is missing. That night when she vanished.' I carry on. 'How could you sleep; how could you be so fixated on the fucking garden?'

Tears glisten on her cheeks. She wipes them away, angry or ashamed, maybe both. Carol looks down, and I see it. The purple marks circling her wrists. My stomach twists. I made those marks with my own bare hands.

'Look at you, what a bloke. What a man.' She taunts me. 'What have we become? I've never felt like this was any kind of a marriage, nor you, any kind of a husband to me.'

'Tell me?' I ask, once again firm. 'What the fucking hell are you hiding from me? All these posters, you can barely be bothered. Why did you even bother to come out all this way?'

She's crying harder now. Shoulders shaking. But her voice, when it comes, is steady as a rock.

'It's killing me, Darren.' She cries. Her sleeve slips. More bruises that are dark and painful looking. 'It's killing us both.'

Her words hang there, I'm desperate for more.

'Lauren.' I ask one more time, showing my anger. 'What did you do?'

I can barely breathe her name out. My girl. Gone. And here I am, drowning in vodka and silence and I know there's more things unsaid.

The air is thick with accusation. My words hang like a noose in the room, tightening with each passing second. Carol's face is inches from mine, her breath shaky, eyes wide with the fear of me grabbing her arm again. I want to rage at her, but I need answers.

'Darren, I don't know where to begin.' She whispers, and the sound of my own name on her lips feels like a slap. 'There's more. More you don't know.'

My heart thuds against my chest. Rage simmers, waiting for an excuse to boil over. But I pause, studying her expression and body language. The desperation in her eye's tugs at me, pulls me back from the edge just enough.

'Fucking talk to me,' I demand. It's not a plea; it's an order. 'What the fuck happened to my little girl?'

She flinches but holds her ground. In that moment, something shifts. The tremble in her voice finds a backbone.

'I can't,' she says, and there's a finality in her tone that pushes me back physically. 'Maybe you'll never find out. How about that?'

'Damn you, Carol!' My anger now feeling like a living creature trying to claw its way out. 'I swear to God, if you don't tell me, I'll make you.'

'Just fucking drink it,' she urges, shoving the bottle toward me. A peace offering or a stalling tactic? I don't care. The burn of the vodka as it goes down is familiar, comforting in a twisted way. I gulp it, welcoming the numbness it promises. 'Do what you're good at.'

She watches me glug another, then another.

'Look, Darren.' Her sleeves are up now, revealing more bruises in different shades of yellow and purple smearing her skin in the ugly truth. 'You wouldn't want to know. You wouldn't want this pain and suffering I've had to live with.'

'See what you've done to me?' She says, but her eyes only show sorrow. And maybe something else. Fear? No, not fear. Determination. 'Each bruise a story of its own. Now I'm beginning to think she really did deserve it.'

'Tell me, what you did with Lauren? Where is she?' I rasp again, grasping for something solid in a world that's spinning

CHAPTER THIRTY-ONE

out of control. 'I would kill for that girl. Kill.'

'Can't you tell?' She's pleading now, pleading for me to understand something that lies just beyond my reach. 'She's been right under your nose the whole time.'

'Lauren, where. What?' Is all I can say, the name a shard of glass in my mouth. I need answers, but I'm fading with every swig of alcohol, with every unveiled bruise. 'What are you talking about? She's our little girl.'

'Was,' She corrected me and the past tense turns my stomach. 'Was, our little girl. And look at all these bruises, she grew up having to watch her dad hit her mother. You ain't even sorry either. Never were, never will be. Not once have you ever meant it.'

'Say what?' My voice is a jagged edge, raw and scornful. 'You want me to say I'm fucking sorry?'

'I'll prove it?' I spit out a bitter laugh. The room spins, my head swimming in vodka and venom. 'What do you want to do, do you want a fucking note to keep as a memento?'

I walk forwards showing her a face she'll fear. This time she doesn't flinch.

'Yes.' Carol replies. Her face taunting me. 'Do it. Prove it. Mean it.'

I lurch up, the movement too quick, the world tilting dangerously. Searching, fumbling. There, on the cluttered sideboard, paper, a pen. I grab them, slam them onto the table. The force feels good, solid.

'Here.' I say, holding the pen. 'Tell me what to write.'

'Write what you feel, Darren. If there's anything left in there.' She replies. Her challenge stokes the rage in my head. 'You're as cold as a brick.'

'Fine.' The pen shakes in my grip, ink ready to bleed truth

onto paper. 'Have this fucking note.'

'Dear Carol,' I say as I scrawl, each letter a struggle against the tide of alcohol that threatens to drown me. 'I don't know. What comes next? Admissions? Apologies?'

Can words mend bruises?

'Go on, and the fucking rest.' She snaps. 'Tell me you're sorry. Write it, read it.'

'Sorry.' I shout, and it finally makes its way onto the page, hollow and inadequate. My confession, a drop in the ocean of our shared pain. I look up at her, wondering how in all the years we've been together that it's come to this. I knew we shouldn't have come here. She insisted on Salcombe, I knew we wouldn't find her.

'Keep writing, Darren.' She insists. But the pen slips from my fingers. 'And the rest. Do it.'

I swig from the bottle, another glug of vodka disappearing down my throat. My head's heavy, like it's filled with lead. The room blurs at the edges, my stomach churns.

'Darren, listen to me. Listen carefully.' Carol says firmly. 'I'm leaving you, and this time I fucking mean it. There's no going back. It's over.'

My eyes squint and the room is spinning. She seems distant, a ghostly figure.

'This time it really is for good.' Her words echo in my mind. I can't stop hearing them over and over.

'Leaving?' I can barely make sense of it. My tongue feels swollen, words slurred. 'You'll never leave me; you couldn't cope without me.'

'Look at yourself.' There's pity in her gaze, but it's hard as ice. 'Get a fucking grip.'

I try to stand, to show strength, to fight. But my legs betray me, stumbling, buckling. A grunt escapes as I grip the table, struggling to stand up.

'You can't even stand up straight.' She says with glee. She's watching me, and there's something else in her eyes now. Not just pity, but something much darker. 'Ten years ago, I nearly walked out on you, but I was afraid back then. I stayed with you for Kieran's sake. I wanted him to at least turn into a decent man, the man that you'll never be.'

'Carol, stop this.' I mutter, trying to reach out, but my hand just waves in the air, useless. 'You know my upbringing. I'm damaged. You knew that when we met. I told you that, remember? You knew what you were marrying.'

She moves closer, the bottle of vodka now in her grasp.

'You should know something,' she whispers, her voice almost tender. 'That she wasn't even your daughter.'

The sentence slams into me like a punch to the gut.

'Wait, what?' I'm gasping, fighting for air, fighting the bile rising in my throat.

'Lauren,' she says. 'She wasn't your daughter. She was Luke's.'

'Luke's?' The room spins faster, my heart's a sledgehammer in my chest. Betrayal tastes bitter. 'You don't mean that. You're still lying. Fucking liar.'

'Here, why don't you have some more of your favourite drink.' She demands. Carol's pressing the bottle to my lips, tilting it back. Vodka flows, burning, suffocating. 'Drink the fucking lot you nasty vile cunt.'

'Stop.' It's a plea, a whisper drowned out by the vodka she's pouring down my throat. It's all down my neck and top. 'Carol, stop. I'm sorry. There, I said it. I mean it.'

'Drink up, Darren.' Her voice is steady, cold. 'It'll help you forget. Isn't that what you wanted?'

My palms scrape the wooden floor, each push a herculean effort. She's there, behind me, silent as a spectre. Her footsteps soft but condemning. The stairs loom, Everest in my bleary vision.

'Up,' I grunt to myself, as I drag my body, one agonising step at a time. My arms shake, elbows locking with each small victory.

'Darren. Take a look at yourself.' She says, now laughing at me. 'You can't even climb the stairs anymore. What are you, a baby. Baby Darren?'

I ignore her. I must ignore her because there's anger, a fire fuelling my ascent.

'Look at you.' Her words are needles in my back. Taking the piss out of me and shaming me. She's lucky that I can't stand up. I'd strangle the bitch. I don't believe for a minute that Lauren is Luke's. She's trying to hurt me, payback for all the bruises.

The top of the stairs seems miles away. My head spins, stomach churns. The vodka, a venom in my veins. I heave, try not to retch, but I keep moving up one stair at a time.

'Lauren is Luke's,' she repeats, closer now. I can feel her breath, cold on my neck. 'We fucked over and over and over. He loved me. We loved each other.'

'Stop...' It's weak, my voice, but she doesn't stop. 'And I killed her when she found out about us. She was going to tell you on the day she vanished.'

Killed? My heart stammers. Lauren. Not just gone but dead. Killed by her own evil mother.

'Ten years,' she whispers in my ear. 'Ten years haunted by all of this. But it's all your fault, Darren. You made me this way.

CHAPTER THIRTY-ONE

It's you, all, you.'

'My fault?' I rasp, each word an effort, barely able to believe it. This revelation bigger than what my mind can cope with. 'How is it my fault? I'm calling the police.'

'Because.' She starts and pauses. I hear a tremor in her voice. 'If you'd been a decent husband, it might never have come to this. Go on, call the police, where is your phone?'

I reach the landing, body sprawling across the cold floor. Something's not right here. I can barely feel my legs; my arms are weakened by the effort of the stairs.

'Carol,' I gasp, 'This isn't true, is it? What's happening to me?'

'Please what, Darren?' Her silhouette towers over me. 'You want forgiveness? Comfort? There's none left to give. Years I've had to put up with your behaviour and it's tormented me. I can't do this anymore, Darren. I'm putting an end to this. Something in me has just turned.'

'Lauren, can't be dead.' I whisper, the pain sharp as glass. 'My little girl. I loved her so much. How could you?'

'She was never yours to grieve,' Carol says, 'You did nothing for this family. I was guilty at first, but the sleeping pills helped. I should have let you die that night you took all mine.'

Grief is a wave, washing over me. I'm slowly drowning in the truth that's been there all along.

My little girl is dead.

Chapter Thirty-Two

Saturday, 10 June 2023
Carol

The chill of the cell sends a shiver down my spine. The metal bars, cold and unyielding, stand between me and freedom. God knows what Brenda thinks of me now, how I've used, abused and tormented her over the last few days. Certain that she knew what I had done, what I was planning, and a fear that she could expose me. And she did, but not in the way I expected.

I wrap my arms around myself, seeking warmth that isn't there. My fingers touch the fabric of my dirty clothes. It's rough, scratchy, still blood stained and fitting for a murderer. I'm a murderer and my stomach sinks when I tell myself. I'm not sure what kind of future I will have next, but it can't be no worse than my past. I've lived a life of pain for so long, that I know no different.

I can still hear Brenda's voice, calm despite the knife I pressed against her side.

'You don't have to do this, Carol,' she'd said. Her eyes showing a mix of fear and pity. That, or understanding?

The police told me her phone had been switched on the whole time. Connected to the police whilst it was under the table,

CHAPTER THIRTY-TWO

on the floor. How could I have been so blind? They heard everything, I couldn't deny a single thing. I knew I'd have to confess about Darren too, the toxicology report will show the bleach I poured into his bottle of vodka.

I slump onto the thin mattress provided, its springs creaking under my weight. My head is a whirlwind of thoughts, each one more torturous than the last. I beat myself up with the words that once Darren weaponised against me. I'm no good for anyone, useless, evil, boring, no one will want me, no one cares. I'm a bad mother.

Darren's face flashes in my mind. His eyes, once filled with love, grown cold and distant over the years. The abuse wasn't just physical. The words he spat cut deeper than any knife. They carved a hole in my soul until there was nothing left but despair. Each year we were together was another year lost of living. We were toxic together and should never have been.

'Insane,' I whisper to the walls. Maybe that's what I am. Insanity would be kinder than the truth. The truth that I killed him. Killed our daughter. My Lauren, my sweet girl, buried under the rose bushes in the very garden where she used to play. We'd sit out in the garden on the anniversary of her disappearance, looking at the roses and wondering where she was, what she was doing now. The lie was so cemented, that there times I actually believed it. I wanted to believe she was out there, living her best life, with her own kids, in a successful job with a husband that loves her. A husband better than mine.

A sob catches in my throat. I miss her. God, how I miss that girl so much. The ache is a living thing inside my chest, gnawing at my heart. I tell myself she's close to me, out there beneath the roses. But it's a bitter comfort. A mother shouldn't lay her child to rest. Not like this. The only connection I have with her is the watering of the plants.

My hands shake as I draw my knees up to my chin. Darren took everything from me. My joy, my sanity. And in the end, I took his life. The price of freedom, paid in blood and regret.

'Are you sorry?' They asked when I confessed.

'Yes, I'm sorry for everything that I have done.' I told them. 'For all of it.'

Every moment, every breath since the day Lauren disappeared has been steeped in sorrow. No one understands me, I barely understand myself.

The cell feels smaller with each passing second, walls closing in as I breathe. I want to scream, to release the turmoil inside me. But the sound won't come. Only tears, silent and relentless. I'm mad, I can feel how crazy I am. No longer nervous, no more anxiety, no more fear.

'Lauren, I hope you will forgive me.' I murmur, 'if you are up there, watching me, communicating to me through Brenda; then please forgive me. I love you, and I'll never stop loving you.'

Outside, the world moves on. Inside, I'm trapped in a nightmare of my own making. And I can't wake up. I don't want to hurt anyone anymore.

The clink of metal echoes, setting my nerves on edge. Footsteps approach, heavy and the sound remind me of Darren's boots as he paced the hallway. The lock turns with a jolt and the door swings open.

'Carol,' the officer says, his voice a mixture of pity and professionalism. 'You have a visitor. Your son, Kieran. He's here with Mrs Mitchell, from next door.'

Kieran. My boy. I shake my head, thinking he'd never want to visit me.

'No, I can't do it. He shouldn't be here.' I barely whisper. 'I can't. He shouldn't see me like this.'

'Are you sure?' He replies, as I keep shaking my head. 'He was insistent.'

'Tell him, I love him, and it's out of kindness.' I say, my voice cracking. 'Tell him he's better off without me. That I... that I'm sorry.'

The thought of seeing Kieran and explaining the world around him that I destroyed would send me further over the edge. The officer hesitates, but there's nothing he can do. He nods and steps out, leaving me alone with the sound of the voices in my head.

Tears roll down my cheeks, my watery eyes blurring the grey walls of the cell, turning them into a watery abyss. I cry for Kieran, for the son who grew up in the shadow of his sister's absence. For the young man who deserved a mother unmarred by tragedy and violence.

I cry for Darren too, despite everything. For the love we once shared before darkness took root and twisted us both into thorns. And Lauren. My sweet little Lauren. The grief is a tidal wave, relentless and consuming. I'll never forgive myself for what I have done.

There's relief, too, a terrible, hollow release. The fight is over; the secrets are out, spilling like blood across the cold floor of my reality. Darren can't hurt us anymore. Can't hurt me anymore.

'Forgive me,' I whisper to no one, to everyone. To the daughter I betrayed, to the son I'm pushing away. 'I love you.'

The burden of guilt is mine to carry, a sentence beyond bars and locks. Yet, under it all, there's the faintest glimmer of freedom. A chance to breathe without fear shadowing every breath. No more lies.

It's over. The nightmare has ended.

Epilogue

Friday, 9 June 2023
Brenda

The living room door barges open and in walks Al, holding a small lap tray. It's as old as I am and tattered as hell, but there's a slice of cake, a cup of tea and some of my favourite biscuits. I sense a bit of tension, but I hope he doesn't moan after the day I've endured.

He puts down the tray on my lap, then walks over to cross the living room curtains, switches on our little lamp, then stands right in front of me, blocking my view of the television. His arms are folded and he means business.

'I told you, how many bloody times didn't I? I said it would all end in trouble and look what bloody mess you've gotten yourself into, woman.' Al says with a stern fierce look on his face. 'I'm so proud of you. I mean, you took some chances, but you got her didn't you. You worked it all out in that head of yours, when no one else ever thought she'd have done it. Carol, playing the victim for all these years.'

I sip my tea, not quite sure whether to have some of the Victoria sponge cake, or a bourbon biscuit, but I look up at my husband to be surprised he isn't starting an argument.

'At least it's just us two now, my love.' I reply, 'what a full on, hell of a week it's been. I'm exhausted, still in pain from my stab wound on my side and giving statement after statement. I'll no doubt still have to go to court, maybe?'

'Nah, she'll plead guilty, won't she? She admitted everything, so why wouldn't she. She can't go back on that now. The police heard everything, they definitely did, didn't they?' Al asks, his voice showing concern. 'You can't tell them you knew all along though with your ghost stories. They'd lock you up and throw away the key too.'

'I always suspected that she knew more than she was letting on. I just couldn't work it all out at first until I met her in the woods that day. The look on her face, the way she was with her husband, the admission of having an affair. 'I reply, saddened that it's all true, 'but, most of all it was the connection I felt with the necklace, the roses and the lack of atmosphere in Laurens bedroom. Someone up there wanted me to expose the truth, I swear it.'

'What do you mean, lack of atmosphere?' Al asks, 'is that your grandmother talking again? Have you thought that maybe you subconsciously picked up on things from her conversations? It might not be spirits at all.'

'I mean, there was no feeling in that room spiritually. It could have been anyone's bedroom. Her spirit wasn't there. I'm not sure how to describe it other than empty. Then I knew, and when I looked out of the window and saw those roses, I sensed she was there. It was a strong connection, a feeling like no other, Al. I knew.'

'Maybe it was all just a nice coincidence.' Al replies. 'Did you ever think of that?'

'There were too many coincidences, too many strange signs,

all that made clear, perfect sense to Carol.' I continue, defending myself against his negativity. 'I know someone was guiding me in the right direction, maybe my gran, maybe even Lauren. Carol was certain I knew something when I hit a nerve. If it wasn't for me, and my instincts, then Lauren's body might never have been found.'

I always believed that she wanted me to find her.

'What brought her out here in the first place,' Al says, lowering the television volume. 'Salcombe is a bit out of the way, and I can't make sense of the bit where she killed her husband?'

'We might never know that part. I've thought about it, and the victim support team earlier questioned me again on what I knew. I genuinely didn't believe she killed her husband; my energy was focussed on Lauren.' I explain, putting down my cup. 'I don't blame him in any way, but I think he drove her to it. I saw the bruises on her arms, I witnessed how he spoke to her and how aggressive he was in drink.'

'Why didn't she just walk away from that monster, then?' Al interrupts. 'Who would put up with that? It's that easy, it really is.'

'Guilt, Al. Pure guilt; nothing more, nothing else. If it was really that easy, there'd never be no women in abusive relationship. It's psychological.' I reply. 'She killed his daughter, was sleeping with his younger brother too. I think in some strange way she felt that she owed him something and was punishing herself. Eventually, tormented by the guilt and the frustration of being in a controlling relationship; she'd had enough.'

'She got away almost with one murder, nearly two, but I don't know how I would have carried on without you, Bren.'

Al says, his look of concern in my direction. 'I'd never have forgiven her. You are very lucky to be alive.'

'Oh, I know you wouldn't have coped.' I joke, 'you wouldn't have forgiven me either, would you? You'd have blamed me for it all. You'd be telling all the neighbours it was all my own fault for sticking my nose in where it's not wanted, like you used to do.'

Al looks at me, gives me a wink and smiles. It's not often he's over affectionate, but we've both been through quite an ordeal. He's been by side through thick and thin.

'I've made a decision. It feels right, and the more I think about it, the more it needs to happen.' I announce, feeling assertive and sure of myself. 'I don't want you to change my mind either.'

'What on earth are you talking about, now?' Al says in his usual sarcastic tone. 'Not like you to make a decision and stick to it.'

'I'm going to quit my job and retire fully. I don't need to be breaking my back up there cleaning all those cottages.' I say through my beaming smile. 'After everything that's gone on, life's too short. I'm sixty-three, not thirty-three. My knees can't take any more of all that vacuuming.'

'What will you do instead?' He asks, 'won't you get bored? There's only so much TV you can watch, so many books you can read. So many crosswords before you get fed up.'

'I won't be doing any of that. No chance.' I say, 'I'm going to do what my gran did, and I don't care if they all want to call me a witch, a fake, a phoney, a weirdo, or whatever the hell they want. I know I can do it. It feels right.'

'Tarot cards?' Al replies, 'Are you going to make lots of money off people who need relationship advice?'

Printed in Great Britain
by Amazon

'No, certainly not.' I snap. 'I want to help people. I want to give back to this community. I found a missing girl, her body. I know I have a gift and I'm going to make full use of it from now on. It's what I was meant to do, it's been part of my family heritage for donkey's years.'

Al smiles, shakes his head and raises the TV volume again so he can hear this program. I'm not fully invested in it, in fact, I'm very tired, but now I've committed myself to understanding my family gift; I'm not going to waste anytime and I'll take myself down to the spiritualist church in Plymouth tomorrow.

'You're going to be a celebrity round here, you know that soon, don't you?' Al interrupts my trail of thought. 'Those papers will be telling your story soon enough. When did you agree to talk to the journalist again?'

'Tomorrow morning, Al. I told you three times already.' I reply, he rolls his eyes. 'A young guy called James is coming with a photographer tomorrow lunch time.'

'My wife, the celebrity.' He mutters. 'Famous.'

I return to my cake and tea. I can tell by the look on Al's face that he'll fall asleep in a minute or two. He can barely keep his eyes open.

'Al?' I say, humorously. 'Shut up, love.'

Here's to new beginnings, however late in life.

The End.

Also by J A Andrews

You Know Who
The next thriller by J A Andrews landing in August 2025. Someone is hiding a dangerous secret...you know who...

Rachael Thompson, a devoted wife and mother, appears to have a perfect life. She and her husband **Chris** run a successful business while raising their three children. However, Rachael's world begins to crumble as she notices troubling changes in her husband's behaviour; late nights at work, hushed phone calls, and suspected lies that leave her wondering if she can really trust the man she married.

Nothing is as it seems in this sinister thriller which will leave you wondering who is telling the truth, who isn't as they seem, and who will survive an explosive ending...

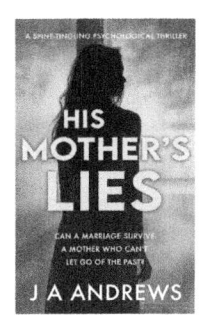

His Mother's Lies
I married her son, but he couldn't see her evil...

Charlotte's dream wedding to **Ethan** was the happiest day of her life. She knew his mother, **Anna**, loved her only son, but her overbearing nature starts driving Charlotte insane. Ethan always claimed his mother accepted her as part of the family, but her gut instincts couldn't be wrong.

To help the happy couple save for their first house together, Anna presents an offer they can't refuse with a rent-free room in the family home. This is when Charlotte suspects Anna wants her boy back for good. Convinced she is out to destroy their marriage; Charlotte has a surprise that was about to bring them closer together or rip their relationship apart.

As tensions mount and Anna digs her claws in, Charlotte discovers a hidden family secret, but Anna's manipulative nature ensures no one would believe her. Charlotte must survive a wave of cruelties and play the most vindictive mother-in-law she's ever encountered at her own sinister game if her marriage is to survive a mother who can't let go of the past.

Anna will stop at nothing to get what she wants...